Grace

ISBN:1492887366

ISBN-13:9781492887362

Lollie

Remembering Grace

The fragrant breeze blowing cooled the warm summer day. Two birds playfully chased each other between a group of trees. The preacher's words fell on unhearing ears. Travis was not a funeral person, and this being an aunt by marriage did not make it that special, but he must be respectful for his daughter's sake.

Out of the corner of his eye, something green blowing in the wind attracted his attention. His interest was drawn to a graceful figure that, while fighting to keep her strawberry blond hair from tickling her face, lighted here and then there planting flowers on another grave. He smiled as a familiarity surrounded his heart.

A teen boy clasping desperately to his young lover's hands, searched his brain for a solution to the problem they faced. Here was the one in a million girl, saying goodbye to him, on what should be her sweet sixteen birthday. A mutual bond promised that they were each other's one and only soul mate.

"I wish there was some other way around this Grace, but there is no other way." He lifted her chin with his fingers. She had been unable to look into his sad brown eyes. "You know I wouldn't go to Wilmington if I didn't have to. It will only be for a year. I will graduate next year, come back, wait for you to graduate the following year, and then we will be married. I promise. Please, don't look at me that way."

A tearful reply was choked back, "How come I feel like we'll never see each other again? A lot can happen in a year. Why don't I come with you? Nobody will care. Nobody will even notice. If you leave me, something will happen, I know it."

"No it won't. Besides, if you come with me, I'll be thrown in jail for kidnapping. I love you Grace. I promise, we'll meet right here, in this very spot, on May 26th. I'll wait on pins and needles for the most beautiful girl in the whole world to keep this rendezvous. Promise me you will come?"

"I promise," she hung her head, "You'll write me? Let me know how you are."

"Of course. I'll call, if ever I can. I'll be staying with my grandmother, so don't get mad if I can't. We'll be on my income, which won't be a lot until I graduate." He

3

embraced her to his bosom, dreading the departure tomorrow. He said goodbye to her, because he would not get to see her the next day.

She could hear the wild beating of his heart through his chest. Why could she not shake the feeling she would never feel these strong arms around her again? "I love you Grace," he whispered in her fiery hair with a kiss. "I'll always love you."

But the tears were rolling down her cheeks at this point, and she could not let him see her cry, so she softly shook her head and muffled a sniffle. The two sat like this until Grace had to make curfew, so Travis took her home.

Travis was unaware of the smile this pleasant memory had caused upon his lips. His daughter, Wendy, was watching him curiously from her aunt's side. "What could Dad be finding so funny?" she thought. The preacher and most of the guests had bowed their heads in prayer, but not the young man to whom this paradisiacal dream had visited.

He watched the fiery red hair bounce contrarily into

her face. There could not be two people in the world with that color of hair. It must be *her*! From a distance, she looked too young to be *her*. Maybe she had a child. Her daughter could have the same strawberry blond color, but could she move with the same elegance as her mother? No! She was leaving. The service was just finishing up. The preacher was walking through the family members, shaking hands. Would he ever hurry? "Wait!" his brain cried. "Is that you? Do not leave yet."

After opening the trunk, placing something in it, taking off her gloves, and putting them inside, the lady mounted her candy apple red Mustang. Much like the owner, the car was sleek and sharp looking. There was not an ounce of dirt on it. The top was down on the convertible and her curls were dancing in the wind. The car slowed to a respectful speed during the passing process of the funeral. She held her head out of respect.

Several members of his former wife's family hugged him, thanking him for coming to Martha's funeral. Still, the thoughts of that young sixteen-year-old girl presided all else. He was itching to step over to that grave, to see who the occupant was.

5

Wendy wondered why her father was procrastinating so. She was ready to go home, and now he wanted to go walking through a graveyard, of all places. She would go sit in the car, and then he would get the picture that she was ready to leave.

Yet the father was not thinking about his daughter. The name on the tombstone read "Billy Jackson". That was *her* grandfather. That must have been her! He had seen Grace! He had been within her grasp. All he had to do was run to her and hold her in his arms. No, that would not be right. She was probably married. Looking like that, she would definitely be married.

His old friend from school, Roger, mentioned to him last week about her class's twenty-year reunion, when he passed him. Roger had attended every reunion, but he never mentioned Grace having ever appeared. Twenty years was a milestone. It would 't hurt to check it out. He wondered if Roger was going to this one as well. Should he dare to call him and ask when he got home?

He decided to keep this a secret. If it ended in disaster, no harm done, and if it ended well, then it would be a wonderful surprise. Roger was thrilled to hear Travis had seen her, and agreed to take him as a guest. He knew the relationship the two had.

Recollecting Grace

The reunion was held at the Grove Park Inn, the most elegant hotel in the western part of North Carolina. Unlike Roger, Travis entered the magnificent tower in awe. The windows stared unblinking while a string of people formed a smile giving the place the appearance of a face. Travis had followed Roger in his own car, but the two walked in together.

Roger was just as anxious to see Grace again as was Travis. He had tormented her throughout grade school, when they attended the same private school. Several years went by before they were reunited at the same high school. They had always been friends until she disappeared quite a few years ago.

The two men searched the throng in hopes of finding a glimpse of fiery red hair. Roger mingled with old friends which left Travis alone. He spotted one red head, but it was the wrong shade. Forty-five minutes later they found their quest. Roger expected to immediately lose his partner, but when he turned to him, Travis was still standing there in a dumbstruck trance.

The green she chose to wear could not have been a

more perfect color. The modestly cut dress expressed every tiny curve. The dress wasn't tight, but enhanced her natural shape. Travis looked for a wedding band, but the view was obstructed by the elegant white gloves on her hands. Her hair was partially falling around her face, framing it in uniqueness. Roger nudged his friend.

"What are you waiting for? There she is!" She had lit into the room with an angelic quality about her, smiling from one former classmate to the next, but not allowing herself to be drawn into serious conversation. Travis remembered her alarming smile, but it metamorphosed into a charming one over the years.

"Look at her. I cannot believe my eyes. Roger, she must be married. What fool would not grab her up? I should not bother her," he stammered.

"You are the only fool I know. I do not see a ring, man. Maybe she is not." He pushed Travis again gently, "Go on. Trust me, if you don't, someone else will be all too willing."

Travis straightened his tie while walking after the figure. She exited the side door, which led to a garden with a fountain and stone benches. He slowed his pace.

Should he follow her? Someone approached him at this point, hindering his chase. It was a few minutes before he dared to continue. He pressed the door open and looked around.

Grace Sorenson perched delicately on a stone bench, conversing with Todd Landrum. The fiery curls bounced in the negative gesture of a shaking head. In order to end the conversation, Grace stood and took a few steps away from the man. She was not paying attention to her steps, which caused her to run smack into someone.

"I am so sorry. Please forgive me?" she asked embarrassedly, while resting her hand on the arm of her collision partner, partly to balance herself, partly to show genuine apology. She gasped when her eyes met his.

"Grace. As I live and breathe. It can't be you. How come you do not look a day older than sixteen, while the rest of us has aged twenty years?" That sounded so stupid. Why had he said that?

Providential Grace

Her melodic laughter had not crossed his ears in so long. "Travis, how are you?"

"I am fine. How about yourself?"

"Great. How are your wife and daughter?"

Ouch. She was getting to the point. "My daughter is well, but my wife is dead."

"Oh, I am so sorry," her answer changed tones. "Was she ill?"

The only answer he gave was, "No. How about your husband?"

"I never married," she smiled.

"Oh?" He questioned with his eyes as well. "I am surprised. How come?"

There was tremendous pride in her answer. She should not show him how he had hurt her. "I am not the kind of person that will marry anybody I do not love. I cannot run off with the first person to come along, just because they are available. I believe that once you have met your soul mate, that person is your soul mate for life. God does not change His plan.

Now she was twisting the knife in the wound.

"Would you like to dance?"

"No thank you. I do not dance. As a matter of fact, I was contemplating on going back upstairs, before I saw you. I remember, now, why I never come to these things."

"Yeah, I never liked this sort of thing."

She flashed her violet eyes, and then turned to leave for lack of knowing what else to say. Travis was overwhelmed. He could not let her leave without explaining everything to her. He must make her understand. He gently reached for her arm.

"I am sorry for not meeting you that night, Grace. I can explain."

Grace turned, lifting her chin high with her Irish stubbornness showing, "It is ancient history. You have nothing to apologize for. We were both young and foolish to think a childish romance could last past high school."

"But I did come to meet you, believe it or not. I was a few weeks late, but I did come. My grandmother had fallen very ill. I wrote and told you to meet me then, but you did not come. I called your uncle's house, but your aunt kept telling me you were never there. She said she would give you the message." His voice softened, "One day I happened to see your uncle at a gas station. He seemed surprised I had not heard about your moving away. He told me you had moved to another city several months ago. I figured it out that if your aunt had been lying about you being there, she probably intercepted the letters. By then, it was too late. The day had already come and gone. He did not give me an address. He told me that he could not legally give it to me. I searched and searched for you. Nobody would tell me where you went. I decided to wait until your eighteenth birthday. I knew, then, you would come back looking for me."

Her expression had softened during his explanation. She should have suspected that Aunt Claudia would be at the bottom of her troubles. Then Grace told her tale, "We had a falling out not long after you went to Wilmington. It was better for me to leave. I don't know why they made everything so secretive. I received two letters from you, and then they stopped. I knew you were working long hours after a hard day at school, so naturally I thought you had no time to write. I did not know you had postponed our meeting. When you did not come and I had not received any more letters, I thought you had moved on. That night, my foster brother agreed to drive me over, under the condition that I escort him to his sorority party in return. I agreed, because it was the only way I had to get there. I am ashamed to say that I probably would have sold my soul to keep that promise. It was the night of my senior prom, so I had this white dress on that I borrowed from a neighbor. I prayed it was not asking too much for you to take me once you arrived. We sat and waited till midnight, but you never came. I thought you must have found someone else, and this was your gentlemanly way of letting me know, because when I moved back after graduation, I ran into Roger Brounden. Do you remember him? He proudly announced your wife had a just given birth to your daughter. I thought I could handle it. I had gotten you out of my mind, but the fear of running into you or your family became more than I could bear, so I moved to Oregon to distance you from my heart."

"Grace, if I had known, I would have…Well, I could

not…How can I say this? I am so ashamed of myself. While I was trying to find you, I was in a bad way. You have to understand, no one would tell me anything. It was as if you had entered the witness protection program and completely fallen off the face of the earth. I truly looked everywhere I knew to look. You were not enrolled at any of the high schools. I thought I was going stark raving mad. When I say I was in a bad way, I mean a real bad way. Roger, Brad, and Tony Lance took me out to cheer me up. I sort of drank too much."

"Travis, no! You never drank. I knew you better than that," she turned away in disgust. How could he face her with that? It must be hard for him.

He dared not touch her hallowed body, but he stepped behind her. "I didn't care. Drinking seemed like a good way to forget you. I cannot even tell you what happened that night, only when she came knocking on my door claiming to be pregnant, what choice did I have? I had to honor my behavior." Tears threatened, as he quieted for a moment. "I am sorry, Grace. I wish I could go back in time and change it all. I would search the world over until I found you. It all could have been so different."

Grace closed her eyes tight to block out what she obviously didn't want to hear. "No, it couldn't. It happened this way, because this is the way God wanted it. His plan was fulfilled, not ours. We could not change one minute of it."

"Grace," he dared to touch her shoulder. He was not sure, but that she was leaving him to his sad lonely world again. He could not allow her to simply walk out of his life again. "Do you have to leave so soon?" He tried to push the despair under a veil.

"Yes, I must," she responded without looking at him.

"Why?"

The cold chills rose on her arm. "Because, I don't trust my judgment where you are concerned."

His voice was but a whisper. She felt his breath on her neck. "So there's a chance you could still love me?"

There was a hurt in the violet eyes he had not anticipated. "As if I could ever have loved another. I made a promise to you one time to always love you. Do you think that I could so easily break that?"

That was more than he could bear. He suddenly succumbed to the battle for control of his emotions. He engulfed her in his arms to accomplish what he had longed to do since first sight of her tonight.

She closed her eyes in submission to his kiss. Her telltale heart announced to the world around of her feelings for this man, as it escalated its palpitations into full blown pummeling in her chest. She threw caution to the wind forgetting the pain she suffered from loving him all those years. For the brevity of those few moments, time stood still. Nothing else mattered.

The man lifted the woman's petite body from the floor's surface absent-mindedly. Losing his balance, the two toppled into the fountain, which broke the magical spell.

Larking Grace

They emerged laughing, while being soaked head to foot.

A voice from the past broke in, "You always were a klutz Grace, for as long as I have known you," the old friend teased with a twinkle.

"Roger," she smiled, "how are you?"

"Dry," he joked, as he walked to her and kissed her cheek. "I see you two ran into each other."

Travis and Grace exchanged glances and burst into hilarity all over again. Grace spoke, "I do not know about you, but I am going upstairs to dry off." She turned to Travis, "If you want to come up, I can have your suit laundered. At least you will be dry."

"I would like that," he expressed his gratitude with a slight pressure to her hand.

Roger assumed the invitation included him, "Let me get Sherry, and we will be up. You remember her, don't you Grace?"

The suite in which Grace was staying was spacious and elaborate. She directed Travis to the shower and linens in the bath and left him to clean up. The magnificent beds were clothed in silk, the towels were fluffy and extremely white, both exemplifying the hotel's extravagance.

Dried and comfortable in the oversize robe, Travis followed her directions to bring his suit to be cleaned. She had already called someone to bring some food up, while she sent the suit to the cleaners with the bellboy.

He promised to have it returned in a couple of hours.

Coming out of the room, Travis confessed, "This reminds me of your sweet sixteen party, when I jumped in the pool and lost my trunks. It was the most embarrassing thing in the world."

"I did not look, I promise. I felt so sorry for you. I had never seen you turn that red before."

Roger and Sherry arrived while she was in the shower. Grace slipped into her nightwear of gray sweat pants and a white T-shirt, and returned in the midst of Roger demonstrating very figuratively some story. He was the type to dominate the conversation.

"Don't you remember that, Grace?" he asked without taking a breath.

She smiled the smile that meant she was enduring some aggravation, "What should I remember?"

"I was just telling them of the time you fell out of that tree when you were a kid. You came to school the next day looking like you hit every limb on the way down. You remember that, don't you? Ed Thomas made faces at you. I will swear you were the clumsiest kid I knew."

Another smile was forced, "No, I am afraid I do not

recall that incident."

"Sure you do. It was the same day Lance Holbert and I stuffed you in Coach Jones's duffle bag and threw you in his trunk," he laughed and poked his date's leg. "She was so little, we actually stuck her in a lot of places. Anyway, old coach did not find her until he got home."

Travis noticed Grace's expression changed. She no longer was smiling nor looking at their friend. Instead, her gaze was directed at the floor. He placed a protective hand on her tightly clenched ones. "Frankly Roger, I think that was a cruel prank. She could have died."

"Oh no. Lance and I did not zip the bag up all the way. Besides, Grace was a trooper. She was a tomboy. She would never rat us out. Isn't that right, Grace?"

"Would you like some more coffee?" With trembling hands steadied, Grace poured more into his upheld cup. "How is your mother, Roger?"

The old trickster couldn't understand Grace's reaction. Her voice wavered almost tearfully. In the good old days, she would never have cried. She had always laughed off all the pranks and clumsy accidents.

Maybe age matured her too much. There was something different in her voice now. Maybe his fun at her expense was more than he had anticipated. These thoughts were pondered over while Grace excused herself to respond to the ringing telephone in another room.

"Excuse me, please," requested the hostess.

"She hasn't changed much," Sherry stated. "She always was an odd girl, but she seemed real nice. For some reason, she disappeared our senior year. There were rumors about her leaving, because she was pregnant or something."

"She was not pregnant!" Travis boomed, "and Roger, your pranks were just cruel bullying. You two boys should have been ashamed of yourselves."

A much more subdued Roger mumble to himself, "Trust me, I am starting to think along those same lines." Out loud, he continued, "Hey Travis, how come Grace left home? I mean when we went to elementary school, she lived with her folks, but when we were in high school, she lived with her uncle."

"Quite frankly, I am not sure," he shrugged. "I

figured you would know that, Roger. You have known her since childhood."

"You know that is the funny part. I don't recall Grace ever mentioning it to me."

Travis was thinking aloud. "The subject was broached a couple of times, but she never gave me a straight answer."

"Someone else told me she was in some sort of mental institution," interpolated Sherry.

The two men stared in unbelief at the girl's ignorance. Roger suddenly became embarrassed over having brought this creature into the picture. He made his excuses after Grace came back in to take his leave. His gracious hostess allowed him the forgiveness necessary to leave with dignity.

Travis was too humiliated in the robe; therefore he remained seated while Grace walked the guests to the door. Roger sent Sherry on to the elevators.

"I will be there in a minute," he called after her. He gave his old friend a kiss on the head, along with a brotherly hug. Grace thought this was so unlike his character. "Grace, I am sorry for all the mean things we did to you. It was not until this very day that I realized our pranks were only fun in our imaginations."

Grace rewarded his kiss with her own, placed on his cheek. Her natural voice was sweet and gentle. "Think no more of it old friend. It is water passed under the bridge and forgotten. You never meant any harm."

"Will you answer me a question, Grace?"

"Sure, if I can."

"Why did you never tell me?"

Revealing Grace

"Tell you what?" she asked innocently.

"Do not play games with me, Grace. I told you, I figured it out a few minutes ago. I may be an idiot, but you are not."

"I still don't understand."

This time he became forceful. He pulled her chin up, trying to gain focus of her averting eyes. "Grace, I have known you since we were five. You have never lied to me, that is, I never thought you had."

As much as she tried, her eyes could not look into his very long. The eyes were the windows to the soul, and he had no right to hers.

23

He continued, "It is ironic how you fell out of that tree the exact same day we put you in Coach Jones's trunk." He paused to examine her reaction to his words. "There was no tree, was there? That is why you left home, is it not?"

"Now Roger, your date is waiting, and you should not keep her."

"What about that time we threw you in Morgan's lake in February? The next day you came to school busted up, saying you ran through a sliding glass door." He waited, once again, for a response, but she only glanced over his shoulder, hoping no one else was hearing his words. "Or, what about the time we put that snake in your pocket? You tore your dress trying to climb out of it. The next day, do you remember what happened?" She shook her head no. "That was the day you were kicked by the horse. You came to school the very next day sporting a black eye. You know what I find odd? Once I put two and two together, it appears that every time Lance and I played a prank on you, you would get hurt somehow. My question is how? Do not ask me to believe any bologna about kicking horses or tree limbs."

24

"Roger, we have been friends almost our entire lives. If you value our friendship at all, please do not do this. Go home. Live your life. You are talking ancient history. I love you no less."

He acted upon two steps, and then turned with one final question. "Grace, why didn't you tell us? We would have stopped."

"Your date is waiting, Roger." She was fighting back the tears, now.

"You could have told on us many times over, but you never did. Why?"

"There was no point in anyone else being punished for it, so why bother?" She, once again, was the recipient of a hug.

"Goodbye Grace. Don't stay gone so long this time."

Travis had watched the graceful moves from the couch. She would shift from one foot to the other, nervously. A twinge of jealousy swept over him, when Roger hugged her. Roger and Grace shared a lifetime of memories that he was not privy to. This made him the outsider.

Upon her reentering the room, Travis stood to greet

her, "How come you look as if you walked off the pages of my yearbook, while I have aged right along with everyone in our class?" He pulled her to him, once they were on the couch again. She was the type of lady that never grinned. Most of her smiles were brilliant, charming, even mesmerizing, sometimes, giving her the ability to entice the receiver. Right now, he was the receiver. "You astound me. I just cannot get over it."

"You are emphasizing this too much. Trust me, I have aged."

"May I call on you tomorrow, take you home to see Renee and meet my daughter, Wendy?"

Soon they were deep in bridging the years that had passed between them. It was during this time of reuniting in which Travis explained how his wife, Linda, had died a lonely death; because he could never love her the way he did Grace. The story was hard to tell. The guilt consumed him. It chipped away at his pride to reveal his shame before this pure woman, yet he wanted her to know everything.

"I can't believe you never married," Travis seemed surprised.

"I knew I could never be faithful to another in my heart. It would not be fair to marry one you could not love."

The humiliation bestowed upon the unfaithful lover was unintentional on the Irish beauty's part. She would not have hurt him for the world. His shame was self-inflicted. Here stood a woman who made an oath in her girlhood, to love him forever, and had maintained that oath for all these years. This was the girl everyone said did not know what love was. They said the two were too young and irresponsible to be in love. Well, they were right about him, but Grace had defied their best arguments. This admission, however embarrassing for her, endeared her to his heart even more. She was more than precious.

Her eyes penetrated the secret place he had hidden years ago from even his wife. He became vulnerable to her scrutiny. How could he take it slow, when she could read him like a book? He tried to look away, but her violets kept alluring him beyond his control.

"Grace, again, I am so sorry for having let you down. I have kicked myself for all these years. Tonight, talking to you, I can honestly declare that I am a fool. Had I ever dreamed you were waiting for me..."

"You would not have changed a thing," she finished. "I don't know, but maybe I am the foolish one. I have been in love with a memory of being in love for twenty years. In love with being in love, I guess. Maybe I am the foolish one for not letting go of what evidently was not meant to be. But, as it stands, I only had one shot at love, and I missed it. Like Paul said, I am content to wherewith I am. I am content to spent the remainder of my life as an old maid."

"I don't know who Paul is, but one thing is for sure, you are definitely not old. Who knows, there may still be a chance for you and I. You have never been far from my thoughts."

She looked down as if she were the one embarrassed this time. "You know, I never dated anyone else after you. Actually, I never dated anyone before you, but I am devoted to another Love. One in which I am not willing to compromise for anything. It is only fair to forewarn you. He runs my life, and I would not want to grieve Him in any way."

Hoping Grace

Accompanying a look of confusion was a fast falling spirit. Then she had met another. Where would that leave him? "Is it anyone I know?"

"I do not know. You tell me. Do you know my Lord and Savior, Jesus Christ? Are you saved by His wonderful grace?"

"Oh, that," he sighed relief. "Yeah. Who doesn't?"

"A lot of people. More people are not saved than people that are."

Figuring she would get better results by taking it easy on the topic, Grace dropped it for the time being. They sat reminiscing through the night hours and into the morning ones. A kindled flame sparked once more.

Travis tarried his leaving until he caught Grace's eyelids drooping over the violet color, even long after he had his clothes returned to him. He did not want the night to end. Before leaving, Travis finalized the arrangements to come for her in the morning. Renee would kill him if he had this opportunity and did not bring her home. His sister and Grace had been very close while they were kids. This parting was easier than the one twenty years ago.

Travis did not see his sister when he got home. She knew it was rare for her brother to ever stay out this late, so she fell asleep on the couch waiting for him. He covered her up and peeked in on his sleeping daughter, before retiring to his own room. It was morning when he excitedly told Renee of his evening before. During his trip to pick up the long lost friend, Renee readied the house, as well as herself, while Wendy made an excuse to be indolent for the day.

The suitor wore his usual jeans and a T-shirt. He was not going to dress fancy just to go back to the posh inn. Grace loved him before when he wore this. He would not put on pretenses now.

Much to his disappointment there was no answer to his knock. Maybe she was out for a walk. He would check the front desk for any messages. He descended the stairs slowly, but the clerk behind the desk informed him that Grace had checked out early that morning. The broken man turned. How could she leave, knowing how he felt about her?

"Excuse me sir," called the clerk, "Is your name

Travis Winston, by any chance?"

"Yes, I am Travis Winston," he returned.

"She did leave this for you." She handed Travis an envelope bearing his name, written in her graceful pen.

"Thank you." He received the envelope, but could not bring himself to open it quite yet. He proceeded to his car, where he sat, fumbling the envelope in his hands, until he worked enough courage to read the words.

My old dear friend,

Forgive me for leaving this way. Duty called me home. I probably should never have come in the first place. Class reunions never appealed to me. Those people did not like me twenty years ago, why should they like me any better today?

Please send my love to Renee and your daughter. Tell Renee we will catch up on the next trip. I am truly sad I was unable to see her again. Maybe I could convince her to come for a visit one day.

I hope you understand what I am going to say next. I

forgave you for not coming that night years ago, so please do not think this has anything to do with that. I have spent my entire life loving one person. One thing I am sure about is my feelings for you. You, on the other hand, have had the opportunity to love another in my stead. I do not begrudge you that love. I know you loved Linda, as you should have. She is the mother of your precious child, and for that I may be slightly jealous, for I probably shall never have children of my own. But that jealousy is toward all women who bear children, not just Linda.

I do not know if there is a possibility of a you and me. I need to know, beyond any shadow of a doubt, that this love you say you have for me is not nostalgia come to deceive you into feeling something that is no longer real. That is why I must know, beyond a shadow of a doubt, that what you say is real.

I will be praying for God's will to be done in our lives, whether it be our desires or not.

Grace

As he read these words, a candy apple red Mustang was flying across the miles with equally red curls blowing their defiance in the wind. The driver sped along with a solemn prayer in her heart.

Explaining Grace

Renee gleefully awaited their return. It had been twenty years since she had seen her old best friend. Grace had disappeared one day without word. Her aunt had been scarce with explanations. Renee had tried to call several weeks after Grace left, but Claudia rudely asked her to not call anymore. She did not approve of Grace's friendship with her.

Years later, Grace had sent flowers when their mother died, but Renee was not able to send her thanks, because she did not know where to find Grace. She seemed to stay ascetic by choice. She could not figure out why her old best friend had chosen exile without her. The years had been lonely without Grace, because she and Renee had a secret bond that would stand against the sands of time.

She ran to greet her brother and long lost friend as soon as she heard the car pull up, but stopped post haste on the porch, when she saw her brother was alone in the car. Perhaps she was following in her car. Yet, no car came in the drive.

Travis stormed by her, throwing her a, "She is not

coming," at her.

"What do you mean? Did she change her mind?" Renee asked following him into the house.

She knew better than to say too much. Her brother had a temper. So when he pouted, she did not push it. "All I know is, she checked out this morning. I am going to the garden. I will be late getting in, so do not wait supper for me."

Presently he emerged from his room in overalls and a ball cap. His destroyed heart could not face the interrogation from his sister. How could he explain why Grace ran off, when he did not even know why? He had his own reasoning: She was still angry with him for not keeping his promise, she hated him for standing her up, she lied when she said she was not in love with someone else, or even she simply could not bear the horrible deeds he had admitted to doing. None of which could soothe the treason of his heart.

True to his word, he did not return till way after dark, when he went directly to bed after a shower.

Renee contemplated what could have happened to Grace. Travis said she had never married. Could she have a boyfriend? That would be understandable. Curiosity filled her mind. Dating back twenty years ago, when Grace just vanished without a trace, the inquisitiveness had begun and grown. Now, with the latest events, the plot twisted even more. Was there more than her brother was telling? Had he done something years ago that would cause her to seek revenge on his vulnerability?

While she was gathering up his clothes to wash, a long envelope fell from his shirt pocket. She recognized the feminine writing. It was from Grace. Should she dare read it? No. That would not be ethical. That piece of paper tortured her for three days, taunting and tempting, challenging her will to withstand. In the end, she succeeded in holding out.

Renee was not the only one that paper taunted. Travis would read it when he woke up in the morning and before he went to sleep at night. He even slept with it crinkling softly under his pillow. He could not bring himself to believe that the Grace he knew and had fallen so hard for could ever be vindictive. No matter how many years passed, she could never have become hurtful. But, then why did she do this to him?

Before long, he began hating himself for having been so stupid as to get drunk that night so long ago. His father had died a drunk. He remembered many nights, when Renee was too little to remember, when his dad would go out every night, while his dear mother cried. He knew his dad had taken the grocery money or bill money to get drunk on. Most of all, he remembered the drunken salivating breath. The putrid stench had never left his memory, causing him to commit his life to never drinking.

Then, one day, in his finest hour yet, he partook of the vile drink, not one or two, but so many that he lost count. Yes, it is true, he did not remember meeting Linda or anything about her, but what he did remember was the sickness that overwhelmed him. The stammering, staggering idiot his father had been had now come home to roost. The horror of that night, along with the repercussions of his dreadful act while under the influence, broke Travis Winston's desire to ever drink again.

How could he blame Grace for hating him? He hated

him. It was not enough that he did not meet her when he promised he would, but now, she knew his dirty little secret. He spent years married to a woman he never could have loved. He always treated Linda well, but he never treated her the way he should. He had spent years withdrawing from his relationship with his wife, because of his distaste for her manipulating and conniving. At last, it dawned on him that she only reacted to his actions. He was the one who caused the trouble. Maybe that was why Grace left. She was not stupid. She could see that he was in a loveless marriage and did not take his responsibilities serious. She was right; after all, he was no man. He was just a coward, which treated his wife and daughter despicably.

Travis was working late at his job and garden, plus skipping meals. Renee worried over her brother's reclusive lifestyle. She watched without saying a word. She was privy to his behavior, and he had never reacted this way, except when he could not find Grace after returning from Wilmington.

"Travis, what happened between you and Grace? You were so excited to see her Saturday, yet she was gone when you got there. Did you say something to scare her away?" she asked, when she could no longer take the not knowing and silence.

He shook his head, "I honestly do not know. Renee, everything was good Friday night. We talked a lot of things through that needed straightening. Least ways, I thought we did."

"Did she say she would definitely come with you Saturday, or did you just assume it?"

"I did not assume anything. We talked about it for thirty minutes, making arrangements and all."

"And she left without word? Have you called her?"

"No. I do not even know her number. Besides, I am not sure she wants to hear from me."

"Why in the world would she not want to hear from you? I think you are overreacting. Where does she live? It should not be too hard to find her number from information."

The brother walked away from her to his room without answering. She heard him call to her behind the wall. "This is why I do not think she wants to hear from me." The voice grew louder as he came back in the same room. "She did leave word. She left this for me at the front desk. Read it and you will see what I mean."

Chancing Grace

The sister took the envelope that had tempted her for three days now. A smile crossed her lips as she read the words. "She left because an emergency at home came up. How did you come up with the idea she does not want to see you? It had nothing to do with you at all."

"That last part sounded like that to me. She hates me for getting married."

"Travis, you are crazy. She does not say that. She may be sad that Linda had the better part of you, but she does not hate you. She simply says that she needs reassurance. It sounds to me like she does not want to walk back into a relationship if you are not at the same point as she is. She has forsaken all others for twenty years because of her love for you. Can you honestly say you feel the same way? There is nothing wrong with her needing to know that. I actually admire her for it. I wish I had the gumption to follow in her footsteps. Maybe then I would not be a divorcee."

"I do feel that way about her. I always have." His response was angry.

Renee laughed, "Then prove it."

"How?"

"I guess that is for you to figure out, dear brother. It is up to you. She wants you to throw caution to the wind, come up with some original scheme, and wow the socks off her. How badly do you want to prove this point to Grace?"

Travis looked stupidly at his sister, "Renee, you have known me all your life. Have you ever known me to be creative or romantic?"

She responded by patting his shoulder. "That is the good thing about having me for your sister. You could not send her flowers. That is not original. You could...no, that would not work."

"Face it sis, I can do nothing to prove myself. She should not have asked that of me."

"I have it!" Renee snapped her fingers as she shouted gleefully. "Why do you not go see her?"

"What?"

"It is perfect. Take next week off and fly out there. You have another week's vacation due you. Go to her. What better way to prove it? Find out if you two are even compatible with each other. Not knowing where she lives is the challenge. It just depends on how badly you want it."

"The reunion committee reached her. Could I find out from them?"

"Ooh. That is a good idea. See, you are more creative than you gave yourself credit for." The wheels in Renee's head were turning fast. "I have my yearbook from her senior year. I know she is not in it, but we could see who the class officers for her grade were that year. It would not hurt to try."

Travis frowned, "I could call Roger, if all else fails, but I really do not want to do that."

The plotting continued until carefully laid plans were completed. Travis was not able to secure the week off on such short notice, but his boss allowed him the following week after that, if no one else was signed up for that particular week. Indeed, no one had.

Travis planned to leave on the next Friday afternoon's flight to Oregon. He would spend the entire week with Grace, if she would allow him the pleasure, then return the following second Sunday. Renee threw in some of her savings for airfare. The only thing left to do was get the pertinent information from the reunion committee. As each day passed without word from Margie Simpkins, the class president, Travis thought more and more of employing Roger's help.

He spent the weekend in anticipation. At least through the week he had his job to keep his mind preoccupied and to settle his nerves, but the weekend seemed endless. The more he thought about it, the more he realized this was a bad idea. Should he call her? If she did not want him to come, she should have the opportunity to ask him not to come. They were not teenagers anymore. He should not act like an adolescent. Maybe he should just forget the whole thing. But, her kiss could not lie. Teenagers or not, it was worth the risk to see her again. Maybe the years had passed, but Grace was the same. She had not aged one bit. She seemed more established, if that was possible, than she did as a teenager. The constant flip-flopping in his mind was enough for him to change it several times. If it were not for his sister's constant encouragement, he would have backed out in the end.

Fortunately, Margie did call him back. On Thursday

of the first week, she left a message with Renee. She also left distinct instructions that no one was to ever find out who they got her address from. She would not want to be exposed for giving out private information. Travis, however, had pulled at her heart's strings with his sweet sentiments so that she could not refuse his request.

Wendy was the only hindrance to the upcoming trip. She made it known very clearly that she was not happy about her dad chasing after some trollop for a week, making a complete fool out of himself. In her heart, she hated Grace. Her mother had always told her about the other woman, the woman that dad would rather have married. She would simply not have anything to do with this woman if he did marry her. Dad would see how much she hated the woman and never marry her.

Renee loved Grace and sang her praises over the years. Wendy remembered as a child, her aunt would tell her about the beautiful red hair that attracted more boys than she knew what to do with. She shared antidotes of courage that caused Wendy to fantasize that Grace was this beautiful fairy-like creature that captured the hearts of all the young men. Renee had even shown her a picture of the best friend. Wendy thought she was the most incredible person in the world. That is, until the day her mom caught her pretending to be Grace. Her mother saw the picture on the dresser, which her daughter was mimicking and fell into a tirade. When Linda accused her daughter of betrayal, she explained how that was the woman that tried to destroy their family. She told Wendy how daddy could never love either one of them as he did that woman. She was a shameless harlot who did not care that she was a home wrecker.

Wendy learned fast how to hate Aunt Renee's dearest friend; therefore, when the aunt asked about her hostility toward her father's trip, she could not tell Renee her true feelings. A couple of times, she thought her plan had worked. Her dad acted as if he had changed his mind about going, then Aunt Renee would change it back.

Chasing Grace

Another exhausting day had passed and Grace came home late, as she often did. The old Mustang seemed to have leapt up the driveway in approval of being home. Samson ran the length of the fence, whinnying to his mistress to pay him some attention. Ginger followed close behind, thinking to get in on the action if Samson succeeded.

The beautiful old house appeared to have been abandoned. No lights were on inside. Grace thought she might have heard Isaiah out in the barn. She assumed Ruth must have gone to the store, because it did not look as though any living person were there.

Grace walked along the fence, patting Samson's shiny coat, as she walked to the mailbox. "Samson, how about a ride in a little while? Would you like a good work out?"

He snorted and shook his head as if he were affirming her question.

She retrieved her briefcase from the back seat of the Mustang on her way in the house. The late afternoon shadows played a foreboding drama across the old wooden floor. She did not even bother to turn the light on in the darkened room. She slipped her shoes off at the door so that her stature shrank an inch. Laying her keys on the table near the door, along with her briefcase, she filtered through the mail in her hands. One in particular, she handled more than the others.

"Ruth, I am home!" She called to an empty kitchen. Her melodious voice echoed in the abysmal void. She dislodged the pins that held the curls in place contrary to the wind blowing through it just a few minutes earlier.

She still studied the piece of mail in her hand, when suddenly a screaming ring sounded throughout the empty house, startling the woman. "I will get it, Ruth," then she laughed. "Talk to yourself much Grace?" She lifted the receiver, giving the traditional, "Hello."

"Grace, I am glad I caught you. You are not going to believe this," came the voice on the other end.

"What is it Stephanie?" her voice changed quickly.

"You are not going to like it either. James left with Amy's dad thirty seconds ago to pick her up. James kept on until he procured permission today."

"What judge is on?"

Stephanie returned, "Moore."

"Meet me in his office in ten minutes. Start on a restraining order. I will bring what we need for proof. I do not need to tell you how fast we need that document. I am on my way." She quickly pressed the button to reset the phone and dialed a set of numbers. "Melinda, do me a favor, please. Get Amy out of there NOW. Do not worry about her things. Hang up, get her in the car, and drive her to my house. Ruth and Isaiah will know what to do from there. Leave now. Please, hurry. Goodbye."

"We are out the door, Grace. Call me if you need me." She, too, ended the connection.

Grace grabbed her briefcase and keys in one swift movement, forgetting to replace the shoes on her feet. Raising her voice louder, turning toward the kitchen, she yelled. "Ruth? Isaiah?" She ran to the kitchen, but no one was there. She could not spare a minute. "Please God, let them be here when Melinda gets here." She prayed aloud.

She raced back through the living room to leave. She stopped short, having sensed the presence of another being, sitting in the shadows, heretofore unseen.

"I have to go. It is important. You may come with me if you like."

No words were spoken as the two ran to the Mustang and sped down the drive. Before they were a mile out of the driveway, the car phone rang.

"Yes?" Grace answered it.

"Lamby, I was in the springhouse. I thought I heard your voice. Where are you?"

"I have to run back to town. Ruth, Melinda is bringing a little girl over. As soon as she gets there, code green. Lock the security behind Melinda. I will see you when I can."

"Gotcha," the Scotswoman replied.

Grace replaced the receiver, and then smiled at her companion with the charm of an angel. "I am glad you are here."

Timeless Grace

Travis sighed his relief inaudibly. She was glad, then. He had feared she would be angry with him for coming unannounced, but she was glad. All the fear and insecurities of the past week fled. She was genuinely glad he was there.

The twenty-minute ride took only eleven minutes. The Mustang almost ran the familiar course on its own. Travis was not sure what crisis he had walked in on, but he was content to be in her good graces. No other words were spoken on the journey. Grace felt inside her briefcase, until her hands clasped the object for which she was looking.

Grace did not even wait for the car to come to a complete stop at the courthouse. She ran up the stairs two at a time. Time was of the essence. Good ole Stephanie was already in Moore's chambers doing her best without being asked.

Moore looked from his desk solemnly, "Grace, why should I restrict this father from his daughter? The mother promises to keep an eye on everything. Tell me why I should stop a father from being with his child."

"If you will listen to this recording of my interview with Amy, you will see why, sir. It contains pertinent information concerning this case. Trust me, if you heard it, you would not let that man alone with his daughter again." Grace laid the tape that she brought from her briefcase on the table.

After listening to a portion of the tape, the judge granted the restraining order. It was unusual for a judge to issue forth one document, only to issue forth a contradiction within the hour, but he had no choice in this case.

"Thank you Judge. You are not mistaken on this one."

"I know. I never miss when you are on the case," he smiled.

Grace expressed her urgency. "Stephanie, how long will it take you to file this with the magistrate?"

"About thirty minutes," she answered.

"If you can speed it up any, I would appreciate it. Can you bring it by my place as soon as you can get it in your hands?"

"I will sprout wings, Grace," Stephanie laughed.

She was the lawyer that worked for Grace's foundation. She had put in as many overtime hours as Grace had for the foundation. Stephanie was not rich, because most of the time she did not get paid much. Jameston Industries paid her a salary for the defense work that went through Grace's office, but comparably it was not much. She was a trustworthy attorney and loyal friend whom Grace depended on.

Grace returned to her car where Travis was waiting patiently for her. Still, she offered no explanation for the bizarre events going on.

The trip home was equally as fast as the trip from home. A large metal gate closed the passage to the driveway. Grace pressed buttons on the pad and immediately the gates swung open. Quickly, she ran back to shut them and secure them once again.

There was no sign of living beings in the house, save for Travis and Grace. To come in, one could not find one sign of the feast Ruth had been preparing forty-five minutes ago. The heat from the eye of the stove had even turned stone cold.

Without explanation, Grace went into her bedroom. She returned in less than a minute in a white T-shirt and gray sweat pants. She unlocked her gun cabinet and carefully pulled out a shotgun. In the drawer below, she pulled out two cartridges and placed them in the weapon. Before she could snap the barrel shut, a buzzing sound came from the wall over the phone.

"Who is it?" She asked sweetly, while pressing a button.

"Grace, this is Deputy Rollins. I need you to open the gates."

"I will be there in a minute Gary."

"Thanks, Grace."

Grace turned to Travis, "I'll be back."

Travis was not about to let Grace face trouble alone. "I am coming along, if you do not mind."

Grace said neither, "yes" or "no". She strolled as if she had all the time in the world, talking to Samson as she went. He was snorting his disapproval at the intruders. Grace approached the posse at the gate with her shotgun posing on her shoulder. Not one ounce of fear could be found in her fiery eyes.

The deputy sheriff had been to Grace's house several times before on similar errands. He was not afraid of Grace. As a matter of fact, he admired what she had done in their community. He knew that if Grace was against this man, then the man was guilty. She had yet to miss her mark.

His co-workers felt the same as he did about Grace. Five others had escorted Samuels and Nicholson to her home. That was all the back up they would need.

"Miss Sorenson," he explained in an unbiased fashion, "Jeff Samuels claims you have kidnapped his daughter. I am afraid I must ask you to let my deputies in to search for her."

"And I am afraid that I must ask you for a search warrant," she replied coolly.

"Gra…Miss Sorenson, I can get one if I must, but I wish you would comply."

"I will be more than happy to, right after I have my hands on the search warrant. I am sorry Gary, but you have no right or reason to rifle through and destroy my place for the likes of that creature."

Grace motioned toward the scoundrel. She ignored the cursing that proceeded forth from his mouth. His commands to arrest her were refused. He grew angrier as each minute passed.

Gary Rollins held his arm in front of Jeff Samuels to hold him back. "Mr. Samuels, we have no legal right to bust up her place. She is right. We cannot force our way in without a warrant. Just settle down. We will get your daughter back, but we will do it the legal way."

Another stream of filth heaved forth from his vile mouth. It was James Nicholson that spoke next. "We will have a search warrant here in the next half hour. We will just bide our time, Mr. Samuels." Then he turned to Grace. "Why do you want to make this hard on yourself? Just let us in for a quick look, and then we will go. What have you to hide?"

The fire in the red head's eyes was rekindled. "James, have you no decency in your whole being? How can you defend a creature that is lower than a snake's belly?"

"I am just doing my job, Grace," he retaliated.

"Then I would seriously consider a new line of work. I do not see how you can sleep at night."

Samuels became irritably violent. He stepped forward. If he could have reached Grace through the gate, he would have strangled her without concern for the witnesses. Grace's response was simply to chamber her trusty companion, which she did with one graceful move of her right arm. The shotgun clicked, reminding the man of his mortality. This was enough to subdue him for the time being.

It had come down to being a race between good and evil. Whichever legal document reached her front gate first would be the winner. Once that paper was in hand, Grace would be forced to let them search for Amy. On the other hand, if Stephanie could only get the restraint, they would have no option but to leave. She was not worried about them finding the child, for she was in a place so secure, a king's army could never find them. It was a matter of teaching this beast he could not implement such abominations on a lesser being without the just judgment of an almighty Judge.

As in any situation, Good will always conquer evil. In the end, it was Stephanie who pulled up in front of the posse first with the restraining order.

She was completely out of breath. "Deputy, I have a restraining order in my hand against Mr. Samuels, here. He is to be no less than five hundred feet from his daughter, Amy. It is time you fellows headed home. Leave Grace to her company." She smiled at Travis.

Samuels lunged at the lawyer. A sharp loud crack

echoed through the night, which stopped the man dead in his tracks.

"I have exactly one more shot, Mr. Samuels." Grace glared him down. "Now, I suggest if you do not want it between your eyes, you leave my property now." He hesitated, but acted as if he did not believe her. "If you think I cannot put it there, you better ask yourself if you are willing to bet your life on it."

"It's alright, Grace. We'll be leaving," Rollins stated. He shooed them all as if he were a mother hen gathering her chicks.

Stephanie was the first to leave. It took her a matter of seconds to hop in her car and get out of this creep's way. Grace watched to make sure every vehicle had vacated before turning toward the house. But, Grace moved not toward the house, but instead, she sauntered to the barn. She placed the shotgun butt end up against the wall of the barn in case she needed to take hold quickly.

Silencing Grace

After about an hour's worth of exercising Samson and Ginger and another half-hour grooming them, Grace fed all the animals. Samson snorted his disapproval at the newcomer. He did not like anyone who would take any of her attention from him. Grace helped birth Samson into the world, and he was very jealous of any other beast, human or not, that demanded Grace. He refused to even nibble the sugar cube, which Grace gave Travis to feed him. He could not be bought for any price.

Not short of two hours had gone by, and Grace made no attempt to explain anything to her guest or to find the now infamous Amy. Upon completion of chores, Grace gathered the gun and headed toward the house where she unloaded the chamber and carefully locked both cartridge and weapon safely away. She tried to work out some sort of sleeping arrangement, but Travis contrarily refused to take her bed. He insisted on sleeping on the couch instead of Grace. She gave him the upstairs room, which was used as the piano and sewing room to unpack and store his belongings. She could not very well move the piano, but she offered to clean the rest out, but he refused.

"The couch is perfect," he assured.

"If I had known you were coming, I would have made a room for you. As it is, Amy will be taking the spare bedroom. The fourth bedroom is Ruth and Isaiah's. I will be more than happy, though, to donate mine to you. Quite frankly, the couch is very comfortable," the hostess offered.

"You will do no such a thing. I told you the couch was perfect. I should not have dropped in on you unexpected," confirmed the guest.

"Then that is settled." Grace would have left him to unpack only he was not about to leave her side. He meant to find out what was going on. From the living room, she went through the kitchen and into another room adjacent to the spare bedroom, except it was separated by the stairs. It had a desk neatly kept, with a computer and several aiding contraptions for an office. A set of windows was on each outside wall. One set looked upon the barn, while the other looked over a large yard, then beyond that a vast woods as far as one could see.

Travis drank in the warmth this old house emitted. It had a homey feeling within its walls. A fireplace on the wall adjacent to the spare bedroom was made of beautiful flat stone. The spare room housed a duplicate fireplace in it as well. Strangely, Grace walked to the right side of the fireplace, put her hand to it, and then she walked into the fireplace, logs and all. To his surprise, the back of the stone wall open at her touch.

She explained, "If ever, when you are here, and anyone tells you 'code green', you are to take any children on the premises and bring them in here. No one knows this room exists, except the people in this house. There is enough food down here to last a month. There are full facilities, such as a kitchenette, bathroom, and beds. You must stay down there until it is safe. It is imperative that no one ever find out this secret. Take along with you any sign of a child having been here. They cannot take what they do not know is here. The lives of these children depend upon fast secretive action. I will come and get you whenever it is safe again."
Grace allowed Travis to assist her down the small stairs,

which were underneath the other stairs. "Ruth, Isaiah," she called.

A small golden blond child came around the corner and leapt into Grace's arms. "Is it all better now?" She asked as if she were an adult, instead of a seven-year-old child.

"Sure is, sweetie." Grace pulled the child close to her bosom.

"Lamby, they didn't hurt you, did they?" A pleasant sounding woman came into view. Travis could not see much in the dimly lit corridor. "Come, I'll finish souper."

Once they had come back out of the dark way and Grace had replaced the back wall, she introduced her old friend. "Travis Winston, this is Ruth and Isaiah. They take care of me. Quite frankly, I would be starving and insane if it were not for them." She lifted Amy's head that was hiding shyly in her breast. "And this is Amy. She is going to stay with us for a few days."

Travis felt the scrutiny of Isaiah's silent inspection. Could he measure up to this man's standards? To break the ice, he challenged the girl first, "Hi Amy. I am glad you are staying for a few days. I am too," he looked at Grace, feeling the piercing eyes of the two elders. "That is, if Grace does not mind."

He could not help but to search for approval from the kindly Scotswoman. Ruth was day and night different than Isaiah. She did not mind offering her opinion on any matter before her, whereas Isaiah rarely spoke a word. Even then, it was never to advise or give opinion. He would make one pull the answer from within himself. We all know what is best for us without someone telling, we just have to trust ourselves to find it.

Another difference between them was Ruth had not educated her tongue in the English way. She still spoke heavily with the Scottish burr. On the other hand, Isaiah enunciated his words carefully, speaking few and without much accent. On rare occasions, when he was upset or excited, he would slip up and slip into the native tongue.

"You are welcome as long as you like. Come on Ruth, I shall help you finish that meal. Isaiah, I fed all the animals and mucked the stalls. It is all finished,"

Grace smiled her charm and gave the tall lean man a kiss on the cheek.

"I need to start on the fence for that lower pasture," he said quietly. "I am going to go to town tomorrow to get the posts."

Ruth fussed lovingly with her husband, "Tonight, you'll make our yoong laddie welcome, won't you, Isaiah?"

He had no choice but to take Travis into the living room, where the two sat without much converse. By the time Grace had escorted her company to the living room, Ruth had already retrieved the meal she had previously begun. When the young woman returned, she was astonished at how Ruth had hidden any signs of cooking before the incident. Almost fully cooked was a ham, with beans and potatoes and carrots. The biscuits were already in the oven baking. When Ruth had time to make the dough was a mystery for Grace.

Ruth asked Isaiah to get a new jar of honey for the biscuits, so he went to the springhouse, where he stored the sweet nectar after robbing the hives of bees he raised.

After the blessing was asked upon their meal, Travis ate the best meal he had ever eaten. He was fuller than he had ever remembered being. He would have to get Ruth to teach Renee how to make biscuits like that. One thing about his sister; she was no cook.

Amy talked excitedly throughout the meal. She kept the conversation lively for everyone. The hour had drawn late and Ruth and Isaiah retired for the night. Grace insisted Amy take her bath and go to bed. She followed suit, and then Travis. Grace tucked Amy in the bed before showering, leaving her some time to reacquaint with her old friend.

While the guest was in the shower, Grace lit a fire in the fireplace in the living room, not so much because it was cold, but more for the comfort of staring into the flames until one was hypnotized.

The two settled on the floor in front of the fire to talk. Travis drank in the reflection of the fire as it caused the red curls to dance with each flicker. Her soft white hands clutched a chain nervously, which hung around her neck. For an instance, he remembered the sweet sixteen as he bid her goodbye. Her violet eyes twinkled merrily in rhythm with the flames. When she pulled her hair back in a band, he wished to take it down again, for he had never seen a lovelier picture before.

"Are you still glad I came?" He asked after watching her refined movements.

She smiled, and with a voice that was soft and gentle, she answered, "I would not have said it, if I hadn't meant it. I am not sure of how much time I will be able to spend with you. I can't leave my job, as you have seen today."

"Exactly what is your job?"

"We help children who have been taken from their homes. Our foundation places them, advocates for them, and tries to give them some level of sanity. We deal with children who have been abused. There are so many of them in the United States. It is a shame that we don't do more to stop it or to protect our little ones. They are defenseless and cannot fend for themselves."

"So you are a social worker?"

Grace shook her head, "No. A social worker does not have the freedom that I have. I have the opportunity to introduce these children to Christ Jesus. The parents know this up front. They would not call Stephanie, if they did not agree to the conditions. That is the only way I am able to help anyone."

"That is admirable," he complimented.

"We do not do it for the admiration. It is my job. I would rather not be admired for doing my job. It is no less than any responsible adult should do. You look at these beautiful children, such as Amy, and tell me you would do no less."

He shifted nervously, "I am afraid I would. I would not know the first thing to do to help them. Maybe you can educate me. How long have you been doing this?"

"Ever since I moved to Oregon. As a matter of fact, this is why I moved here. I adjured to several different large companies to set up a nonprofit organization to help these children. Mr. Jameston was pleased to take me up on the offer. He gave me a choice of where I wanted to live, and here I am. I suppose it is a boring story, yet, this is my life. I would not trade it for anything. We do not win them all, but when we do, it makes it all worthwhile."

"I do not think it is boring at all. Frankly, I think it is

incredible. I think you are incredible."

"Not very likely." Her head fell in humility.

A small voice, barely audible interrupted, "Grace, I'm scared. Can I sleep with you?"

"You sure can. Would you like to sit with us by the fire for a while?"

Amy sparkled, "Can I? You wouldn't care?" Grace nodded. "Oh goody!" She piled into Grace's outreached arms.

"Would you like some hot cocoa?"

"Oh boy! Would I? Can I please?"

"You sure may. Would you keep my guest company, until I return, please?"

The girl looked warily at Travis. She was not sure she should be left alone with him. Finally, she responded, when Grace was half way in the kitchen. "Yes ma'am."

Grace returned shortly with three steaming mugs of cocoa to find Amy had now piled her little self into Travis's lap. He was showing her some new trick. This made Grace feel secure. If Amy gave her approval, then she should not have to worry. He was safe.

They sat, drank cocoa, and talked as children having a sleepover, until after midnight. Grace watched Amy sparkle and twinkle all night. Her fair hair and blue eyes made her golden, thus Grace begun thinking of the girl as her golden child. For having gone through the horror in which she had gone through, Amy still had so much life and kindness inside. She bubbled with life; something Grace had taken for granted and lost years ago. It was renewing to watch Amy's animated converse.

"Well Amy, I am sure Travis is very tired. Did you know that the time is different by three hours where he lives than the time here?"

"No. What time is it there right now?" asked the curious child.

He looked at his watch. "Let me see. It is one thirty here, so it would be ten thirty at my house."

She giggled, "So we are actually going to bed early." She lit up as if a light bulb had lit in her head. "And then we can get up ten in the morning and really be getting up at seven."

"That is very good math, young lady, but for now, we

shall sleep." Grace turned to Travis. "Why don't you take my bed? Amy and I can crash right here in the floor. It will be a lot of fun. I promise it will be fun. We'll not be put out at all."

"Yea!" Amy cried.

"I cannot argue with you both. I shall take the bed and leave you lowly females to sleep on the hard floor," he laughed. "Good night you two."

"Good night," said Amy.

"I will be back in a moment, Amy. Let me show our guest where everything is."

She quickly, yet neatly, spread clean linens on the bed and pillows. She pulled some extra blankets from the closet shelf, along with extra pillows. Then she took the mugs to the kitchen and washed them.

"Come Amy, brush your teeth again."

"Aah, do I have to?"

"Yes ma'am. You had cocoa. If you do not brush your teeth, you will be sure to get a cavity."

"Okay," she sulked into her room.

Once all teeth were brushed and all were snuggled safe, Grace sighed a tired silent relief. She was worn to a frazzle. Her head had begun to ache. She was almost in the capacity of slumber, when she heard a tiny whisper.

"Grace, I don't want to go home again. I love my mommy, but I hate my daddy. My mommy says my daddy loves me and that I am wicked, because I lied on him. I don't want him to love me."

Amy's Grace

"I am certainly going to do everything in my power to prevent you from living with that man again, but I would like for you to understand something. The things your daddy does to you are not love. Love should never hurt you. A parent that loves their child is willing to lay down their life so that child does not hurt. A parent would sustain any adversary to protect that child. Love is not hurtful. It is good that you love your mother, but she is wrong. Do not feel you owe that man a thing." She kissed her golden head. "Sadly, I can make you no promises about going home. Sometimes, I have not the support necessary to protect all children."

The seven-year-old asked. "What do you mean, support?"

"By support, I mean evidence. It is utmost important that you give me anything you can remember, whether you think it is important or not. Sometimes, you may think something is not worth mentioning, but it is the little things that can make or break a case."

"Can I tell you now?"

Grace had done this long enough to know that when a

child was ready to talk, you do not throw away the opportunity. Her philosophy, and probably the reason she was so good at what she did, was that she would wait until the child was willing to talk about it.

"Now is good." Grace left the warm side of her bed partner.

"Where are you going?" asked the golden child.

Grace retrieved something from her briefcase and came straight back. "I was getting my tape recorder. I would like to record everything you tell me. If I miss something the first time, I would like to be able to go back and hear it again. This aids me more than any other instrument. Do you mind?"

"No. What do you want me to say?"

"Just a minute. Let me get this new tape in. There we go. Now, start with what you want to tell me, whether it is from the last thing you experienced to the first, or the first to the last. Anything you can remember will be most helpful. Like I said a minute ago, you may not think it is anything, but that wee bit of information can make or break a case."

Amy shared many things with Grace of the horrors

she had endured over the last years. Grace's heart broke as she listened to the vivid descriptions that no seven-year-old should ever have knowledge of. Then, anger consumed her. This was the one part of the job she had trouble with.

"Grace," Amy began timidly, "does it still hurt?"

Grace returned with a confused expression. "I beg your pardon?"

"I mean, will it always hurt this bad?"

"I do not understand what you mean."

Then Amy explained her question. "My dad told my mom that the only reason you were trying to destroy our family was because your daddy did mean things to you. He said you lied on your daddy like you made me lie on him."

"So that is what your dad said, huh?"

Amy continued, "But, I know it happened for real, and I was just wondering if it always hurt as bad as it does now."

"Well now, do not listen to everything you hear." Amy's reaction was one of disappointment. After witnessing the forlorn look, Grace pulled the child close and whispered. "It hurts no longer. Once I gave that burden to my heavenly Father, He took all my pain from me. It is a comfort to rest in His peace."

"I don't understand. I thought your father did those things to you."

"Not my earthly father, Amy. I have a heavenly Father. His name is Jesus. He lives in heaven. He willingly died for me that I might have everlasting life and be free from all my pain. Once I asked Him to enter into my heart, He washed away all my sins for good. He does not remember the wrong I have committed, whenever I ask Him to forgive me. In return, He covers me with His love which soothes away all my hurt."

"What does He look like?"

"I have never seen him."

It was Amy's turn to look confused. "Then, how do you know He is real?"

"Because, my dear, He lives inside of me. Faith is, believing without seeing. One day, I will see Him in all His glory. Until that time, I know He is real, because He talks to me, and He walks with me everywhere I go. He lives inside of my heart. Can you understand that?"

Amy nodded, "I think so. He sounds real nice, even if He isn't a real person."

"Oh, but He is. He is as real as you and I. He left heaven around two thousand years ago. When He left, He left as King of Glory. A King, who left His Home to come to earth as a lowly man, so that He may save a wretched sinner like myself. He lived as you and I live for about thirty-three years. Then, the time came for Him to be crucified. He let them hang Him on a tree until He died. Three days later, He came back to life. Forty days later, He ascended to heaven, where He now sits on the right hand of God, His father."

"Is that really true?" Amy asked in disbelief.

"Every word of it. We all have to make the choice of whether or not we believe and accept Him as our personal Savior before we die. Once we ask Him into our hearts, He feels every bit of pain we do. One day, He will come back to take all those who believe to heaven, where we shall live forever."

"Can I believe it?"

"It is your choice."

Amy sat quietly for a few minutes with her head

resting on Grace's lap. At first, Grace thought she might have fallen asleep. Then in a still small voice, Amy replied. "I see how much you believe in Him, Grace, but I don't understand how Someone that loves me could let me be hurt."

"And I cannot force you to believe. It is you that must come willingly, as He knocks at your heart's door. He will drag no one against his or her will. Maybe when you are older and fully understand it, you will ask my Savior into your heart."

Another five minutes of silence passed, then Grace heard the softest sniffles. Her hand instinctively caressed the golden head. She prayed in her heart for the angel child in her arms. Life could be cruel sometimes even for the most innocent.

"Grace," she whispered, "I don't want you to go to heaven without me. My grandmother told me about heaven. She's going there, and I want to go too."

Grace proceeded to show Amy the way to the old rugged cross. Before the new day dawned, Amy was born again. That night, her sleep was the most peaceful it had been in a long time.

Wavering Grace

The morning, however, came too soon for Grace Sorenson. She dragged her weary aching body out of the comfortable makeshift bed she and Amy were sharing and began her duties for the day. She ignored the aching in her brain which told her to sleep longer.

She had made arrangements earlier in the week to go fishing with Isaiah this morning. They usually left about five thirty, in order to catch a good amount. Isaiah had the forethought to see that his gear was prepared before the morning. For this reason, he caught over double what Grace did, because she spent the first twenty minutes preparing her line and pole.

Next, she made her way to the barn. Samson did not get ridden yesterday, so she would begin with that chore. He kicked and bucked like a wild yearling, because he was so pleased to have his mistress on his back once again. He was happy she had chosen to spend time with him, instead of the new guest.

The fresh air did not relieve the pounding in her skull. It throbbed with every stroke on Samson's shiny coat, and bending over to clean his hooves intensified the beat. However, she continued her duties oblivious to the sound of the bell beckoning all to come eat breakfast.

Before too long, Amy came bounding through the barn wanting to help Grace. Samson agreed to carry the light load, while he followed his mistress while she completed her chores.

The shrill ring of the phone in the barn could be heard from the pasture, but Grace did not hasten to answer it. She knew Ruth would answer it inside, but it was not to be ignored for very long. Shortly, the Scottish companion was heard coming across the yard, when Grace had finished putting the hay in the rack for the cows.

"Lamby, telephone. It is Stephanie," she called.

"Thank you, Ruth." She held the phone in one hand and shielded her eyes with the other. Ruth watched as the beloved pressed her temples with her thumb and forefinger. "Stephanie, is there any news about Amy?" She asked quietly so that Amy would not hear.

"I am afraid there is, but it is not good. Amy's grandfather found out what Jeff Daniels had done to Amy last night. He killed him."

Grace reeled in dizziness as a curtain of darkness fell over her. She slid to the ground in a heap.

Ruth retrieved the phone. "I'm sorry, boot Lamby will have to call you back later." With the click of the button, she ordered. "Land sakes, Laddie, you go get a cold cloth."

Samson sensed his master's need, and walked carefully with his load to the fallen woman. He gently folded his knees beneath him, allowing his passenger to dismount. He nudged Grace with his muzzle. "Put her on my back. I will carry her home." He was snorting. He looked at the Scottish woman for obedience. Amy panicked and ran after Travis. Neither understood what was happening.

Ruth caressed her charge's hair. "Coom on Lamby. We'll be getting you in bed. Wake oop and coom on. I knew you would have woon of these confounded things. You never learn, Lamby. You aren't superwoman. Here cooms the Laddie now."

Amy ran faster than the older man, so she arrived first with the cold cloth. Isaiah was not far behind. Ruth compressed it to the girl's head. It was not long before

Grace was reaching for her splitting skull again.

"Okay, Lamby, let's get you in the bed." Ruth was pulling her to her feet.

The migraines came randomly for Grace. They were excruciating to say the least. Grace refused to get medical diagnosis, accepting this as part of life. Lack of sleep would bring them on, so would stress, but the two together was a tremendous combination. The solution would be a darkened room with quiet rest.

Walking was not easy for Grace. She blindly allowed Ruth to lead her. Ruth understood that words were magnified in her Lamby's state and kept quiet. Amy, however, was not knowledgeable of this information, so she chattered frantically.

"What's wrong with her? Is she sick? Did I make her sick?" Ruth remained silent, but Isaiah pulled the golden girl back from the patient.

In his usual calm voice, he explained, "You did not make her sick. She gets bad headaches. If we keep quiet, she will get better quicker."

"I can do that," Amy whispered aloud.

When Travis reached Grace, he lifted her easily into

his arms and carried her. She moaned a few protests, but was rendered helpless. She allowed them to place her in her bed with the blinds pulled.

After making sure no one would reenter, Grace slipped quietly into the bathroom and soaked in a steaming bath. This usually relieved some stress. She slept in the tub, until the water turned cool. Much to her chagrin, Grace lost a valuable day. She had so many things to accomplish, and she did not have time for this stupid headache. Ruth brought in some aspirin on several occasions throughout the day, but it was too little too late.

Isaiah was convinced to put Travis to work in the field, when the Scottish couple was left to entertain the two visitors. The grass needed cutting for hay, and that was something he could do. In the kitchen, Amy was being taught to cook beans and potatoes with pork chops and spinach. Bread was made from scratch, which enthralled the seven-year-old. Neither minded Grace sleeping through the day. They would much rather have spent this time with her, but the elders kept them well occupied.

The day turned into night without Grace's knowledge. She slept straight through till Sunday morning. This Lord's Day was beautiful with a surprise summer rain, which replenished the greenery around the farm. Unfortunately, the hay field, which Travis cut yesterday, would now be used to straw the stalls. No one minded the rain.

Travis attended his first church service in many years. For Amy, this was a completely new experience. Christ used the preacher to reach places in both hearts. Amy had already prayed the sinner's prayer, and this sermon taught her the first steps of growing in salvation.

Isaiah treated the crowd with some homemade strawberry ice cream at dinner. Grace's headache had subsided, and the three younger people played all day. Grace tried to make Amy's last day the best. Somehow she would have to break the news to her about her dad; however, the woman did not want to break the news on the Lord's Day. She prayed that it would not hurt to wait another day.

Knowing Grace

"Would you like to keep the car today?" Grace asked Travis Monday morning.

"Can I not go to work with you?"

She laughed, "You would probably be bored senseless."

Travis's hand slid down her braid. "I would rather be bored senseless with you than spend a fun filled day without you."

"It may not all be fun. I have to break the news to Amy about her dad."

"What about her dad?" he frowned.

"Oh, I guess you do not know. When Amy's grandfather found out what he did to Amy, he went crazy and shot him. I am not sure of all the details myself, but I cannot put it off anymore."

"I am starving for Ruth's pancakes." Travis spied the golden child coming and changed the subject.

Grace picked up on it. "Our Ruth is the best cook in the world. I do not know what we would do without her. Good morning Amy. Hungry?"

"No," came the sad reply.

The caregiver knelt to Amy's level. "Why the sad face sour puss?" She hoped the girl had not heard the converse about her father.

With a pouting answer, she mumbled, "I don't want to go back to that group home. I love it here. Why can't I stay here? Did I do something wrong?"

"Oh Sweetie. You did nothing wrong. We made plans, when we got you on Friday. Until things get settled, you must go back there. You may be going home at some point soon. Would you like to go back home, again, if things were different?"

"No." Grace enveloped her in her arms and lifted her from her feet.

"Come on. Shall we go get some of Ruth's famous blueberry pancakes?"

Amy buried her head in Grace's shoulder. She did not eat a lot of breakfast. She gathered her meager wardrobe from the weekend. Grace's heart was breaking. How could she drop this other news on this sweet child? "Oh God, help her please. Give her strength, I pray."

Sunday's rain left a fresh smelling day ahead. They

let down the convertible top before leaving. Contrary to Amy's expectations, Grace did not drive to the home. Instead, she drove to the mall.

"What are we doing here?" asked Amy.

"Someone I know needs some new clothes. When she stayed at my house this weekend, I realized she did not have enough."

The girls shouted gleefully, "Me! You mean me? Do I get new clothes?"

"You sure do Sweetie. Ready to shop?"

"Yea! I've never been shopping before."

As usual, Amy walked between the two adults holding each hand. Grace made short work of getting the best bargains. She knew how to get more for less, because this was something she did often. Next, she bought some necessary utensils such as toothbrush, hairbrush, fingernail supplies, etc.

After a quick lunch, Grace's office was the next stop. She still had to break the bad news to Amy, and this would be the best place. The building was an old two-story office building that was built some thirty years ago. The bottom floor was not in use anymore, so it appeared spooky with the huge columns shadowing eerily. The old elevator creaked lazily under the strain of being pulled. There were two rooms on the top floor: an outer office that held dust from being neglected, and a private office that was specifically organized.

She explained, "I lost my secretary about a month ago. She ran off to get married and left me stranded. One of these days, I should take the time to hire someone else. If you will come in my office, we shall finish up and get you home."

"It smells old in here," stated the child.

"You think so? Well, you should smell the stairway. It is worse."

"Travis, can we go see the stairs?" she pleaded.

"Sure Squirt." She led him off by the hand to explore.

Grace pulled down her books in order to report her expenditures for the day. She was constantly praying for Guidance. She took this opportunity of privacy to return Stephanie's call. "Stephanie, can you give me any more information on Amy's grandfather?"

"Hey, are you feeling better?"

"Yes, much. Thanks for asking."

"Good. Listen, they have released him on bail. Trust me, it was not cheap. He is not a flight risk or anything, plus it was a crime of passion, so they agreed to let him out on his own recognizance. He is home with his wife."

"Do you have his number? It would make telling Amy a lot easier if he could help."

"Yeah, his name is Duncan. The number is 720-2287."

She repeated the numbers she had written down. "Thanks."

"Any time. If you need anything else, call me," offered the attorney.

"Will do." The conversation was completed just in time, for the duo returned as she hung up the receiver. "Travis, will you two run around the corner to the newsstand and get me a paper, please?"

"Sure. Glad to be of service madam," he laughed as they left.

Once again Grace reached for the phone and dialed. "Mr. Duncan, please. Thank you. Mr. Duncan?"

"This is Mr. Duncan."

"This is Grace Sorenson. I am working with Amy on her…"

"Did you say your name is Grace?" the grandfather interrupted.

"Yes sir."

Accommodating Grace

He did not give her the opportunity to continue. "I thank you for what you are doing for my granddaughter. You will never know how much it means to me that you got her away from him."

"Yes sir, but I must ask you a huge favor."

"Name it little lady."

"I have not had a chance to tell Amy about her dad. I was wondering if I might enlist your help. She could use an ally in the family right now. Her mother does not seem to be applying for that position. No offense, I know she is your daughter."

"She is no daughter of mine, letting that scum do that to her own little girl. I am at home if you want to bring her over now. I would appreciate the opportunity to tell her myself."

"Great. What is your address?"

He was in the process of telling her, when Travis and Amy stepped off the elevator. She bid a hasty goodbye to the man.

"Well, I am ready to go. How about you two?"

"We are ready," they chimed.

Amy got excited when they drove up in her granddad's drive. "Am I going to stay here?"

"Your granddaddy wanted to see you."

The front door flew open, and a doting set of grandparents ran to Amy. The grandfather hugged her tight. "My, my, look how much our baby girl has grown. How tall are you, Amy? Five or six feet?"

"No," giggled the golden angel.

"There is some ice cream with your name on it. Hi," he turned with extended hand to Grace. "You must be Grace. I am Duncan Gillespie. This is my wife, Charlene."

"It is very nice to meet you. This is my friend, Travis Winston."

With the introductions made, the entire group entered the house. While Amy worked on her Popsicle, the adults worked on telling the truth.

Duncan began, "Amy, we know what your dad did to you." The child ducked her head in shame. The grandfather lifted her chin with his finger. "Now, don't you go feeling sad. You have done nothing wrong."

"You are not mad at me?"

"How could I ever get mad at that face?" Relief passed her angelic face. Duncan looked to his wife for support. "But Amy, I have done something to be ashamed of. I am afraid you will be mad at me."

"I won't get mad at you Grandpa. I love you."

Tears filled the old man's eyes, and then Grace's. Her heart broke for the man. She wanted, more than anything, to not have to do this.

"When I found out what your dad did to you, I got real mad. I mean really mad, crazy mad. Before I knew what I was doing, I lost my senses and committed a horrible act. There is no justifying my actions." Her trusting eyes were piercing his, "I...I..."

"Sweetie, there was an accident. Your dad and granddad got in a fight. There was a gun. Your dad was shot. It was an accident." Grace helped out.

"Did he die?" she asked with bated breath.

"I am afraid so, Sweetie."

"Good." She jumped into Grace's arms. "I hate him. I know Jesus said not to hate, but I can't help it. I hate him, and I'm glad he's dead." She was sobbing now.

The grandfather simply patted her head. "I am so sorry Amy. I did not mean to kill him."

After a long pause, Amy spoke into Grace's shoulder. "Oh Grace, can't I stay with you tonight? Do I have to go back to that home? I promise, I won't complain."

"I do not see why we cannot work that out." She looked helplessly at Duncan. Even though she did not express it, she could tell Amy was angry with him.

The trio left shortly thereafter. Grace went by the home to make arrangements for Amy to stay another couple of nights. Grace took this opportunity to speak privately with the little girl.

"Sweetie, I have a lot of work to finish at the office. Would you mind going home with Travis? If you do not feel comfortable, just say 'no', it will not hurt my feelings at all."

"I like Travis. I do not get that icky feeling around him. Can I help Ruth cook again?"

"You sure can. I think she would enjoy that a whole bunch. Come on. Let us go."

Back in the car, Grace directed the vehicle toward the courthouse. "Travis, do you know your way around town yet?"

"A little, why?"

"I thought you and Amy could go back home, while I finish up at the office. I am swamped, since my secretary left. It would be a great help."

Travis was disappointed to end their time together. "Yeah, I could do that. I would rather hang out with you, but I do not suppose Amy would. I could take her home and come back."

"Tell you what, you two come back around seven, and we can grab some dinner," she suggested.

"Seven! That late?"

"Yes. It will take me that long to finish up. I have a better idea; I will meet you two around seven at Henry's. We passed that down the road as we came into town."

"I can show him where it is," piped Amy.

Grace hugged Amy. "Great! It's a date then. I shall see you two around seven."

Each one received a treasured kiss on the cheek, and then they watched the woman disappear up the courthouse steps. Travis reluctantly drove the red trophy out of town toward the house.

Grace needed to report to Stephanie the plans for keeping Amy a little longer. As her lawyer, she needed to know all details of the girl's life. She stepped into the lawyer's office with a bounce to her step, which quickly faded at the sight of Beth Samuels.

"Oh, excuse me." She started to slip back out.

"Oh no, Grace. Come back," called Stephanie. "Grace, you know Beth Samuels? Beth you remember Grace Sorenson?"

The glare that bore through Grace was filled with venomous hatred. "I know her. She's the one that filled Amy's head with these lies about Jeff. I'd like to know how you sleep at night."

Grace stepped forward with her head held high. "And I would like to know how you can live with yourself, knowing what he did to your child. How do you sleep at night after turning your back on your own little girl?"

"Just how many kids do you have, Miss Sorenson? It kills me how you people who don't have kids try to tell us how to raise ours."

"Stephanie, I can come back later." Grace was not

going to stand here and fight with this woman.

"Please wait," Stephanie called after her. "Mrs. Samuels is here to sign the papers allowing the state to take custody of Amy. She finds it difficult to raise her considering the problems." The lawyer was disgusted, yet had to maintain an impartial status. She knew Grace was sickened by the news as well, but would remain discreet as usual. This was par for the course in these situations.

Grace's tone was harsh. "That is probably best. Are you aware, Mrs. Samuels, that Amy will be available for adoption?"

"I could care less. She's your problem now. Since you think you can do better than me, why don't you raise the trouble maker, *Miss* Sorenson." With having said that, she signed the papers before her, snorted, and stormed out.

"Wow!" exclaimed the lawyer. "How come people like that are allowed to have children?"

"I am sure I do not know. Amy will be devastated. Duncan Gillespie told her a few minutes ago about her dad. She loses her mother, father, and grandfather in one day."

"She will be better off without that mother and father. You know why she is really dumping Amy, don't you? She has a new man in her life. Her husband's been dead how many hours?"

"How utterly sad. Maybe she will be better off without them. Nonetheless, they were her parents. She will feel responsible for both of them. If she had kept her mouth shut, her dad would still be alive and her mother would still love her."

Stephanie retorted, "And he would still be abusing her. Do we not have such fun jobs?"

"Not hardly."

"We are supposed to be helping these children. How come I feel like we are failing miserably?"

Grace fell wearily into the chair across from her friend. "We are not failing. In the long run, Amy will be better off. It is just important to get her over the rough bumps. That is why I came by. I want her to stay over with me a few more nights. She wants to, and I want her to."

"Fine with me. Do you need anything?"

"No, we are set. She went home with my friend."

They bade farewell, and Grace walked briskly to her office. The four blocks gave her enough fresh air to clear her mind. She was now ready to stare at the computer the rest of the day.

Dating Grace

She had tapes to audit and file, calls to make for updates, and reports to make. The fiscal year for Jameston Industries was ending in less than a month. She had to make the annual financial budget, along with the annual performance graph. Since Penny had run off to get married, she would be required to put in overtime galore.

She desired to take a week's vacation in order to be able to renew a kinship with her old friend, but knew it was out of the question. He had come across country to be with her and was not getting to see much of her at all. The woman shook off the memories. Time would not allow her to harbor such thoughts.

There were nine tapes which she listened to, took notes, and then filed away. One task down, only a million to go. She decided to wait until tomorrow to make the phone calls, so she skipped to making notes and reports for Stephanie's use in court.

The phone kept ringing, so she removed it from the cradle. She would never get any work accomplished this way. With the recorder taping messages to herself,

Grace dove back in to her work. Relentless obsession with meticulousness drove the woman into a world of timelessness. She worked through the seven o'clock hour and on into the eight. Time was the farthest thing from her mind.

Meanwhile, her two dates waited patiently. After they had waited an hour, the waiter kindly asked them to leave if they were not going to order. Amy wanted to wait for Grace, but Travis knew the girl needed to eat sometime soon. He ordered very little for himself. He was worried about Grace. Where could she be? He excused himself to call her office. All he got was a busy signal. Surely, she was not still working.

"Tell you what Squirt. We will run by her office. I bet she is still working. What do you think?" he suggested upon returning to the table.

"I bet she forgot. We should take her something to eat."

"Good idea. I will order something." Travis left again to speak with the waiter.

It was eight forty-five when they took their leave. When they pulled up in front of her office building, they could see dim lights. They found the front door unlocked and climbed the stairs to the second story. In the darkness of the night hours, the huge columns seemed to come alive. The creepy shadows sent the duo running into the stairwell.

They found their quest engrossed whole-heartedly in her work. Her braid from this morning had since been released and replaced with a pencil for a bun holder. Several curls were awry. A pen protruded here and there in the mass of fiery strands. She was caught red-handed talking to herself. The two watched her silently for a few minutes with smiles on their faces, while forgetting to be angry with her.

They remained unseen until Grace said, "Memo to self. If you want to preserve your sanity, hire another secretary. Now, ASAP." A stifled scream sent the observers into hysterics. Grace whirled, as if a snake had bitten her. "Oh my word! You scared me to death. What are you doing here? We are supposed to meet in another…" she glanced at her watch.

"Another what?" prompted Travis.

"My watch is wrong. It says it is after nine o'clock."

Amy giggled, "Your watch is not wrong. You forgot us."

"No. Tell me you are joking," her eyes pleaded with Travis's brown ones.

"Sorry, but she is right."

"I am so sorry. Oh, I am so sorry. Can you two forgive me? I had so much to do. I did not realize it was this late. I am so sorry."

Travis smiled generously, "It is okay. Just do not make a habit of it."

"I shall not. I hate that I missed it. I was looking forward to it."

"So were we. Are you ready to go home?"

"I suppose I had better be. Did you guys eat?"

It was Amy who answered, "Yes."

Amy was fast asleep, by the time they arrived home, and Travis lifted her to the bed. Grace decided to wait until after she had lunged the horses before eating what they had brought for her. The horses needed to be exercised daily for half an hour. This was solely Grace's responsibility. She would not push it off on Isaiah to do. No matter what hour she came home, she still had a job to do. The metal turnstile enabled her to get this job done twice as fast.

She hooked them to the turnstile and then prepared the brushes for the grooming, followed by measuring their food and pouring fresh water. The summer had allowed the animals the freedom from their stalls, so they did not need mucking.

Halfway through these duties, Travis snuck up on her for the second time that night. "You know, if you had told me, I could have done this while you were at work."

"Oh no, it is my responsibility. I do not mind. Again, I want to apologize for missing dinner."

"Stop apologizing. I understand. Come here." He gently pulled her hands, drawing her close to him. "Do you realize that this is the first time you and I have been alone since I have been here?"

"True." Grace looked up into his strong face. "Please try to understand. I will not have a lot of free time this week. Actually, I will not have a moment to spare until the end of the month."

"Well," he kissed her forehead. "We better make good use of our alone time then."

Ah, but he spoke too soon. "Lamby, there's a lass on the phone for you." Grace retrieved the receiver of the old barn phone. While Grace gave blunt affirmatives and negatives, Ruth turned to Travis and lowered her voice. "I'm afraid the Lamby doosn't get mooch free time. You moost feel froostrated having coom all this way for her to be gone all the time."

"Yes ma'am, a little. But I do understand her job is very important. I would not have it any other way." A revelation was suddenly exposed. If he wanted to find out who the real woman he loved was, there was no better place to go than the people around her. Those that lived with her would know her best. Standing in front of him was a woman who could do that. As a matter of fact, everyone who knew her well seemed to think highly of her.

"Be patient with her Laddie. She is worth the wait. You have strook her fancy, or I'll miss my guess. I never saw her with any oother man."

Grace returned the phone. "I am so sorry. I must go." She headed to the horses.

"Now?" Travis was devastated.

"Now, so late in the night, Lamby? What's so important you moost leave now?"

"A young girl tried to commit suicide tonight," sighed Grace. "It does not look good. I really hate to have to leave you again, but I must." She did not realize her words were directed to her male friend.

"Oh Lamby, go on. I'll finish the horses," offered Ruth.

Travis stepped forward, "No such thing. I will finish up here. I think I can brush them and feed them. You two go on. Ruth, I will be in the house in a while." He was rewarded a prize kiss from the Scottish woman and a 'thank you' from Grace, as he watched the two disappear into the night.

Ginger was a breeze to brush. She lazily awaited for the human to finish. Samson, however, refused to budge. Travis stood arguing with the animal for thirty minutes.

"Listen," he was saying. "I do not know what your problem is, but cut it out."

"Snort."

"You know, I think you are jealous."

"Snort."

That's it, isn't it? You are jealous. Listen, Bud, you do not have anything to worry about. I could not change her feelings for you, Old Boy."

"Snort."

"Hey! What was that for?" Travis asked, when Samson nipped at his arm.

"Snort."

Hopeless Grace

The hospital loomed eerily in the night. The quiet halls were contrary to the action of the emergency room. Denise Bishop had called Grace, knowing she would be beneficial in this situation. She met Grace in the emergency waiting room.

"Hey Grace. Thanks for coming in."

"How is she?"

"Not good. The next twelve hours are critical. We should know something by then." Denise explained.

"What happened? She seemed fine last week. I spoke with her at the home, and she was actually happy. Why now?"

"Did you not hear? They sent her back home."

Fury raged inside. "No! Why would they send her back? We presented them with more than enough proof. I do not understand."

"James Nicholson is good at what he does. His defense brought forth an alibi. They had to throw it out. I tried to call you yesterday but could not get through."

"Oh my word. I took the phone off the hook yesterday in order to get some work accomplished. How could I be so stupid? What was his sudden alibi?" A guilty wave consumed her.

"His wife. He did a number on her, because she changed her story and swore up and down that he was not even home that night. They had no choice, but to throw it out."

Grace mused, "When I interviewed her, she was angry about Shannon's accusations. She had no problem believing her daughter. I cannot believe she changed so insistently."

"Well, she did. Grace, since you are here, I am going to head home, if you don't mind."

"Sure. You go home and watch your babies sleep. I will call you if any changes occur."

"Thanks, I will see you later."

"Oh, by the way," Grace called her back. "Did her parents bring her in?"

"Yes. They are with her now. I would not suggest you going back there while they are here."

"I won't, trust me. I will see you."

"Bye," she repeated.

Left alone to do nothing but think on this tragedy, the

fiery temper flared hot like the curls on her head. She procured her tape recorder and prepared it with a blank tape. She laid her weary head back and closed her eyes briefly. The thoughts rushed in.

Two hours later, she was still wide-awake, and there was a strong need to stretch her legs.

"Excuse me, I would like to check on the status of a young woman brought in through emergency a few hours ago," she asked the nurse at the desk. "Her name is Shannon Randall."

"Are you a relative?" questioned the nurse.

"No. Here is my identification." She handed the woman the card that identified her position.

"Sure, Miss Sorenson. Let me check." She disappeared behind two swinging doors and returned several minutes later. "Shannon was taken up to ICU about three hours ago. She hasn't regained consciousness, yet."

"Three hours? Are her parents still with her?"

"No. She's been alone, since she was brought in."

Grace was confused. "Are you sure? I was under the impression they were with her."

The nurse shook her head. "I'm sure. I remember thinking how sad it was that she had tried to end her life, and no one was with her."

"May I go up?"

"I'll call up and let them know you are on your way."

"Thanks."

Shannon appeared lifeless, with machines protruding supportively from her small mouth. The telltale bandages on her wrists screamed their pathetic story. Her sunken eyes bore dark circles of restlessness. How could they not tell she was sick? Why could they not hear her cries for help? It was so obvious. Curse James Nicholson. He should never have sent that child back home.

She stepped into the ICU waiting room. The chair invited her to rest her exhaustion in its lap. Before long, sleep had overcome. It was a brief interlude, but helpful nonetheless. She took turns placing her elbows on her knees, with her chin in her palms and pacing back and forth in anxiety.

Seeking Grace

Travis went back in the house through the kitchen. On the table lay the supper he had ordered for Grace. She had not eaten a thing all evening. He just shook his head and went on to prepare for bed. Tomorrow, he determined to set out to find out what kind of person Grace was by interviewing her loved ones. Tonight, the memory of the smell of her hair when he kissed it, would lull him to sleep.

A fire was burning on this cool evening. The shadows on the wall danced without any pattern in order to hypnotize those who watched. For the first time since his arrival, Travis felt the deafening silence of the farm. An occasional wild animal would sound its cry, and except for Chief, the family dog, breathing heavily, there was only quiet.

Sleep finally swept him, only to be erased again shortly by a whisper. "Travis, are you awake?"

"What is wrong Squirt?"

"I went to Grace's room, and she wasn't there. Where's Grace?" Amy sleepily rubbed her eyes.

"There was a little girl that was hurt. Grace went to

the hospital. Is something wrong?"

The golden head shook slowly. "Can I sleep with you? My stomach hurts."

"Sure." Travis puzzled as the child began taking the cushions from the couch."

"Whatcha doing, Squirt?"

"Making us a bed on the floor. That's how Grace does it."

Travis laughed, "Oh she does, does she? What else does Grace do in these situations?"

"She gives me that pink medicine in her bathroom to make my stomach feel better."

"Pink medicine? Wait here." He went and searched the bathroom cabinet. He found two pink bottles. He read the labels carefully before deciding which one to give her, but by the time he walked back into the living room, the girl was sleeping soundly beside an empty spot just for him.

***

Ruth wakened him with a gentle tap early the next morning. "Laddie, I'm going to take Lamby soom breakfast. Would you like to coom?"

"Yes. Can you spare me five minutes to get ready?" He forced himself to rise up, because his body rebelled from lack of sleep. True to his word, he was standing in the kitchen five minutes later.

"There you are. I thought we could eat with Lamby, instead of making her eat alone." She held up a picnic basket, which was permeating with the aroma of biscuits and bacon.

The always-quiet Isaiah spoke in his strong low tongue. "Remember to ask her about the float. Do not forget." He kept sipping his coffee.

"I won't Isaiah. You make sure the Lassie eats her breakfast that I put in the warmer."

"Go on now. Here," Isaiah spoke in an even lower tone, while slipping some money into his wife's hand. "Give her this."

Ruth took the money discreetly with a huge smile on her lips. Dear old Isaiah. He loved Lamby as much as she did. Travis carried the basket to the small blue car in the carport for his hostess. She allowed him to drive according to her directions. Seven o'clock was not early for Ruth, but evidently it was for the hospital, which was virtually empty. After asking a couple of workers, the two were directed to the ICU waiting room.

Grace, with her hair still thrown up with a pencil and elbows on knees, with palms containing her chin, was barely able to hold her head up. Ruth knew another headache would pursue, therefore came prepared with a bottle of aspirin. She knew what Lamby needed and was there to see that she needed for nothing. The old woman found new sympathy for her Lamby, but Grace did not see her guests. She may have been sleeping with her eyes open for all she knew.

To Travis, the fatigued woman was a picture of perfect womanhood. Most women who had not slept could never look this beautiful. He looked to Ruth to interrupt Grace's dazed condition.

"Lamby, how is she?" She spoke as she touched Grace's arm.

Grace started, "Ruth, I didn't see you come in. Travis, hey. Shannon's not doing well at all. I went in about six, and she seems to be fading." At this point, Grace could not, nor did she want to stop the tears from falling. Travis had never seen her cry before. This new experience endeared her even more. "It does not look like she is going to make it."

"There, there, Lamby. You go ahead and cry." The mother figure cradled the broken woman to her bosom, petting any stray curls.

"I failed. I could not save her," sobbed Grace.

"You can't save them all, Lamby. Look at all the ones you did save."

"But she could die. We may not get them all safely away, but we have never lost one like this."

Travis watched the expert soothe his broken hearted friend. Ruth was wise beyond the normal mother realm. "Lamby, it's not your fault."

Grace tried to wipe her eyes in vain. The tears refused to stop. "Ruth, if she dies, you know what that means? Her blood will be on my hands."

"Did you witness to her?" Grace nodded affirmatively with a sniffle. "Then how can you be responsible? Salvation is a personal choice. Only she can make that decision."

"I just cannot help thinking I didn't do enough."

"That's joost stoof and nonsense. You'll not be

responsible. We are each held accountable for our own choices. She has to be the one to choose. You can't choose for her."

These words did little to comfort Grace. She could not help believing her guilt. However, a nurse entering the waiting area interrupted these thoughts.

"Excuse me, Grace. Can I see you a minute?"

Grace swiped the tears quickly from her cheeks. Being caught off guard was embarrassing. She briefly glanced at her guardian for encouragement. "Yes Dorothy. I am coming."

She rose to follow and Ruth pressed her hand softly before letting go. It was as if she had not even seen Travis sitting in the same room with them. He did not mind being ignored as much as he minded the feeling that he was eavesdropping on a divine conversation. Even after her departure, words were inappropriate. The solemn discussion penetrated his own heart. What if that were his own Wendy? His own child had been protected from all such atrocities. It brought to light a hidden secret about his beautiful Grace, which he never knew before. The ugly truth was bitter to taste. She had never told him of her horror and had bore her pain all those years. How could he ever question and help her, if he could not admit that he had heard Amy and her talking the other night? Would Grace hate him for snooping? Ruth had not acknowledged him, since Grace had left. She was rocking back and forth with closed eyes. In his ignorance, he did not know that she was praying.

Deciding Grace

"Grace," the nurse was saying as they walked. "Shannon's mother came in about ten minutes ago. At first, Shannon did not respond to her presence. Then, her mother started screaming at her. We tried to calm her down. She was disturbing the other ICU patients. We called security, but they are slow. Meanwhile, Shannon has come to in an agitated state, and we cannot seem to calm her. Do you think you can help?"

"I do not know. I will try."

The two followed a man in a security uniform into the curtained room. Shannon's mother was loudly pulling tubes and wires from her daughter and insisting on taking her daughter home.

"It was a mistake to bring her to this no account place in the first place," she screamed.

The man calmly grabbed the woman's arm and twisted it in an agonizing hold. The way it was held left her with the inability to function. She could only move her mouth in protest. "Ouch! You are hurting me. Get your hands off me!"

"You were asked to leave. You have disturbed every

patient in the intensive care," responded a solid masculine voice.

"Who do you think you are? Get off me!" She shrieked while being led away.

Grace witnessed the nurses frantically running around the patient to replace the life supporting equipment. Hopeless fear and despair filled Shannon's eyes as she watched Grace. Those eyes pleaded with the friend to understand her pain and just let her die. Grace was hypnotized by their drawing magnetism. She felt the tears threaten to surface again, but fought hard to prevent that from happening. She tried to turn and escape the piercing into her soul, but was unable. Soon, Shannon closed her eyes and fell into a deep sleep. The nurses knew the coma would not likely pass over, so they sent Grace away until the normal visiting hours. They fought a long time in order to stabilize the patient, until she was finally comfortable and her vitals were down to semi-normal.

Ruth and Travis had, meanwhile, spread their small feast for the noble princess. Ruth prayed continuously in her heart. When the family of another ICU patient dolefully watched the sweetness of the Scottish woman's preparations, Ruth politely offered them of her bounty in which they accepted.

Travis wandered into the hall to avoid the interruption. Benevolence was fine, but for him, it was not appropriate at this moment. He wanted to be with Grace. Tears blinded her vision when she left Shannon which caused her to collide with his willing arms. There was no need for apologies. Grace was familiar with the cologne of the one she encountered, and contented to rest in his supportive embrace. This alone was worth Travis's trip west. He stroked her back until the sobs subsided somewhat. Words need not be spoken.

With a gentle swipe, Travis conquered a tear on her cheek when the embrace was finally broken. With gentler cadence than Grace remembered hearing, "Is she…?"

Grace shook her head negatively. "Not yet. Would you mind? I need some air."

"Ruth brought you some breakfast," he reminded.

"Oh, I couldn't eat a thing."

"We will stop by and give her a report of our actions,

and then we can go." This they did with Travis's arm protectively wrapped around her shoulders.

The cool morning air revived the tiredness in Grace but did nothing to rejuvenate her spirits. The soul of this girl lay heavily on Grace's heart. She had failed to save this girl from her heinous father. How could she wake up in the morning knowing this child would not, because of her?

They had silently strolled along for about thirty minutes when Ruth met up with them. She knew Lamby would not eat anything in this condition. However, she did worry about another episode of that wretched headache. "I am taking off now. You make sure you don't make yourself sick, Lamby. Take you soom aspirin. Tell her Laddie. She is already roobing her head."

"Ruth is right. Take you something or you will get sick," he reiterated.

"Now, Laddie, are you going with me?"

"I would like to stay, if you do not mind." He looked to Grace for an answer. "Unless you think Amy needs me there."

"Don't ya mind the lassie. She'll be fine with Isaiah and me. Oh, speaking of Isaiah, he wanted me to ask you about the float. I know it is hard to think at a time like this, boot, soomthing needs to be dune before Saturday."

Instinctively fingers rubbed vigorously upon aching temples. "The float? The float! Are we still planning on the barbeque Saturday?"

"That's oop to you, Lamby."

"Alright. I will get the foundation business finished this week, and Saturday we will bring the children over for the decorating party. We could park it in the barn until Labor Day. That is only a week."

"Oh, Lamby, don't bite off more than you can chew. Don't forget you have that speech in the mornin'. When do you think you'll have time for the float?"

"The speech! I forgot about it." With a heavy sigh, "I don't know. I will get to it, though. I…I…I need to…" more vigorous rubbing of the temples ensued.

"You need to slow down," Travis interpolated.

"Aye. He's right. Isaiah would be more than happy to help."

Grace surprised them both with a sharpened response. "Isaiah will do no such thing. He does not need to work himself into the grave, because I'm too lazy to carry out my own responsibilities. He has enough to do on his own. I mean it Ruth. Please do not bother him with this."

Ruth understood the extreme tension Lamby was under. She watched approvingly as Grace swallowed some aspirin, and then kissed her goodbye with a prayer.

It was shortly after the next visiting hour that Shannon slipped into eternity. Grace had tried to witness to Shannon. As far as she knew, the child had never accepted Christ as her Savior. When the Great Judgment Day came, and all are held accountable. Shannon would face the consequences of the choice she had made here on earth. Likewise, Grace would watch Shannon's blood drip from her own hands. She had failed God in letting that man steal the girl's life too soon.

Casing Grace

She asked Travis to drive. These were the only words spoken during the trip to her office. Her friend respected her loss and remained silently in thought. He wanted to comfort her, yet he was found lacking. He did not quite understand the converse between Ruth and Grace. He knew about God and Jesus and all, but what did that have to do with dying? Dying was simple. Living was what was hard. One had to live a good moral life, and when they die, they go to Heaven. If you believe in God, then you try to be kind and generous.

Grace entered her office and secured Shannon's interview tape and listened, still crying. How many times had she heard the girl's pleas? There must be something she missed. Something that could have prevented this tragedy must be found. She must be the responsible party. She reread the files. To save her life, she could not find anything she could have done differently. "What did I do wrong, God? How do I prevent it from happening again?"

"Did you say something?" Travis asked, stepping from the outer office.

"No. I was just…" the ringing phone disrupted the moment and Grace was busy with her work for a while. This job did not leave much for personal time. "Are you bored?" she asked him after hanging up.

"Not a bit. Is there anything I could do for you?" He asked, as the phone rang again.

"Excuse me. Hello," as she lifted the receiver.

"Grace, I have another case. How soon can you start?"

"I can be over in a minute, Stephanie." She turned to Travis after replacing the receiver. "Would you like to drop me off at the courthouse for a while? You can take the Mustang and do some loafing. I should be at the courthouse most of the day."

"Could I hang around the courthouse with you?" he asked.

"I suppose. There are always hearings going on. You could check some of them out. The courthouse is across the street from the library, if you would like to go there. There are several places close by to get you some lunch, as well."

They were already on the elevator, going down.

"Sounds good to me, only if I can pick you something up for lunch also."

"Sure. You could pick me up a sandwich. I would appreciate it. If you get bored let me know. Will you do that for me?" Grace smiled through the threat of tears at the chivalrous gesture of his holding her door open.

"You got it. I believe I will find more than plenty to keep me busy though."

"Good. Oh, by the way, would you like to take a day trip with me tomorrow?" Life was finding a way back into her voice.

Travis tried to continue the cheering, "A day trip? Where to?"

"The coast. I have an appointment. I would really like it if you would drive with me. The appointment may be boring to you, but the road trip will be long and boring without you."

The car had stopped in front of the courthouse. The driver had received a green light to pursue a courtship with the maiden. His fingers danced lightly on her hand. "Count me in. We could make a day of it. I will bring you some dinner in a while, okay?"

127

"Check my office first. I may end up there. If I am not there, check with Stephanie's office, here."

"I will see you." He threw open his door and ran to the other side in order to open hers.

Travis walked her into the lobby of the courthouse. He had an agenda of his own. He intended to investigate the character of Grace. He could find a lot if he looked into the law library at Grace's professional history or ask questions of the people she worked with daily. He waited for her to disappear up the steps, and then proceeded. It was a simple task asking someone where to obtain these records. He engrossed himself for hours scrutinizing old records and questioning different workers. All brought a good report about the woman he loved.

Grace stepped into Stephanie's office, dreading to face yet, another case. Exasperation of this never-ending job seemed to be getting the best of her. "What do you have for me, Stephanie?"

"Grace, please, sit down." She placed a file before Grace. "This is Leslie. Her parents came to me today. They are bringing charges against Paul Murphy. Here are the notes on the interview. Murphy was Leslie's softball coach. There are specific details that are directed in proving his guilt, but Grace, I have a huge favor. Mr. Murphy was my teacher, when I was little. I know this man. He is not capable of what they are accusing him. He is kind and gentle. He would rather give his right arm than hurt any child. Please, prove his innocence. Will you help?"

She sighed, "I will look into it. Does he have any priors?"

"Not that I know of. I have not researched it much. I just know he did not do it. I have known him all my life. I hate the thought of someone trying to falsely accuse him of something this horrible."

"Well, I am off. I will get as much done today as possible. Would it be possible to interview her today? I will not be available tomorrow."

"I suppose you could. Let me know. I would offer to go through all that paperwork with you, but I am due in court in seven minutes. Thanks again, Grace."

"Any time. Knock them dead in there."

She had to keep this migraine minimal, so she

stopped by the water fountain to swallow a few more aspirin, when James Nicholson startled her.

"Hey Grace, who was that clown with you at your house the other night?"

The violet Irish eyes fired darts at the twinkling blue ones belonging to James. "I hope you are happy James Nicholson."

"If you are talking about Shannon, I am truly sorry."

"You are right," she spat, "you are sorry. How could you send her back, knowing what he was doing to her? You just as much cut her wrists for her."

"Grace, I was only doing my job. I do not get the choice of being the good guy like you."

"I do not care. I work my tail off trying to get these children safely away from these stinking perverts, and you just throw them back into the pack of hungering wolves. You do not care about the consequences. How do you sleep at night?"

"Grace," he started, but stopped suddenly when the fiery redhead placed her dainty hand across his cheek in anger. It did not hurt, but it shocked him into silence.

"That is for Shannon. Maybe you should look into

finding another line of work," she flared, as she whirled around and left.

He stood there smiling, while his co-worker snickered at the scene. The two continued to the men's room.

"Who is that spitfire?" asked the companion.

"You mean Grace?"

"Sweet name for such a devil."

James defended, "Quite the opposite. She is an avenging angel."

Fred laughed, "Well, that angel packs quite a wallop. Your face has a handprint on it."

"Grace couldn't hurt anybody. One of the little girls under her watch just committed suicide. Unfortunately, she blames me for defending the girl's father. I know the people are guilty, sometimes, but this job puts us on opposing sides. I hate it."

"You are sweet on her, aren't you?" observed Fred.

"Not that it counts for anything."

"You are not messing around with a married woman, are you?"

They were at the door. "Not likely to ever happen. She only has eyes for her kids."

The silent witness on the other side of the wall remained unseen.

Informing Grace

Grace did not have time to interview Leslie on Tuesday. Her research lasted into the closing hours of the courthouse. When Travis met up with her for dinner, she suggested he come back at five o'clock, which he did, and took her back to her office to gather some needed materials before going home. Grace worked late into the night to prepare the speech for the morrow and the crucial budgets for next Tuesday's board meeting. She still had not had time to complete this task.

That is why she asked Travis to drive the next morning. She needed the five-hour journey to work on the speech she was about to give. She had roughly thrown together a quick outline of what she wanted to convey to the auditorium of high school students. This was her first opportunity to reach out in this medium to a large group of children in order to offer a helping hand. If she could get more schools to accept her proposal, maybe she could help more children. Maybe, they could even set up similar facilities in different counties across the country.

The only opposition before her was the fact that

Grace could not speak in public. She was more of a one on one person. Crowds intimidated her. Her brain refused to function. Nervousness had already rooted, causing her concentration to flee.

There was a break in the monotony when the car phone rang. It was Amy who answered, "Hello."

"Lassie, is Lamby too busy to talk?"

"Hold on please," responded the grown up little girl who handed the phone to the back seat. "Grace, Ruth wants to talk to you if you aren't too busy.

"Thank you, Sweetie," Grace reached for the receiver. "Ruth, is something wrong?"

"There is not, Lamby. Isaiah told me to ask if you thought you're a sly woon?"

Grace smiled, "I do not know what you are talking about."

"And pigs fly." When the elderly Scottish couple came down for breakfast, an envelope containing two tickets for a three day Alaskan cruise pleasantly surprised them. There was extra cash for spending, as well. This was a gift from Grace in appreciation of all their hard work.

"Happy anniversary! You give Isaiah my love and enjoy your trip."

"God bless you Lamby. You'll be blessed for your kindness."

"I love you guys. You better take off if you are going to make it in time. See you Saturday."

"Will you three be okay while we be gone?"

Grace laughed, "It will be hard, but I think we should be able to manage."

"Alright, tell Lassie and Laddie goodbye."

Two hundred and eighty miles never seemed so far before. With each mile of US 101 came more nervous tension. Astoria was comparably larger than Springfield, and most likely, the schools would be much larger. "God give me the words and strength, I pray, please," her mind kept repeating.

Travis understood her need to finish her work and was content to develop a relationship with the awesome machine he was maneuvering while answering Amy's thousand questions. If Grace did not need those papers laid out in the back seat, he would love to put the top down and watch the beautiful cliffs pass by. One thing he had learned in all his research was that this woman worked hard. He wished she could take a break, but understood why she could not.

He was somewhat surprised when he looked back and saw her working herself into a panic. After the three hours of sleep she might have gotten last night, he would think she would be sleeping.

Because they had skipped breakfast, they stopped for an early lunch. Grace only pushed her food around, but ate nothing, for fear it would not stick with her in her nervous state.

The school was large, and the auditorium echoed its immensity. Looking out into the bleachers, Grace could see it was full. The principal escorted Grace to the back row of chairs on the stage and quickly added two more for Travis and Amy.

Grace knew her business. To a board meeting, she would wear a business suit, flat simple shoes, hair up, and a briefcase. However, to reach a child, you must be read as understanding. In order to achieve this, Grace knew to wear her fire red curls cascading down her shoulders, a simple yellow and white summer dress, and sandals. She was attired to perfection.

During the opening introductions, Grace watched the students, which had filed in by the droves. Travis placed his hand over her trembling one. Her face, which was void of makeup, had turned pale. A cold sweat had broken across her flesh, joined by a queasy stomach. Again, she prayed for strength. Her friend cupped his other hand on hers in order to calm the quivering. He had never seen her like this before.

Finally, the speaker was introduced to the student body. Her short walk to the podium intensified her fears. Several boys yelled and whistled, screaming obscenities in her direction, while her legs threatened to give way beneath her. Nonetheless, when the woman began to speak, the fear in the voice was deeply hidden. Her voice did not shake a bit.

"What Door allows you entrance, but no exit? It has no hinges or knobs and is always open. On the outside is total darkness. On the inside is Light. You must die in order to enter this Door, but you gain Life after passing through." Even though she portrayed youth, there was an unspoken command for respect from her composure. The boys who previously were yelling were now silent. Actually, the entire auditorium was filled with silence while the question was being pondered. She knew just how long to pause before continuing with their undivided attention.

"If you would like the answer to the riddle, I will be happy to tell you afterward. For now, I would like you to look at the girl sitting closest to you. Picture that girl in your mind for the next few minutes. One girl in every four is sexually abused by the time she is eighteen years of age. Could that girl I told you to look at be the one? How can you tell? One boy out of eight is sexually abused before the age of eighteen. How many boys are you acquainted with are being abused? The Worldwide Legal Information Association reports these very real statistics. Sexual abuse is a very real problem in this country. Eighty-five percent of the victims know their offenders. That is an astounding number. Eighty-five out of every one hundred cases, the child knows the perpetrator and usually well. Most of these offenders include the child's own father or even brothers. Some are teachers or coaches. Basically, anybody that has continual access fits in this eighty-five percent. One study showed that out of twenty-four rape cases, sixteen were incestuous. That is sixteen girls out of twenty-four were molested and/or raped by their own flesh and blood. Incest is a heinous and unnatural crime. Who could possibly commit such an abominable act? Nine of the sixteen girls were raped by their fathers, four by their stepfathers, and four by their blood brothers. Two grandfathers, two uncles, and one adopted father took the dishonor of perpetrator for the other five. Do you still think it does not happen? Do you think it could not happen to someone you know? Fifty percent of the offenders were the fathers of the victims. The one person in the world given to love and protect a little girl from all harm is the one raping that little girl. These offenders are good at what they do. They know how to get the job done without letting anyone find out. They are experts at intimidation. They know that at eleven years old, a child can be manipulated or threatened into keeping "daddy's secrets". Intimidation is the key to keeping a victim quiet. In one case, the father and son were raping the twelve-year-old daughter and sister.

139

Think about that a minute. Imagine the horror of that poor girl. How many of the girls in your class, remember one out of four, are in that number of victims? Could the one sitting next to you be the one?

Another powerful pause followed. Then at the precise crucial moment, she continued. "An abused child is not going to announce it everywhere she or he goes. They will not tell at all. Could the child you are talking to between classes every day be suffering in silence? If you could understand the pain these children suffer, you would cry real tears. If you are being sexually abused, or you know someone who is, then I adjure you, please call for help. A child is one hundred percent not guilty of any wrongdoing in this situation. The offender is the one that has done wrong. You have done nothing to be ashamed of. We cannot help you, if you do not allow us the knowledge. It has to be you. Simply call your local Child Advocacy and they will get you the help you need. Out of the twenty-four cases I mentioned, eleven perpetrators are still free, living, as they have done nothing wrong, while the child, who was robbed of her youth and innocence, lives in constant fear and destruction. If you know someone who is abusing a child, please, help that child and call for help. We all have the power to stop sexual abuse. What will you do to change the statistics?" She folded her paper and retraced her steps to her chair. A single clap of hands led to the entire congregation in applause. Grace's legs finally gave way as she reached her chair. She refused to allow herself to pass out, as a sick feeling passed over her. Travis slipped his arm around her frame for support and she leaned in to accept.

Rachel's Grace

The principal expressed his appreciation before dismissing the assembly. Grace resigned to accept her failure. Not even the principal appeared to have been affected by the speech. It was a big waste of time. The guests lingered on the stage, until the classes dwindled into scattered clusters.

Several students approached the speaker for the intriguing answer to the opening riddle. She had left them hanging and curious. All had to ask the solution save for one young lady.

"I know the answer," she exclaimed excitedly.

"You do?" Grace smiled into her eyes. "I believe you do."

"It is Jesus, isn't it?"

Grace quoted, *"I am the door, by me if any man enter in, he shall be saved and shall go in and out, and find pasture.* John 10:9. Those were the words of Jesus. That is right."

Grace watched a young girl a few feet away. A familiar sadness portrayed a silent prison within. The obvious screamed loudly. One could tell she wanted to come to speak with Grace, but fear held her at bay. With a few nods and smiles, Grace distanced herself from the present conversation. Travis and Amy were left to chat with the eager riddle solver, while Grace flowed tactfully to isolate herself. At first, they did not observe her departure.

Once she neared the frightened child, Grace solicited a water fountain from a nearby student. She spoke loud enough to announce her solitude to the young girl. After thanking the informant, she proceeded in the direction of the fountain. Much to her disappointment, though, the girl did not follow. Another sign of a failed operation. "Oh Lord, I did not reach one child."

She found a secluded bench outside the building. Here, she was drawn into retrospection. Grace felt the chill of hot breath on her face. "You will not tell Daddy's secret, will you Gracie?" The wind whispered. Repugnance filled her soul. The reminder had escaped from the safety of deliberate inclination, somehow.

"Excuse me," came a faint utterance. "Miss Sorenson, my name is Rachel."

Grace was thankful for the interruption and

judiciously slipped her hand into her pocket to turn on the mini tape recorder hidden inside. "Please call me Grace. It is nice to meet you."

"Can I ask you a question?" The pitiful despondent eyes grasped for some life saving conclusion.

"Anything."

"Um, what would happen to a person, you know, if they needed help? Not that I need it or anything. I just wanted to know what would happen, in case I ever met someone who needed help."

Grace descended to the girl's level of mentality. "It depends on the situation. If it is a family member, the child is removed from the home immediately. It does not matter who the offender is though, there will be a thorough investigation, along with arrest and prosecution, if guilt is proven. No child should ever feel responsible."

"If no one saw it, how do you prove it?"

"There are ways of identifying sexual abuse. There are people trained to reveal the truth. Tell you what, Rachel. Here is my personal number at home. I am available to you twenty-four seven. If you need any help at all, call me," Grace finished, because Travis and Amy were approaching.

"Thanks." She reached for the paper being handed to her.

"There you are. We were wondering where you slipped off to," Travis smiled, "Are you ready?"

"In a minute." Grace turned to introduce Rachel, but she was gone. "Well, I suppose I am finished here." She reached in to turn the recorder off.

Sheltering Grace

Travis asked, "Are you feeling better?"

"Yes, thank you."

"Your color is back. I thought we would grab a lunch and maybe stop along 101 at one of the turn-offs. We could have supper on the beach."

"Yea!" Cried Amy, who wedged between the interlocked arms of the adults.

It was unanimous with Grace's approval. "Sounds good to me. Let us do it."

They released the top to the Mustang, stopped at a restaurant for food, and headed on their way. The wind blew the fire from the pins placed in it prior to leaving Astoria. They drove for three hours before pulling over for the much-anticipated picnic.

With blankets and basket in hand, Travis helped his two ladies down the rocky embankment. Grace spread the blanket along the sand, then the three sat down to a meager supper. Amy was obsequious when Grace asked her to ask the blessing over the food. They must have been hungry, because they did not stop until all food was gone. Amy finished first and ran to play. It was not

146

long before Travis had the privilege of leaning back on his elbows to watch these two angels gliding on the sand.

They were examining a jellyfish that had washed ashore, when Amy spoke seriously, "Grace, what is going to happen to me, now?"

"Well, Sweetie, I am not sure. What would you like to happen?" Again, she slipped her hand into her pocket to roll the recorder. This was customary for any such conversations. You never know when a very important piece of information will accidentally be released.

"Mommy hasn't come to see me all week. She doesn't love me anymore, does she?"

"I am sure she still loves you. She just cannot have you with her right now, but it is not your fault."

"Yes it is. Daddy told me she would hate me if I ever told."

"No Amy. It is not because you told. You did the right thing by telling. Sometimes, moms need to grow up before they can help their child grow up. Her problem is, she cannot accept what your dad did to you. She failed to protect you, and for that, she feels responsible."

"Couldn't I live with you? I would help out with the chores and I wouldn't eat much. Please?"

"It is not that simple, Sweetie. I am not married. They frown upon single foster parents. I am not a legal foster parent, either. It would be complicated and take an awfully long time, if it ever happened."

Amy frowned deeply, "You don't want me either."

Grace enclosed the golden girl in her arms from behind, pulling her close, while rocking. The golden strands were blown by the wind into Grace's face. "Amy, do not ever say that. I want you very much. I just do not want you to get your hopes up for nothing. Let me work my end, but do not put too much faith in me. I do not know that they will allow it. It may take some time, but remember, I do want you."

"Really! You mean it? You want me to really live with you?"

"I would love nothing more," she finished with a tickle to the girl's side.

She immediately stood up and fled, lest the child should advance retribution for the tickle. Travis intercepted the chase by grabbing Grace, until Amy caught up to exact her revenge. The playful banter continued till Amy became allured away by some thing or another.

Grace smiled grandly at the reclining friend and fell with an exhausted sigh to the ground. "She is so happy. I never thought she would be."

"She owes it all to you," Travis responded, placing his head across the yellow clad lap.

"No, she owes it all to God. I did not do a thing."

"Have I told you how incredible I think you are? You should be proud of your speech. I believe you reached those kids."

Her dainty finger danced delicately over his forehead, removing the brown wisp of hair, which rebelliously fell. "You think so?"

"I do."

"I do not. I think it went terrible. We will just have to present a better speech, if there is a next time."

The time was right. From what he had seen, Travis felt safe in pronouncing his devotion to the old flame and friend. She was exactly the way he remembered her: kind, loving, gentle, smart, and funny. He knew he would always treasure his beautiful Irish lass. "Grace, is it possible for one to fall in love with the same person two times in a lifetime?"

"I think the ocean is so beautiful. To me, it shows the immensity of God. It defines, 'forever'. No matter how far you look, there is no end. Do you know what I mean?"

"It is a gorgeous view. When I moved to Wilmington, my grandmother and I used to watch the sun set in the evenings. It was a sight to behold."

"Have you ever listened to the words in the last verse of, *Amazing Grace*?" she asked with a faraway expression satisfying her countenance.

"Sure hasn't everybody?"

She quoted, "*When we have been there ten thousand years...We have no less days to sing God's praise.* The earth has been here for nearly seven thousand years, from the creation till now. That is a long time to us. To think, all the time passed, several thousand lifetimes ago, it is the first day of forever. Time will never run out. I get so excited thinking about it. I mean, seriously, think about it. We will not have these same bodies, with all the aches and pains of this world. We shall live forever in perfect bodies, and no perverts can enter there."

The brown eyes could almost see the halo of the angelic lover. His lips reached up to hers in a tender love token. He was not sure she heard the words he breathed. Time alone may be limited, but the quality of this time alone was worth waiting for. It defined his feelings for this woman.

Grace pushed him gently, "Ummm, if we leave now, we can still make it to church."

"Okay. If you will gather up Amy, I will collect the blanket and basket."

Because the clouds had shadowed the sun, they thought it best to put the top back on the Mustang, which was good, because three quarters of the way, the heavens opened up and poured a cleansing on Oregon. Ten hours of travel in one day was more than enough for the three weary travelers. They did not mind running to the shelter of the house through the downpour, after all that riding.

Requesting Grace

Grace was welcomed home with a note from Isaiah, which permeated his love, before the words were even read. In his unique way, he was expressing his thrill for the surprise she deposited. He finished it up by enlisting her aid with Ginger. It seemed Ginger had been favoring her right hind leg, leaving the caregiver concerned. He had rubbed liniment on it before he left, and wanted her to continue.

"Travis, would you mind terribly taking Amy to church? I have to feed the animals and doctor Ginger's leg. I am not sure how serious it will turn out to be," she asked after reading Isaiah's words.

The man hesitantly agreed. He would really rather Grace take the girl to church and he stay here. Not that he knew anything about lame horses, or anything, but to please the woman he loved, he would have agreed to the moon.

Ginger was laggardly waiting in her stall, where Isaiah had left the outside doors open for them to get out of the rain. Sampson snorted his welcome, "Where have you been?"

Grace measured out the grain for each beast and poured it into their feeders. She would wait to see if the rain would slack off before feeding the cows. She opened the door to Ginger's stall and examined the injured leg. It was indeed swollen and hot to the touch. Ginger did not mind the woman touching her sore leg because she knew she would get a good rub down from it. Perched upon an upside down bucket, with liniment in hand, she began the doctoring process of massaging the ointment on the white stocking. This, Samson objected to highly and made his opinion known loudly.

"Sampson, if you do not stop being jealous, I am going to put a flowery bonnet on your head and ride you through the parade on Monday. Then, what will all the fillies think about you?"

The creature gave what sounded like a neigh of pain and shot into the dark, wet night. He would get her attention one way or another. Now, she would have to brush him, at least.

An ice pack was alternated with a heating pad to Ginger's swollen leg, which was wrapped snuggly by a bandage. Grace, working with crepe paper to adorn the flat bed trailer for the Labor Day parade, filled the long intervals between. Few idle moments were ever found in her life. So much had to be accomplished in such a short time.

For a good hour, she managed to work hard and uninterrupted. It was time to rub ointment on the leg again and switch the ice pack to the heating pad. The swelling was already coming down, but the leg was still very tender to the touch. It was while she was rewrapping the leg, that she heard the familiar engine of the Mustang in the drive. It must have been a short service.

The ancient phone in the barn clanged loudly, startling Grace. Isaiah and Ruth were not in the house, so she responded to the clamor with a, "Hello".

She assumed it would be Isaiah or Ruth calling this late, but was surprised when her grandmother answered. "Grace? This is your grandmother."

"Yes ma'am. I know. What is wrong?"

"Does something have to be wrong for me to call my granddaughter?"

"No ma'am, but you usually do not call unless

something is wrong."

"Then, I need to remedy that. It's your Uncle Jerry, Grace. He's real sick. That stinking war is killing him. They don't expect him to live longer than two weeks. I know you would never forgive yourself if you don't come see him before he dies." This was her not so subtle way of ordering people around.

"Where is he?"

"The VA hospital. He looks like your granddad before he died. Grace he looks bad."

"Okay, but I am not sure he wants me there. We have not spoken in a long while."

"He's changed, Grace. Two weeks ago, he got saved."

"Did he really change? Is it for real?" she questioned anxiously. She had had experience with members of her family doing cruel things under the claim of being a Christian. She should not be such a doubting Thomas, but experience out-ruled spirituality.

"He really did. You would just have to see for yourself. Do you think you will be able to come?"

Grace was motioning a welcome to Travis and Amy

155

who had just stepped into the barn. "I have to come east next week. I will try my best to get by."

"Do make it Grace," insisted the old woman.

"No promises, but I should be able to."

Grandmother sighed her frustration, "I would think you would be more respectful than that Grace Sorenson. After all he did for you, and he, on his deathbed..."

"Fine. I will be there Monday, if I can."

"Why can't you come now?"

"Because Grandmother, I have responsibilities here, that I cannot just walk away from. There are people depending on my being here. I could possibly push it up to Sunday, but I do not know."

"For the life of me. I cannot figure what would be more important than family, Grace."

Grace had reached her limit. She did not want foreign ears to fall upon the conversation, so she lowered her voice. "You are preaching the value of family to me? I am sorry I do not have the same impress on family as you do Grandmother, but this is the best I can possibly do. I love you but I have to go for now."

"Well, I didn't mean to make you mad. I love you,

too. Goodbye." A snippy hum finalized the call.

Declaring Grace

Samson had come in when he heard the approach of the newcomers. He knew how to demand attention. Per the animal's request, Travis sauntered to his stall while Grace was still in converse. Samson sulked that *he* was the one to pet him, but *he* was better than nothing.

Samson proudly held his head high. His master was finally giving him sole attention. Hey, what was she doing looking at *him* that way. This was his moment. He nuzzled Grace for full attention.

She conceded to his nudge and walked him out of his stall. "I have to wipe him down. I will be in there in a minute. Will you get Amy started on a shower for me?"

"Sure. Promise you will not take too long?"

Grace favored his cheek with a soft kiss. "I promise. How was the service?"

"Fine, I guess. I'll see you in a few minutes."

Samson loved his thirty minutes of full attention. She rubbed him with towels until he was warm and completely dry. Then, she brushed his coat for it to shine. His mane and tail were combed perfectly. She locked the outside stall door before leading him in for the night. Last, she bestowed upon him the carrot, hidden away for the right moment. Of course she received a horse hug for gratitude.

When Grace entered the living room, a comforting fire was burning bright in the fireplace. Amy was crawling into Grace's bed. "Can I sleep in your bed tonight, Grace?" She asked sheepishly. The truth was, Ruth and Isaiah were not going to be sleeping upstairs, and she was slightly frightened.

"Sure can, Sugar Lump. I would kiss you goodnight, but I smell like horse. Let me slip into a shower, then I'll tuck you in."

"Okay with me! I love you, Grace."

"I love you too, Sweetie."

The shower soothed the soreness of driving all day down the drain. The problems that had previously plagued her brain washed away with the soap and water. Her grandmother should have understood her position better. She knew how things had been. Grace loved her uncle very much, but many years had festered the sour ending between them. Why could people not understand that sometimes, in order to get along with people you love, you must separate yourself from them? She owed it to Uncle Jerry to visit him, as she intended, but what a Pandora's box it would open.

Amy had fallen fast asleep the minute her head hit the pillow, forcing Grace to give her a kiss unawares. She pulled the blanket snugly around her golden girl with a smile. For now, her angel was safe. Clad in a clean pair of sweat pants and white T-shirt, she joined Travis in the living room.

He had prepared two mugs of hot cocoa after his shower. He watched her from where he was sitting on the hearth. The loveliness he beheld took his breath away. Grace seemed lovelier each time he laid eyes on her. What was it about her that induced full captivation of his soul? At some point, she transcended time an became immortal in his mind. She defied age with her youth, while dispelling instability in her mind. He felt revered to be in such close bondage with this creature.

His brown eyes were the initiation of a smiling face. He beheld the vision before him, photographing it in his mind. He held a mug out to her. "I made some hot cocoa. I figured it would warm your insides."

"Thank you," she smiled, and then seated herself opposite him, holding the heated cup between her palms. "Mmmm. This is delicious."

"Living with my sister teaches me all kinds of neat tricks."

"Renee is a very wise young woman."

Travis shifted closer, "Grace, I love you. I know we live on opposite ends of the continent, but we could make this work. I do not want to lose you, when I leave in a couple of days." Grace sipped her drink. Travis frowned, "Grace? What is wrong? "

"Nothing is wrong."

"Did you hear me? I love you, and I want to know if you feel the same about me?"

Rejecting Grace

"Lord God, help me, I pray." She prayed inaudibly. Her feelings for this former lover was just as real and strong as it always was, but as it was now, this love was forbidden. Grace was a Christian. The Word commanded that she be not unequally yoked with anyone. Travis may believe in God, but according to what he had told her, he was not born again. There was no way she could share a love with one who did not belong to her Savior. She had prayed for his salvation for two weeks, but God was working in His time, not hers. Now, she could not put it off any longer. Truth demanded to be revealed, but he would not understand the truth. How could a lost person comprehend this?

She delicately touched his sun bronzed cheek, a touch that thrilled them both. "Travis, you worry too much. When the time is right, all things will fall into place according to God's will. Don't rush..." the ringing of the phone tore into the silence of the night. "Excuse me," she requested and rose to answer, before it woke Amy. "Hello."

"Grace, this is your Aunt Janet. I hope you were not

in bed yet. I would have called sooner, but I just got home from work."

"I was still awake."

"I wasn't sure if anyone had called you about your Uncle Jerry. He is in the hospital. This time, they do not expect him to come home."

"Grandmother called me earlier. How is he? She said he got saved. Have you been to see him?"

Janet sighed, "I have not had a chance yet, but I am going tomorrow. I guess I'll find out if it's real. Not to be ugly, but I will believe it when I see it."

"Is it the cancer from Vietnam?"

"Yeah. It has progressed pretty far. You know for years he complained of stomach pains. They told him it was just ulcers. Well, it turned out to be cancer all along."

"What about surgery?"

"There is really no point. The side effects are killing him quicker than the cancer. It is like Daddy with his leukemia. The aplastic anemia is hereditary."

"What have they done about the aplastic anemia?" She inquired.

"There is not a lot they can do. They have done the blood platelet transplant several times, but to no avail. A bone marrow transplant would be best, but so far, no match has been found. He wouldn't do it if he could."

"Could I be a match?"

"I doubt it. The best match would be a sibling."

Grace didn't need to ask if any of the sisters or the brother had been tested for a match. This *family* of hers would rather see the last one dead than to forgive long enough to save a life. Her heart cried for the once beloved uncle and his deathbed tragedy.

Aunt Janet continued, when the break in conversation occurred. "If you want to see him before he dies, I suggest you get here soon. They have given him two weeks but I don't know if he will hold out that long." Janet was not known for her compassion. It was true that her brother had not been nice to her for years which made her feel entitled to hold onto her resentment.

"I told Grandmother I would try to get there Monday. I have a business meeting on Wednesday in New York, but I could come by beforehand."

Travis had gathered the empty mugs to the kitchen to

wash. It was at this point that he had come back into the living room. He saw the weariness cross the beautiful features and placed his hands on Grace's shoulders to massage the tense knots that were almost visible. A brainstorm had occurred in his mind. She was coming to his home. He could have her as a guest and bring her home to Renee.

"Do you have any arrangements yet?" asked the aunt.

"No, I am not sure whether I can make it Sunday or Monday. I will probably know something definite Saturday."

"Well, if you need a place to stay or a ride, just give me a call."

"I appreciate it."

"Well, I better get off here. Time is money, and this call is not cheap." As usual, the ever-thrifty aunt was worried about the dollar.

Grace refused to allow her head to ache. How many loving family members must she endure before this was over? She thoughtfully hung the phone up, but continued to allow the magical fingers to work the tension. She smiled her gratitude, "If you keep this up, I may make you keep doing that the rest of your visit."

"My pleasure. You are so tense. What is going on?"

"My Uncle Jerry is on his deathbed. They do not give him but a couple of weeks."

The rough strong hands, which showed signs of a lifetime of hard work, guided Grace back to the hearth. "You are going home to see him?"

"Yes. I cannot let him go without making things right. No matter what has transpired between us, he tried to love me."

"Then you will come to my home," he said decidedly. "There is no need shaking your head at me. It is settled. Renee would literally have my head on a silver platter if I allowed you to stay anywhere besides with her."

"I do not know. It would, perhaps, be better for me to stay in a hotel. My plans are tentative at this point. I am not even sure when I shall get to go."

"Why waste money on a hotel? I know my sister, and she will not take no for an answer. You can meet Wendy, and I know she will love you," he was excited.

"We will see. It would be good to see Renee again. I wish she could have come with you this trip."

Completely seduced by her grace, Travis could no longer contain the kiss he placed on her lips, which displayed his token of love. The exotic dance of the firelight had worked its magic. No matter what words she may or may not utter, she could not deny her love for him, which was manifested in that kiss.

Grace made the goodnight exit on weakened knees. She was supposed to be forbidding this love. This was certainly not the way to do it. How could she? She had prayed for God to help, but she was acting on her own emotions and not allowing God's help.

She berated her actions all through her sleep. Her dreams replayed the pleasure over and over, until the morning broke with the warning blaring louder than any alarm clock, "There are pleasures in sin...for a season."

Proving Grace

Amy and Travis were still sound asleep when Grace slipped out to begin her day. She wanted to, no she needed to, remove herself from temptation. She checked on Ginger's leg and fed the two horses, releasing their stall doors to the open. Then, she waited at the end of the drive for Stephanie, whom she had called for a ride.

She had wanted to leave Travis and Amy a way to get around.

The sanctity of the office, by means of quiet and loneness, soon overcame her racing mind. Once she could sweep all other thoughts away, she was able to concentrate on the interview at hand.

This meant a lot to Stephanie. Grace must know beyond a shadow of a doubt before going to her friend. She had been uncomfortable with some information she uncovered the other day, but a man is innocent until proven guilty.

The process of the interview took most of the day. Although the girl was a bit obnoxious, the truth could not be hampered. It took the whole return trip from Eugene, in the back seat of the cab, for the woman to conclude that she must tell Stephanie, now. She wouldn't wait to fill out the reports. It would be better to get it over with.

Grace paid the cabby at the courthouse, but before she could make it to Stephanie's office, she was jolted from her own little world by a boyish, deep voice.

"Grace, are you still mad at me?"

"Of course, I am James. As long as you work against the children, I probably will be."

"You cannot hold that against me, Grace. That is my job."

"I have told you before. If it were me, I would find another job."

"Are you offering me a job?"

"Not likely," she scoffed.

"Do you see my dilemma? I want to please the lady, but I do not have any other offers on the table. How can I ever hope to gain your respect, if I cannot provide financial stability?

"Get a life, James."

"I have a life Grace Sorenson, and it includes a trip east next month with a beautiful redhead."

"What are you talking about?"

"I am talking about the senate hearing, my dear. I am going with you."

"Why?"

"I have been asked to represent the other side. I guess they figured someone should challenge this cause to make it sound real. So, what are your reservations? I thought we could keep each other company."

The Irish temper was fueled. He made her life's work sound trivial and insignificant. This was a game to him. How dare he? This was the most serious thing in the world for her, and he was trying to make it sound "real".

"My boss makes all the arrangements, and I'll need no company, thank you very much." She spoke plainly before, storming off.

Stephanie was not in her office. This was good, because Grace could sit to recollect what she had planned to say. She did not read the clock, which told that it was half past five and Stephanie would probably be gone for the day. When she finally did notice the clock, it read six minutes after six, and she felt foolish for having wasted so much time, for naught. She was leaving a note for the attorney, when Stephanie entered. Both were surprised to see each other.

"I was just going to leave you a note. What are you doing in the office so late?"

Stephanie reclined in her chair behind the desk with a slight sigh. "Court ran over. We were working on the

Laughter case. You have found something. I can see it in your face."

"You are not going to like it. I thought Leslie might have blamed the wrong person, but it is undeniable. The distinctions she made in specific details do not lie."

"I trust your judgment, Grace."

"But?" Grace prompted.

"But, I just cannot believe it is true."

"Why is it so important for him to be innocent? I understand he was a favorite teacher, but even they are not infallible."

Stephanie fiddled with a pen between her fingers. "Because, I had a friend from grammar school that confided in me certain things he had supposedly done to her."

"Missy Watkins?"

"No, Sandra Hollis. I refused to believe her. He had been the best teacher I ever had. I could not believe that he would do such things."

"You made a bad call, when you were a child. Why beat yourself up over it still? It is not as if you could have stopped it."

"She told me, Grace, and I told her she was crazy, and no one would believe her if she said anything."

"You were a child, Stephanie. How could you know? Why does this make you responsible for her? If it was really happening, she could have gone to an adult. An adult would have known what to do."

Tears had actually formed in the lawyer's eye. "But, *I* did not believe her. Since her best friend could not believe her, who would?"

"Whatever happened to her?"

"Two weeks later, she killed herself. I tried to tell myself it had nothing to do with what she told me. If he is guilty this time, then that means he was guilty then, and I am responsible for Sandra's death. How do I live with that?"

"My friend, I do not know if words could ever make it better. It is not easy to deal with."

"Grace, who is Missy Watkins?"

"I found her in the archives. She was a girl that brought charges against Mr. Murphy a few years ago. He resigned from his teaching position, and then the Watkins family dropped the charges and left town.

Nothing else was ever said about it."

"Oh my goodness. I cannot believe I was so very blind to it all. I enabled him, in a way."

Deceiving Grace

Travis and Amy were disappointed to awaken and find their hostess missing in action. The ham, biscuits, and honey she had left on the table, contented their hungry bodies, but her vacancy starved their craving soul.

Amy needed some semblance of security, since her mother had deserted her, thus needing to physically be with Grace was something no one else could give her. On the other hand, a yearning to love a child and prove to herself that a mother's love is unconditional had been a subconscious need for Grace. The fact that she had never married or given birth prohibited that need. That is why, when Amy became orphaned, she had the ability to fulfill a need in which Grace was not even aware.

The two houseguests busied themselves around the farm. Travis raked the field of grass which was nothing but straw, since the rain. Amy made rounds feeding the dog, cows, and pig. They were excited by noon, because they had worked hard, and were now planning to surprise their beloved with a picnic lunch. They cleaned up all shiny and new and drove to town in the Mustang, thinking they were something special.

To the dismay of both, their guest of honor never appeared. They were the ones surprised when, at two o'clock, the only ones in her building were themselves. They were forced to take the cold rubbery pizza and eat it glumly without her.

"Well, Squirt, that is that!" Travis said with frustrated overtures.

"Yep, that is that," she repeated, while pondering the thought with a frown. "Travis, Grace works too much. Ruth told Isaiah so, too. She should not work so much."

"Maybe, but are you going to be the one to stop her, Squirt? She is not the sort of person who will slow down voluntarily," Travis informed.

"We could try, you and me. If she became my mom, she would have to be home more."

"Well, now," Travis paced a couple of steps. "What about the other children who need her help?"

Amy looked toward the floor shamefully, "I didn't think about them. I guess my mother is right. I am just a selfish little girl, always thinking of myself."

"No you are not! You are worried about Grace. How

is that being selfish? You were not thinking about Amy
or what Amy wanted. Sounds to me as if you were
being pretty selfless, if you ask me."

She awarded his kind tone and words with a radiant
smile. "We could kidnap her and make her take the
night off," she giggled mischievously.

With some thought, "Hmm, you may be onto
something there, Squirt. If we could catch up with her,
we might do that tonight. We could take her away
somewhere quiet."

"No, not tonight. The carnival opens tomorrow night.
Couldn't we do it then? Couldn't we, huh? Please? We
could take her to enjoy the rides. She'd have fun. We'll
make her."

"It is a deal, but mum is the word," he laughed.

The golden child had worked her magic once again.
No longer was he glum and frustrated, as they drove the
distance back home. He was actually looking forward to
tomorrow night. Over the next twenty-four hours, the
two exchanged sly glances and secreted smiles with the
knowledge of their hidden agenda. Travis determined to
make this work. He was going to be leaving too soon.

Grace called a cab to drive her home, and only Samson's snorting escort interrupted the silent walk up the drive. Travis was startled at the opening door. He was not quite sure how she had intended to get home or if she planned on coming home at all. He was angry, because he felt she was avoiding him. He promptly relieved her of her briefcase and maneuvered her to the couch before exiting to the kitchen. Grace took advantage of this time alone to slip out and freshen up. She found Amy in the comfort of slumber in her bed. She bent to distribute a loving goodnight kiss on the child's head and pull the blanket snugly around her.

Travis heated the plate that her two keepers had kept for her. He sat his princess down to her awaiting feast, when she came back out of her room.

"We were starting to worry about you," he commented in a gruff way, after Grace asked her blessing. He tried to keep the annoyance from being heard, but found it hard.

"Why in the world were you worried? You knew I was at work."

"Because, Grace. We have not seen or heard from

you all day. We waited at your office for three hours in order to have dinner with you, but you never showed. It is almost twelve thirty now." This time, he could not hide the agitation.

The lady swallowed her bite, and then smiled her charm. "Did you not get the message?"

"What message?"

"I called to tell you I would be late. When no one answered, I left you two a message. Did you not check the machine when you came in?"

The frown that creased his forehead smoothed into a half smile, half guilty look. "No, we did not. We...you...uh...Well, why are you having to put in so many hours?"

"I was just given a new case on top of the one I was trying to finish up today. Then, there is this board meeting next week. Everything has to be in meticulous order, and I have hardly begun. Plus, I have this presentation to make in a couple of weeks. There are a lot of things needing to be done at one time. This is my life. Most of the time, I have everything hitting me from every direction." She put her fork down and touched his hand. "I am sorry I have not been able to spend more time with you this week. You took all this time off to spend with me, and I have not been in a position to accommodate you."

"Stop that right now. You certainly cannot leave your work on a whim for some hair brain idea I had. I understand how important your work is. You would not be the grand lady I know if you did."

"You better stop spoiling me. What am I to do when you go home?"

"That is my aim," he laughed. "To prove to you how much you need me."

"Be that as it may, if I do not get busy, I shall never get finished in time. Thank you and Amy for the delicious supper. I appreciate you saving it for me."

"What do you mean, 'get busy'? It is bedtime. Grace, you have to rest."

"There will be time for rest next week. Until then, I must get these reports completed. Since my assistant left, there is no one to do the work, but me."

He offered, "Can I help?"

"How fast can you type?"

"About a letter a minute. If Renee were here, she could type real fast."

"That would be a Godsend." Grace sighed.

Travis was not sure what hour he fell asleep. The clackety clack of the keyboard lulled him into the world of dreams. Grace typed, until she could no longer hold her eyes open. The pounding pulses had begun to throb her temples, so she laid her head across her arms momentarily to ease the pain, but ended up sleeping into the morning hours.

Forcing Grace

This is how Travis found her when he came in. An innumerable amount of pages contained the letter 'f' on them where the pressure of Grace's arm lay on the keyboard. To incur further setback all her work was stained dark brown, where Grace's nose had bled during the night. This was the zenith of her frustration. What a day, and it had not even begun yet.

A debate was in process whether she could actually get any work accomplished, if she worked out of the house today. Of course, Travis and Amy supported this idea whole-heartedly. Grace had to take Amy shopping for school supplies anyway, so the decision was that she would work at home.

She gave strict orders that were followed specifically. "If you distract me, I will have to go to the office." So Travis and Amy worked in the field and barn, leaving their quest in total solitude. In this time, she managed to type eighty percent of the individual reports on the children, which had come through their office.

She made the necessary phone calls to order the supplies sent for tomorrow's cookout. The children from the home were coming to design the float, and they were going to barbeque a feast for the little ones. Isaiah would be back in the morning, and she did not want to leave him with any last minute worries.

Amy slipped in silently with a lunch tray, but Grace did not slow enough to eat a bite. The golden child and Travis held their breath in hopes of a perfect evening plot. The shopping trip made it possible for the two to get Grace in their mercies. It worked perfectly.

Amy strutted in the stores obsequiously. For all the world knew, she was with her natural parents, and they were shopping for their daughter. Even her own mom had never done this with her. It was exciting buying new things.

Grace carefully pocketed each receipt, although she was not planning on turning this shopping spree in to her work budget. She had every intention of making this child her child, so she might as well be responsible for her now.

It was only after the last pencil was bought that Travis and Amy apprehended their victim. Travis was driving, which fit in perfectly with the plan. They swept her off to a quiet Italian restaurant lit by candlelight. Grace had lived in Springfield for fifteen years, yet had never been to this place before. Of course, it was in Eugene, but she had never occasioned the place. Sharing this with these two particular individuals made it very special.

Travis's brown eyes twinkled with delight for pulling off his coup. In all her glory, Grace was completely his tonight. Amy flitted around as if she were a fairy, sprinkling fairy dust to mesmerize the woman she wanted to be her mom, into a pleasant evening. Travis could see a dull pain behind the darkened violet eyes, but Grace did well to hide it from Amy. Her head insisted on aching.

She was completely surprised, when they ended up at the carnival. The blaring music forced them to speak in louder voices. They strolled together, with Amy in the middle, holding both hands. All the pain and suffering in her young pitiful life had flown completely from her memory for the time being. She was the happiest kid in the world tonight.

It was on the merry-go-round that she met up with a

schoolmate. Bonnie Johnson wanted Amy to stay with her, so she would have someone to play with, but Grace was downright hesitant. She was not comfortable letting her go off alone in a place like this.

"Please, Grace. Can I? I promise I'll be good. I'll do what Bonnie's parents tell me to do." She did not care a whole lot about running off with Bonnie, but this fit in perfectly with her own agenda. Travis and Grace needed to be alone, and she knew it. If she could work things out, she would not only get a mom, but a new dad in the process. And it was safe to say Travis was her choice.

"I do not know, Sweetie."

The girl pleaded, "You'll still be here. You can keep your eye on us. Come on, please?"

Grace could not refuse the golden charm much. A couple of pleas with that pouty expression and forget saying no. "Come here," she gently pulled Amy to the side. "You remember what I told you? If you come across any person, no matter whom, that gives you that icky feeling inside, you scream for help and run. How about Bonnie's dad?"

"He doesn't give me that feeling. I promise, I'll kick

and scream and bite, and anything else. Can I go?"

"Meet me at the gate at ten o'clock. Be careful, Sweetie. Behave."

Amy planted a hug and kiss on her cheek before running off in delight. Grace nervously watched her ward fade into the crowd, then sent up a silent prayer for protection of her little angel.

Gifting Grace

Within two hours, Grace was having some difficulty carrying all the stuffed animals that her gentleman had won at different games. Because of the size and number, they almost refused to allow her on the Ferris wheel. When Amy spotted them from the Scrambler, Travis had slipped his strong hand over Grace's. It was working!

The slow mounting of the huge wheel allowed Grace to search the park for Amy. From the top, she could watch fairly clearly all the happenings below. Amy seemed to be having a blast, but that did not stop Grace from fretting over the golden sweetheart.

After riding it several times around, Travis reached into his pocket. The chair began swinging erratically. "What are you doing? You are going to flip us over." Grace held on tightly.

"I have something for you."

"Something for me? You did not have to give me anything."

"Actually, it is something I bought for you years ago. I intended to give it to you on your eighteenth birthday."

He held a tiny box in the palm of his hand. The faded velvet made his hands look large as he held it out for Grace. She reluctantly was forced to at least look at it. Releasing the spring exposed an elegant gold band supporting a simple diamond. She gasped, "Oh my! You should not have."

"Yes, I should have." He argued. "You and I were to be married, Grace. I loved you. I worked for the entire year in Wilmington earning enough to buy my girl an engagement ring. My grandmother helped me pick it out. We both thought it would be perfect for you. I know you never met her, but she felt as if she knew you well. She hoped that you would come to Wilmington for our wedding. Here, let me put it on." He pulled her hand in his and placed the ring on the appropriate finger. "It still is a perfect fit. It was made for no other hand."

Grace was lost in the sweet memory and glitter of the jewel. She had never owned anything so gorgeous. The ride had stopped, but Travis motioned the conductor that they wanted to remain for yet another turn. The conductor shook his head and motioned, "One more time."

"It is truly beautiful, Travis, but I cannot accept it." She shook her head, while removing it carefully. She feared she might drop the valuable token.

"I do not understand. Of course you can. It is yours. It was bought for you. I hid it away all these years, along with my love for you. You cannot not take it."

"But taking it would be sending you the wrong message," protested the girl with a plea for help from her Heavenly Father.

"Wrong message? Grace, it is simple. I love you. Either you love me or you do not. If you love me, terrific. I will love you for the rest of my life. I will take care of you for the rest of my life. I will take care of our children for the rest of my live. I will do anything you need me to do, but please, tell me you love me. If you do not, then I will leave you alone and never bother you again. Either way, the ring is yours. You do not have to wear it, but it is yours." His apparent frustration was showing.

Grace prayed for the words to speak in order to finally put this issue to rest without breaking the man she loved. Her heart was crying forth, "Oh yes, I love you! I have loved you since we were babes. I have loved no other, nor shall I ever. I love you so much that it physically hurts. I love you Travis Winston! Do you not know how much?" but her lips were forbidden to speak these words. It did not change the fact that he was not a Christian, and they were of two different worlds.

"Travis, it is not that simple. I know you do not understand my reasons, but that does not change their legitimacy. We could not be happy, because we are not the same. You want things I do not and vice versa. For example, I am content to live only to serve my Lord. I have to put His will first."

"I do not mind you doing His will, Grace. I just do not see why He would care if you and I got married. I came to Oregon to find out what kind of person you are. What I found out, proved beyond a shadow of doubt, that I have always been right. You are the only one for me."

Grace produced a sweet, soft smile. "You see, that is the difference between us. I do not have to find out about you. I already know what a kind, generous, wonderful, good-hearted, loving, and perfect man you are. I would never have loved you in the first place if you were any less than that. You could never have changed, no matter how many years passed. You possess qualities rare for a common man."

"Then, I do not understand the problem. Are you mad because I checked you out?"

"No. Maybe, a little disappointed because you felt you had to, but I am not mad at you about anything. That is what I have been trying to get you to understand." She could not simply give him the ultimatum to get saved or they could never be together. She knew if she did, he would do it just for her love, meaning he would not get the real thing. He had to be drawn by the Holy Spirit, or he could never find what it was she had. "I will tell you what, when the time is right for us, I will be wearing this ring on the proper finger. Until that time comes, we had better get off this ride, or we will certainly be late getting Amy."

The gentleman was not pleased with the outcome of this interaction, but she had not shot him down completely. At least he was still in the game. He would win her heart somehow. There had to be a way.

Someday, Grace would come to her senses. He knew she loved him.

Amusing Grace

By the time Ruth and Isaiah arrived, the barbeque was well on its way. The children had arrived early in the morning and worked all day on the float. They laughed, ran, rode Samson, and played all day. Many of the children had never experienced this kind of fun in the entirety of their young lives. The food was excellent, and the day, in general, was pleasant.

Isaiah sauntered all day with a niche in his step that always displayed his satisfaction. His little girl had sacrificed for the vacation he and Ruth had been on. He knew she had scrimped, saved, and done without a lot of needful things in order to make them happy. She would never discuss with another living soul one ounce of discomfort she suffered for them, and he knew it. That was the way Grace was. Doing without Ruth and him for three days was, in itself, costly to her. He only wished she would take some time off for herself. The weekend of her reunion was not nearly long enough and besides, she was called back early from that. Maybe he and Ruth could manage to get her sent off for the weekend.

Travis talked to Renee to let her know of the plans for the trip east. She agreed to pick them up from the airport, when it arrived about midnight that night. Grace could spend Monday at the hospital, and then fly to New York on Tuesday. That would give her a day to rest before her board meeting.

Mr. Jameston had paid for her first class plane ticket, but Grace traded it in for a cheaper seat. She hated him spending so much money on trivial things as such.

The plans were thrown awry, right about the time to leave for the airport. Grace answered the phone not long after the vanload of children drove away. Giles, one of the workers called to warn them that the new girl, Michelle's, father was waiting with a lawyer. If the van had not left yet, they needed to stay put. The father had papers, and they were going to take the girl back home, but it was too late.

Grace fled as fast as her Mustang would allow, giving Travis barely enough time to jump in the passenger seat. By now, Travis needed no explanations for her spontaneous adventures. Grace drove as hard as she could to pull up only minutes behind the van; however, the children had already unloaded and were scattering in diverse directions.

Grace hid the Mustang behind Michelle's cottage. Using her key to slip in the back unnoticed enabled her to hear the male voices down the hall. The order came to the frightened ten-year-old to get her things from her room. She was going home. It was too late to intercept. "Drat! Lord, be with me, I pray. You know my heart, and I believe the girl's in danger. Show me how to protect her, please. Thy will be done, Father, not mine."

Michelle slowly walked the gauntlet-like hall. Any way she turned would be her doom. She did not know how to pray to a God that had, heretofore, been cursed to her. Tears of deathly fright rolled down her cheek, as "Hurry it up" followed her sharply.

Grace could hear Mrs. Basil pleading for them to wait. Something did not feel right about this to the housemother. The strange masculine voice had now become irate.

When Michelle walked close enough, Grace seized the moment and Michelle. She clamped her hand over the child's mouth to prevent a frightened scream from escaping. With her other arm, she pulled Michelle through the back door and into the car.

Escaping Grace

Travis quickly slid behind the wheel and started the Mustang's engine. When Grace and the young girl slid in the back seat, he sped away. Although Grace and Michelle hid in the floor, the men in the cottage caught a glimpse of the curious car.

The lawyer that was with Michelle's dad turned out to be a judge. He knew exactly who drove the car and suspected what she was up to. He urged the housemother to check on the girl.

Mrs. Basil came back without much surprise. She, too, knew what had happened. This was her thirteenth year as a housemother. She had witnessed what Grace was capable of doing to protect these children. It was no surprise that Michelle was gone. She told the two men the results of her search and made a hasty exit.

The judge had to procure an address on the child advocate, which bought her enough time. Ruth and Isaiah had already prepared to code green, after Grace received the first phone call. All signs of existence were minimized.

Amy was taken to the secret shelter to await the

inevitable. The Scottish couple was at the car door hustling the child into the house, before the Mustang came to a complete stop.

Once the fireplace was restored, Grace breathed easier. She and Travis went ahead and loaded their luggage into the trunk. They had to act normal. Showing no signs of knowledge was imperative. They even began their drive to the airport, when the posse, led by Judge Harris, pulled them over. At least they deflected the authorities from the house.

"Is something wrong, Officer?" she asked sweetly.

"Can you step out of the car, please?" commanded the young officer.

"Sure."

"Slow. Where I can see your hands. You too, Sir. Slowly."

Another officer was opening the passenger door and forcibly ejecting Travis.

"Is something wrong?" challenged Grace.

"Step over here, Grace." It was Sheriff Coates that was speaking now.

"Bill, what in the world is going on? I know I was

not speeding or breaking any laws."

The prominent judge emerged from his fancy Cadillac with an air of self-appointed authority. A glare intended precisely for Grace found its mark. She could feel the ice prickles creeping from one end of her body to the other. What was Judge Harris up to? It was odd that a judge would be executing his own court orders. Usually James, or some other fledgling would be employed for this task, let alone the fact that this was a Saturday. Maybe this little girl was related to him. He may have a personal interest in this case.

"Where is she, Grace?" he commanded.

"Judge," she nodded, "it is good to see you again. For whom are you searching?"

"Don't play games. You know exactly who we want," interpolated David Bradley.

"David, go wait in my car. I will handle this." He waited for the man to comply.

Grace had set the ground for the challenge. He knew it, and so did she. In the courtroom, he had total control, but here, they were in her domain. She need not threaten or say specific words. He knew she would not give the child up, even to him. He accepted the challenge and returned the fire in his stare.

"Where is Michelle, Grace? I saw you leave the orphanage with her. Now, we can do this the hard way, or we can do this the easy way. It is your choice. I have the papers ordering you to release her. It is all nice and legal, because I know how you like everything to be legal. So what is it to be?"

"Judge Harris, if I took off with her as you say, where is she? My friend and I were on our way to the airport. I truly am sorry, but I do no see her anywhere, unless you want to check my trunk."

The police radio burst forth with loud static, and then came, "Search of the house came up negative. There is no sign of anyone having been here at all."

"Did you search the barn and fields?" asked Bill.

"Negative."

"Then report when you are finished," he turned to Grace. "Grace, if you know where she is, I suggest you tell us. I am going to have to arrest you, if you don't, and then we'll find her anyway."

She held her hands out in a gesture to be handcuffed.

"Then, I suggest you start arresting, because I have no intentions of being bullied, even if I did know where she was."

Arresting Grace

"Hold on a minute," boomed Harris. "Grace, I promise the girl will be safe. Nothing will happen to her. Her dad is worried sick. You have no proof of her allegations; therefore, it is your civic duty to return her home. You have no choice."

"Let me see, I have no choice in allowing that sick pervert in your car to rape his own baby again? I know he did it. What's more, so do you. So, I ask myself why you are sticking your neck into the hangman's noose for this condemned man."

"Watch it, Grace. You are treading on thin ice. I may not be in a courtroom, but I still *am* a judge with a lot of power. It sounds an awful lot like you are accusing me of something sordid."

The look Grace distributed to Harris could not be duplicated. It was a mixture of confusion, but just underneath the surface, she had figured it all out. Several ideas crossed her brain, but it stayed just out of reach. She simply held her hands out to Bill and quietly spoke, "Do your job, Bill. Take me in."

None of the officers were willing to arrest Grace.

They had seen her showdowns before, but Grace had always prevailed. She was a good figure in the community, helpful and honest, so how could they put handcuffs on her and treat her as a common criminal?

Bill forewent the handcuffs and placed her in the backseat of the patrol car. Harris was angry. A lot of good it did to arrest her, when they still did not have the kid.

"What about him?" Harris pointed to Travis. "You should arrest him as well."

"For what Sir?" The officer asked.

With a menacing gleam, Harris charged Grace. "You are a fool, Grace Sorenson. Why would you go to jail for some kid who is more than likely making it all up, because she did not get her own way? You just remember, you will be in my courtroom, and I will show the same mercy you have shown me today."

A long discussion ensued. He returned to his Cadillac, because the two men were still sitting there when the last squad car pulled out, followed by Travis.

Grace prayed Travis wouldn't lead them back to the house. God answered. Her long time friend was not going to leave her side. He didn't know how long she would be here, but he did not intend to forsake her.

They refused him permission to see her for the longest time, because she had to be booked, photographed, and locked securely behind bars before allowing him a few minutes with her. This was the time her mind was racing for a contingency plan.

"I'm sorry you were dragged into this. You can still catch your plane, " she informed through the bars.

He bore a wounded expression. He leaned his head on two bars and reached for her hands. "Is that what you think of me? Do you think at the first sign of trouble, I'd leave without a second glance? Grace, if that is how you feel, then maybe I should leave. Is that what you want?"

"No, I don't want you to leave. I was impelled to offer you a way out, before things go bad. I don't know how long this will last, and I know you have to get back to your own life in North Carolina."

He kissed her forehead through the bars. "Grace, without you, I have no life at all. I would go back to living the life of a zombie, like I did before you came back into my life. I will give every bit of that old life up, willingly, if you would just say the word."

Grace wanted to cry. Why was she being so sappy? That did not change the status of his soul. He must be born again. "Then will you help me, while you can?"

"I have been waiting for my orders, my lady."

"Do you have a pen and paper?"

He pulled a pen and cash receipt from his front pocket. "Will this work?"

"Perfect. Here is Stephanie's number. Would you call her and inform her of what happened? Tell her that Judge Harris is overseeing this one personally. She probably will not be able to turn his decision over, but we must try. Michelle's dad is trying way too hard to get her back. I fear for her life. At some point, I need you to swing back by the house and set the security. I do not trust this man. First, go by my office. It may take a little time, but if you would not mind, I have some files. Look for the one labeled, 'Michelle Bradley'. Make copies of everything and bring me copies. In my left hand desk drawer are some cassettes. I do not know if hers is even labeled. If not, listen to the ones without a label. At the beginning of each one, I will have said the name of the child interviewing. I do not have another copy of any of these, so please; do not let anything happen to them. There has to be something I missed. You can call Stephanie from my office."

"Got it. Anything else?"

"Oh! Here, let me see that paper. This number belongs to the assistant district attorney. I am surprised he is not in on this deal, but because he is not, it might work to our advantage. Will you call him and explain what happened? Tell him I want to know what is going on and explain to him what has happened. Tell him I want to know why Harris is in on this one. Maybe for once in his miserable life, he can do the right thing."

"I will hurry back." He rushed another kiss by pulling her face to the bars. "Are you going to be okay?"

"Don't worry about me."

Investigating Grace

The sight Travis walked into, when he arrived at Grace's office, was not the one he expected. First of all, the door was not locked or shut. The creaking elevator drowned out the footsteps in the stairwell and the closing of the outside door. Next, the outer office had papers strewn all over the desk and floor. The door to Grace's inner office was shattered into huge splinters. The handle still remained in tact from where the bolt refused to release. Finally, the inner office had been ransacked. Files were thrown hinder and yon. There were no unlabeled tapes. There were no tapes at all, save four.

He dug for the phone, which had been buried. It had been off the hook long enough to stop the signal. Impatiently, he hung it up to wait for the reconnection. Then, he called Stephanie, but there was nothing but the answering machine. He called the sheriff's department to report the break in.

"Hold on," Bill told him. Shortly he came back to the receiver. "Grace asked if you would bring all the remaining cassettes with you. I will send my deputy over. Wait on him, would you?"

Travis disconnected that call and began to dial the other number. He did not mind that James Nicholson was the one to answer. He explained the events and waited for the reply.

James jumped in. "Tell Grace, I will be there ASAP. Does she need anything from her office?"

"I am there now, waiting for the police," he responded.

"Why?"

"There's been a break in."

"What about her house? If they broke into her office, who is to say the house is safe? Did she put her security gate up before she left?"

"No. I must get out there to do that, but I can't leave until the deputies get here."

"Do you think she would trust me enough to do it for her? It is on my way, and if you will tell me what to do, I can do it."

This brought mixed emotions. "Thanks, I appreciate that. I am afraid you may be right. What if they did not find what they needed here? The house would be next."

The officers arrived and began surveying the damage. They took pictures of all the doors and locks, dusted for fingerprints, and scrutinized every detail for an initial investigation. At long last, Travis was given permission to remove the cassettes and leave. He dreaded going to his beloved after having failed his mission.

Meanwhile, Grace paced the small cell floor like a caged animal. If the file and tape were gone, she would have to give Michelle up. She could not interview her again without bringing her out of hiding. She could not expect another judge to overrule Harris's order on her whim. Either way, Michelle would be exposed. "God, was I wrong?" yet she knew she was not. The devil would not be fighting so hard, if she were wrong. "Please, help me in Thy way." She fell to her knees beside the small cot and began an earnest supplication with her Father.

This is how Travis found her. At first, he did not want to intrude on what he did not understand. Prayer was not occasioned at the Winston house. Sure, Thanksgiving Day, they always gave some sort of prayer of thanks, but that was the extent of his prayer life.

She did not respond to his clearing throat, thus he waited for her to finish. He was not expecting the radiance she wore as she stood. There were no tears of defeat or sad lines of anger, only a twinkle in her violet eyes and a smile beaming. She knew God had taken care of the problem, even before it became a problem.

He explained in disappointment, "I was not able to get a hold of Stephanie, so I left a message on her machine. That guy from the second number said he was on his way. He offered to stop by and lock your gate. I hope, that it is okay for me to let him. We were afraid whoever broke in at your office might try the house before I could get there."

"That is wonderful. I really hated to lose you that length of time. You are far too important to me here and now. Thank you."

"I brought a box with the tapes in it. There were not a whole lot," he explained.

"That is because I had most of them at the house, working on my annual report. Oh! Oh! Oh! Thank you, Jesus! I forgot! That tape was not on my desk. It is in my briefcase. I was going to include the preliminaries in my report. My briefcase should be in the trunk. I did not have the file in there, though."

"I will go get it." He quickly gave her hand a squeeze.

"Thank you Jesus for reminding me."

"All this prison time has made you start talking to yourself, Grace. I do not think I have ever found you more attractive than at this moment. You are in total submission." James entered candidly.

"James! What is Harris doing? Why is he out on a Saturday throwing his weight around? Why would he chase this little girl all over the place on a weekend?"

"Grace, you tell me, and we will both know. I was not included in this one. I am curious to find out myself. What was the name of the kid again?"

"Michelle Bradley. She is ten years old. She has only been removed from her house three days. I did a preliminary with her the other day. It was not thorough, but enough to find out she does not need to go home. Harris was adamant about getting her returned to her father. I want to know why."

"Grace, that case has not come across my desk at all. I do not recognize the name. It is highly unusual for a judge to issue an order without my office knowing about it. I can call Greg to see what he knows, but I would not count on it being much. It sounds as if we were all kept in the dark. I find it hard to believe Harris was there personally."

"Travis, good, you are back. Have you met James? James, Travis Winston, Travis, James Nicholson. James is the assistant district attorney. Thank you for bringing my briefcase."

Bill escorted Travis to the cell. His job required him to search anything brought in to a prisoner, before allowing it. James walked out with the sheriff to call his boss.

"I do not know what I would have done without you. Thank you so much for all your help." Grace blessed her long time friend with an enchanting smile.

He reddened at the public gratitude. "I hope you get what you need from these. What now?"

"I have to find something I missed before. Just one little detail to get Harris's order turned over."

She sat down on the floor with her opened attaché case. She was hesitant about allowing other ears to hear the private conversation, but desperate measures took desperate means. Travis paced along the outside wall, with one ear clinging to every recorded word.

There was the focus. Whenever a child has truly

been through a traumatic experience, they focus on one thing: whether it is a smell, or sound, or something seen, or even heard. In Michelle's case, it was his wristwatch. The elastic band flashed horrors, Grace remembered. Michelle had trembled with chill bumps until a large tear fell helplessly down her cheek. Grace could see the girl sitting before her. This had been the first red flag. The answers were hard to voice, yet specific, nonetheless. This, too, was normal for having survived such atrocities. Obviously this was not enough to keep him from her, or Harris would not have issued an order. She needed more.

"Greg was handed Michelle Bradley's file yesterday morning with a note from Harris attached saying it was a rush case." James reported, as he came back in. "He requested, in a not so nice way, that we find a way to fix this broken family. Greg pushed it through to Harris's desk. The court order did not come down by closing yesterday, so he left it at work. He was curious as to why Harris was out on a Saturday doing civil labor too."

"Well, I suppose there is nothing to do, except wait. I will have to get Stephanie down here to help get a reversal. You two should go ahead and get some rest. I appreciate everything you did to help James. I will not forget it."

"My pleasure. Are you sure I can't do anything more? I know we butt heads professionally on occasion, but I always hate seeing you behind bars. I'm not the one keeping you here this time. Why not tell them where she is? It is not likely that her dad would do anything to her under the hot seat of this case. Too many people are watching."

"It will be more than the night," pronounced Stephanie at her arrival. "This is Saturday before Labor Day. It will be Tuesday, before they will hear your case. You better settle in. James, it is good to see you in the enemy camp. So, what have we found out so far?" She listened as the story, so far, was told. "Well, she was right about going home. There is nothing you guys can do for her tonight."

Coveting Grace

"What about the girl, Grace? Where is she? If you produce her, they'll let you go."

"James, I cannot believe how incredibly ignorant you are. Do you honestly think I would turn that child back over to the man that raped her?"

"What? I am just trying to get you out of jail. Even if he did it once, he would not be stupid enough to do it again while all this heat is on him," he defended.

The Irish temper reared. "I am not willing to risk it for any price."

"Fine, then I can post bail? Stephanie, could we not get a judge down to night court?"

Stephanie shook her head. "Not until Tuesday. This is a holiday. There is a slight possibility we can get Judge Moore to open shop long enough on Monday, but I would not count on it."

Grace sighed her frustration, "It will not do any good, if we do not sift through this information and find something concrete. I will either have to produce Michelle or probable cause."

"We have two days for that, and I have no doubt you

can pull it off," Stephanie encouraged. "Where is her file? I could take it home and research it."

Travis started another explanation of the other incident. "Whoever broke into Grace's office took any file she had on Michelle. We went through every one of them and came up with zilch."

"I am sure David Bradley had everything to do with that. What were you able to salvage?" this from Stephanie.

"You can comb through this cassette. It was the initial interview with Michelle. I can get the basics, but nothing that would get one judge to overturn another's ruling. You can see what you come up with. Guard it with your life. It is the only copy I have."

"Great. I will get on it. I will be back in the morning." Stephanie closed Grace's case to take with her. "Could I bring you something in the morning?"

"Nothing, thank you. I only pray you find something salvageable."

"Okay then, I left Fred with the boys, and I know he is wishing I would hurry." She hugged Grace through the jail bars.

"I will walk you out," James reported. He thought about trying to give Grace a hug as well, but decided against it. "Grace, if you need me, call. I will be here in a minute."

"Thanks again, James. I appreciate you both." She waved them goodbye and then turned to Travis. "You need to get some rest, too. You are going back to the farm, aren't you?"

He lowered his voice, "Should I? I mean, would it be wise?"

"You will be the only one at the house tonight. I am sure you can fend for yourself."

He understood her meaning. The secret they shared could not be uttered, even in the mind. He did not want to leave the side of the woman he loved, so he lingered as long as Bill allowed, clinging to her hand through the bars. It was not until Grace reminded him that they were suppose to be landing in North Carolina any minute that he remembered to call Renee. She would be greeting their plane and be angry they had not call.

Travis was at the jailhouse before visiting hours began that next morning. He wore the haggard look of not having had much sleep. On the other hand, Grace had slept soundly, after taking her burdens to her Father. Travis handed her Bible, which she requested he bring last night. He was not allowed to stay with her all day, but what time Bill did permit, he was by her side.

Stephanie did not come by that morning. It was after Travis had already gone that she made it. The reason for her late night visit was because she had been investigating a lead she picked up from the recording. Michelle mentioned ever so briefly about where the incident sometimes took place. She said something about her dad's work. Jumping on the long shot, Stephanie drove out to his office building and managed to interview the security guard, who confirmed the presence of David Bradley on the night in question. There was some hobnob meeting. He remembered it well, because Bradley's daughter was with him. She had been crying and carried a pitiful plea in her eyes, yet he had felt helpless. The guard said he could not get that frightened face out of his mind for some reason.

This should be enough evidence to get eradication. This, along with the other information Grace had extracted, would be sufficient to present to Moore in the morning. She was still awaiting his return on whether he would convene court long enough to free Grace or not. Meanwhile, the lawyer had all the proper paperwork drawn up into legal documentation.

To her surprise, James showed up Monday morning to advocate for Grace's release. It was not often that he could side with her, so he wanted to support her whenever the opportunity arose. Between Stephanie and James, and the fact that Grace was Grace, Moore signed the reversal. He was so angry that he almost ordered the arrest of David Bradley, but could not do that quite yet. Judge Harris still played into this scheme, somehow. Crossing another judge would most certainly cause trouble for him, but he did not mind in the name of justice.

Judge Moore agreed that Michelle could live with Grace for the time being. Ruth and Isaiah would keep her safe, while Grace was gone, yet she did not want to risk Harris or Bradley getting their hands on the child in their absence. At the first sign of trouble, they could go back into hiding. The advocate wanted to make sure that

Harris did not try to legally outmaneuver Judge Moore's ruling.

Before leaving, she made sure the supplies at the house were sufficient. They should not need for anything, until Grace came back from New York. She wanted them planted safely behind locked gates, while she was gone. Back at the farm, she unloaded the groceries and put them up. Next, she walked the entirety of her land to check for any intruders. Her nonchalant stroll was made hand in hand with the man who stood by her for these last two days. Lastly, she went into the secret room to release the prisoners inside. Ruth and Isaiah breathed easier, but knew the danger that still lurked about. They would protect this child with their very lives.

Traveling Grace

At long last, Travis and Grace were aboard the plane. The delay cost them two days, and because of the uncertainty of their plans, they had not even called Renee to meet the two a.m. landing. Both were exhausted mentally and physically. These last few days of constant stress had fatigued their nerves, and the

Winston couch was a haven for the weary Grace, who refused to take Travis's bed. That was the condition of her agreeing to stay.

The two travelers were awakened by a piercing squeal. The sleeping sister had awakened to find, to her pleasant surprise, that her brother and long lost friend were home. If that was not enough to bring Grace to full awareness, Renee's arms around her neck and screams in her ear did the trick.

"Oh my goodness! I cannot believe you are here. I have missed you so. You look wonderful! Oh, my, I can't believe you are finally in my living room!"

A sleepy Travis stumbled from his door, rubbing his sleepy eyes. His brown locks mussed from the hasty arousal. "For the love of Pete!" he growled. "Do you have to be so loud so early? Grace and I are tired. We need sleep."

Grace smiled forgiveness to all. "I really need to be up. I should have been up hours ago."

"See Travis, just because you are a grump, doesn't mean we all have to be a grump. You have to get ready for work, so what are you complaining for?" Renee teased.

He turned, grumbling, and shut his door. He had forgotten about work. Labor Day was over and so was his vacation. He would be unable to be with Grace their first day in his home. The old lover did not want to leave her side for a minute. He begrudgingly dressed in his jeans and work shirt and presently exhibited a sullen face to his two ladies.

Renee was occupying Grace's attention and time trying to catch up on twenty years, while her brother tempered. His moments with her were precious few and far between, and now he was forced to share her with Renee. He could not even tell her goodbye. Well, he could, but not the way he would have chosen had they been alone. With a mumbled "Bye" to Renee, and a "Grace, I will be home around three thirty. Will you be here?" he left sulking.

Renee had to be at work by ten, so she offered Grace to keep her car for the day. The two talked and laughed all morning. It was a reminder of yesteryear, when the two had been teens.

Grace rearranged her flight schedule in order to stay

with her uncle overnight. The meeting was scheduled to begin late morning, so she could wait to fly up early in the morning. She knew this would be the last time she would have to see her dear uncle on this earth.

The first thing she must do is to visit her grandmother. She knew this was not going to be a pleasant experience. Grace was a day late, and grandmother was not happy, so for several hours, the granddaughter listened to condemning criticism. "Why aren't you married?", "What's wrong with you?", "You should call more often.", "You are too thin.", "You should visit more.", "You are too quiet.", "How do you expect to find a man if you're never available?", "Your cousin found her a nice husband and has three kids.", "Don't you want kids?", and "Why not?" were just a few. The questions and criticisms were truly heartfelt gestures spoken out of love. Grace knew her grandmother really loved her, and she could not help being the gossip that she was.

The frustrations of the day and previous weekend wore on Grace's already fagged nerves. A migraine was onset, so she swallowed a handful of aspirin in hopes of controlling the severity of it. The blurred masses of bright spots had already taken possession of her sight.

She was later than Travis, who had showered a night's flight and a hard day's work from his body. The fresh, clean, gorgeous man welcomed her with an incredible smile. Nostalgia overwhelmed the Irish lass temporarily. His presence did something. For the first time, this feeling inside was made manifest. The week spent together had woven the threads of these two would-be-lovers together into one fabric. She enjoyed his company. Her heart seemed to stop, when he was not near. He literally took her breath away. She did not mean for it to happen, but somehow, it did. A longing to run into his arms and cherish his love, brought her to a repentant prayer. Only God could prevent this from happening now.

"I was worried when you were not home. Have you had a good day?" he greeted.

"I spent it with my grandmother. I have not been to the hospital yet." Grace tried to keep the thrill of seeing him from her voice.

"I could go with you, if you would like me to," he

offered with the hope of acceptance.

"I would like that very much. How about you, how was your day?"

"Suffice it to say, I could tell I have been off for a week."

Forgiving Grace

Grace made one stop prior to going to the hospital. She had wanted to do something special for Amy, so she came up with the idea to purchase a charm bracelet and fill it with specially made charms. Tiny gold rings with the engraving of each place Grace traveled would fit perfectly on a gold bracelet. The charm had to be ordered because of the engraving on it, which meant she would have to pick it up the next day, which Travis volunteered to do in her absence.

The hospital loomed ominous in the evening hours. The stench of death lingered in the halls. Veterans from the long years lined the walls, each with their own tale of terror to tell. Scars from their battles informed of their torments suffered for their country.

Jerry lay in a pitiful heap. His thin frail body used only a small portion of the bed. His once fully bearded face and head were bare. For the first time, Grace recognized how much he favored his dad. Jerry had always been a strong handsome man, but the frail being before her contradicted that. He had contracted cancer from the Agent Orange sprayed over Vietnam during the war. For many years, even back when Grace lived with him, he suffered with problems in his stomach, which was misdiagnosed as ulcers for all the years. By the time they decided it was cancer, the disease had infiltrated his stomach to the point that no surgery would be possible.

To add fuel to the fire, he was stricken with aplastic anemia. This is a disease that attacks the blood. Grace could barely stand to look at the once vigorous uncle. She entered as if on razor's edge.

"Jerry," she spoke softly.

"Grace, I knew you would be here. I was just thinking about you."

Like the prodigal son, she fell upon the neck of the man who had taken her in his home and loved her. Tears fled their ducts. Afraid she would hurt his fragile body, she touched him lightly, but she could not control the compassion that passed between them. He expressed in his touch the realness of his salvation. No words were necessary. When Grace moved from North Carolina, things had soured between uncle and niece. Fifteen years is a long time to allow this kind of anger to fester, but anger was not what either was feeling. The presence of Deity was undeniable.

"Uncle Jerry, I am so sorry for everything I have done. I was a rotten kid. I was selfish and angry and generally a pain in the neck. I exemplified pure heathenism for over twenty years. I plead for your forgiveness. Can you ever forgive me?"

"That is funny. You are asking me, when I should be asking you."

"No, dear one. There is no excuse for my behavior. I was saved and knew better."

"You were a little girl. I was the adult. You owe me nothing. It is I that begs your forgiveness for years of hatred and disowning you."

Grace smiled tearfully. "You were forgiven of all the day Christ forgave you. His absolution is what counts. He cast it all in the sea of forgetfulness, never to be remembered anymore."

"You may not realize it, but you were an influence on my life, even back then. Believe it or not, you left that impression on Lynette and Claudia as well. I thank God for taking care of you, when I did not have sense enough to do it myself."

"He sure has been so very merciful to me. Had it not been for Jesus, I would be in hell today, literally. You know that, as well as I do. He saved me from so much more than a burning hell."

"I regret so much in this life." Jerry's frail voice seemed to give away.

Grace broke the embrace while clearing her throat. She needed to change the mood, quickly. "Uncle Jerry, do you remember Travis Winston?" She presented her friend, as if she had just remembered his presence.

"Of course I do. How are you, Son?"

Travis responded to his outstretched hand, "I am fine, thank you, Sir."

"Have you been taking care of my Grace?"

"As much as she will allow. She is pretty stubborn," he laughed.

"She gets it honestly. Her grandfather was stubborn too." Travis bowed out of the picture, henceforth forgotten. "Grace, are you being difficult for your young man?"

"Probably. I always was a difficult child. You

should know that. The question is, how can I make things easier for you?"

"There is nothing you can do, Grace. It is just a matter of time." Grace noticed how he constantly pressed the morphine button. It would only send the relieving juice periodically, but the pain was so excruciating, he begged for it sooner. "Oh, there is one thing you could do. I need to change the beneficiary of my insurance papers. Could you witness them and get them sent for me?"

"Sure can."

He struggled toward a case, but Grace intervened. She recovered his satchel for him to pull out the necessary papers. They signed the appropriate lines to make the documents legal. Grace being a notary provided a legal assurance, unexpectedly.

Jerry breathed a sigh of relief. "I am glad that is done. Will you get these mailed for me, please? If they do not get sent, Myron will control everything. You know how terrible that would be."

"I will overnight these, when I leave, so you have no worries."

"There is something else I want you to do for me, Grace."

"Name it, dear uncle." Grace touched his arm delicately.

"I want you to promise me you will stay away from Shawn. He is dangerous."

"I know."

"No you do not." Grace saw a fear in her uncle, heretofore unseen. "Grace, you have not seen him for thirty years. I have. He is consumed with evil."

"Jerry, he lost the battle a long time before that. A person has the choice of good and evil. Sometimes, there is a fine line between the two. Shawn made his choice, when he allowed Satan to possess him. You do not have to worry about me ever getting around him, again. I am no fool."

"Good girl. I am so sorry for not believing you, then. I am sorry about a lot of things. I allowed Claudia to change my ideas in a lot of things, and for that, I shall never be absolved. I know what he did to you. I knew then. I should have done something to protect you."

Grace released a captivating smile for him. His eyes

closed slowly in weariness. "Do not beat yourself up for something you had no control over. It was all in the hand of God. I would not be the person I am today had things been different."

"My amazing Grace. Do you see good in everything?"

"You rest now. You are tired."

Jerry opened his eyes abruptly. "Do you have to leave?"

"No. I will be here when you wake up."

His lips quivered a smile of comfort. "I'm so tired. I don't want to go until Claudia and Lynette get in."

"You know you cannot do that. *It is appointed man once to die. After that, the judgment.* When your appointment is here, you must go. You can claim your family for the Kingdom, but you can't miss your appointment." She touched his arm as a feather. "I am envious. You will be resting in Him and going to the first day of your forever in your new and perfect body. I would love to go in your stead." She caressed the brow over his closed eyes.

"Go on. Tell me more."

"You know, when Stephen was being stoned to death, the Bible says that he looked up into Heaven and saw Jesus standing on the right hand of the Father. He was entranced in the vision. He was not aware of the rocks piercing his flesh. That is how I want to be. When my time comes, I want to be so close to God, I can see into Heaven. I do not ever want to alter my faith." Travis witnessed a surreal, faraway expression on her face.

"Not you, Grace." His words came amidst heavy breaths.

"Oh yes, me. You put too much faith in me, I am afraid. Look at you. You have suffered so very much for so long, and you found faith. You are ready, should He call tonight."

Parting Grace

"Grace Sorenson!" came a shrill agitating voice that opened Jerry's eyes and made both faces grimace. "What in the world are you doing? If you can't stop being so morbid, then you don't need to be here."

Travis had seen Claudia enter the door so quietly, but he did not have the opportunity to forewarn of her arrival. Grace bit her lip in prayer of not saying the wrong words. A weary look came over Jerry's forlorn face. Their holy communion had been defiled.

Grace reached to his ear to kiss him goodbye. "I will return later. You rest. I love you."

"Claudia, for crying out loud, do you have to be so loud?" Jerry chided as the two shut the door behind them.

Travis could feel the trembling creature under his arm. He felt as if he had eavesdropped on something so private, yet he dared not acknowledge to Grace that he had witnessed.

The stairwell door closed behind the couple, when Grace stopped in her tracks. Travis complacently enveloped her within his strength, where she collapsed into uncontrollable tears. She knew with him, she need not explain. He would understand completely. She contented to rest in his arms, while the tears insisted on flowing. His soft lips comforted her head with a gentle kiss. Soon, she forgot how Claudia had reverted her back to being a naughty child needing to be disciplined. Soon, she forgot the penetrating words of her aunt. The exhausted Irish woman would have been satisfied to remain in his strong arms forever in this solace.

Grace knew how important it was to send the insurance papers, so they mailed them first thing. She sent them overnight to their destination. Next, Travis took his would-be-lover to dinner. She mainly picked over her plate without eating much. Her mind was concentrating on Michelle, Jerry, and the final touches of her report that needed completing.

After a meager supper, they returned to the Winston home. Grace put Travis to work double-checking her figures, while she finished up the reports. Renee found them absorbed in work, when she got home from work, and threw in her assistance. Before long, it was finished.

Travis required sleep before his long workday on the morrow, so Renee offered to drive Grace back to the hospital. She had planned to spend the night with Jerry. Travis would pick her up before going to work in the morning, so that he might drive her to the airport.

The reunion of old friends had Grace trying to persuade Renee to make the New York trip with her. They could make a day of the Big Apple. A thought had occurred to Grace when Renee was helping. She needed an assistant, and if Renee had no commitments here, she would love her to consider moving to Oregon to become her assistant.

The night was short. Jerry kept trying to wake up and tell something important to Grace, who shushed him back to sleep. "You need your rest. Get some sleep, Sweetie," she would say. Then, his eyes would close in a restful slumber, for a while.

When five o'clock came, Travis appeared with his sister, who decided to take her vacation money and time and join Grace on her trip at the last minute. The suite was still reserved for a second night, so they decided to stay over after the meeting. Travis regretfully hastened goodbyes, because he had to get to work. He felt some better that his sister was going with Grace. Since her breakdown yesterday, he was concerned about how much more she could tolerate. Oh, how he hated not being able to go along.

Like Grace, Labor Day had gone, leaving a chill in the air and in Travis's heart. What was he to do when she went back to Oregon for good? He had failed at making her fall madly and passionately in love with him.

Actually, the only thing he succeeded in doing was rooting her irrevocably steadfastly within the confines of his soul.

The holy discourse he witnessed in his hospital room gripped his conscious like a vice. She had a perception, which, though he could not understand, he revered. Wisdom was a far better quality to possess than even beauty, and she possessed both. What tormented the man was that for twenty years, she had loved none other, save him. She could have had any man she wanted, including that James character, but she loved *him*, yet now, she held back. Why? She had spoken as if it was a Spiritual thing, but he was a Christian. He may not practice all the rituals, but he believed in God. He was always a good person. He did not lie, cheat, or steal. He never drank, except that one time. Yet, with all this admission, there was an unexplained pulling at his heart. The converse between uncle and niece had been poetic. They spoke of Jesus, as if He walked among them, and God as if He had always guided their lives. Now, he did not necessarily believe that. God never seemed to have cared about him or Renee; yet to Grace, it was real, undeniably. Travis Winston pushed these thoughts from his mind. Confound Grace, if that was her excuse for not loving him, then he was not sure he wanted this religious stuff. It was too complicated.

Grace and Renee appreciated catching a few winks on the flight. Neither had slept much the night before with all the anxieties going on around them.

New York was huge. Renee had never seen anything like it before. The tall skyscrapers loomed ominously, blocking out the sun from many parts. People overcrowded the streets, while cars were bumper to bumper. The two took breakfast at a little sidewalk café nearby the Jameston Industries building.

"I am so glad you came." Grace said excitedly. "I will be in this meeting all day, but afterward, we will have a blast."

"Yes, we will. There is so much I want to see, I do not know where to begin."

"We can go ahead and check into the hotel before I go. We probably will not have time to do much tonight, but tomorrow the possibilities are limitless. Our flight does not leave until nine o'clock tomorrow night. What are you going to tour today?"

Renee shrugged, "I don't want to go sight seeing

without you. The Statue of Liberty won't be the same, if you are not there to share it with."

"Oh, Sweetie, you enjoy your day. I am just glad you are here. It will give me time to try and persuade you to relocate to Oregon. I could sure use your expertise in my office."

"My expertise?" came the surprised response. "I'm hardly qualified for what you do. I would scare the bajeebers out of those kids. Kids and I never got along too well."

"I do not believe that for a second. You have more in common with those girls than you know." A somber attitude fell. "Did you ever have any more trouble from your uncle?"

"No, thank God. He ran like the dog he was with his tail between his legs. He did not even come to Momma's funeral; not that I am complaining."

"Did she ever know?"

"No."

Grace was fiddling with her cup. "Did you ever tell Travis?"

"Do I look crazy? Travis would have killed him long

before he died, if he ever found out. I never told another living soul except you."

"You dear sweet child. You have been so strong and brave. See, you can be an incredible asset to children who have been through similar situations. Think of how much you can benefit these girls. They need you. I need you. Please, think about it."

Renee laughed, yet pondered the idea all day. Renee's father died, when she was ten, and her mother's brother moved in with them three years later to help her mother out. This was part of the reason Travis moved to Wilmington. Uncle Robert had made life unbearable for him.

With Renee, it started out with 'accidental' touching in wrong places, and then graduated into more. Renee's mother was working, when she came home from school, but Uncle Robert made sure he was there, especially after Travis moved out. It was then, that he felt safe enough to advance his actions.

Renee had been devastated. She turned to the only one she knew she could trust, and Grace proved to be a worthy ally. She came up with the plan and helped in the execution of it. Renee came home from school, as usual, only, this time Grace was in the closet. She stayed out of school and hidden there all day. Uncle Robert went out around eleven that morning, so Grace let herself in with Renee's key. She had a Polaroid in one hand and a tape recorder in the other. This was where she learned the trick of taping everything. Renee allowed him to make his move, while Grace recorded his words. At the right moment, Grace cracked the door and snapped the camera three times. Two pictures fell to the floor, but the one in the camera stayed in her hand, along with the tape recorder, which she threw in her pocket. The flash had momentarily frozen the man, giving Grace the opportunity to flee. She ran, like the wind, the two miles between their houses and hid the picture and tape where no one would ever find them. Meanwhile, Renee challenged her molester.

She told him that if he ever dared touch her again, she would take the pictures and tape to the police, right after showing them to her mother. The two pictures lying on the floor showed him that she had enough proof to pull it off. He thought of threatening her, but thought better of it. He quickly redressed and stormed out.

Within a week, he made his excuses to move away. Renee never saw him again. She did not even join her brother in attending the hateful man's funeral. He had stolen her innocence and stripped her of her purity; things she would never regain. The things she held most precious to her, her treasures for her husband were stolen away. She hated him.

Meeting Grace

The annual company meeting was actually in its third day of convening. The many diverse branches of such a corporation required several days to filter. It was not important for Grace to be in attendance, except the tail end. All charity work usually went last.

She sat through the grueling hours of tortuous business jargon wondering how Ruth, Isaiah, and the girls were. She wished she had called them again this morning. Last night, the Scottish woman had sounded chipper, but Grace questioned if she should try staying the night, or go on back home early. At the lunch break, she phoned Ruth, who assured her of their safety. They had not had to open the security gate for any reason, yet they were prepared to code green at any point. She insisted Grace stay and not worry.

At three, Renee came to the office to collect Grace, but since the meeting was still in progress, she sat in the lobby to wait.

It was nigh four fifteen, when Grace presented her

divisional report. It took all of twenty minutes to conclude to the satisfaction of Mr. Jameston. He waited till last for Grace, because he knew her work would be precisely accurate, ending the meeting on a good note. If all his CEO's maintained their divisions like she did, he would not have as much gray hair.

He gave an ending speech of encouragement instruction, and criticism where it was needed, and then adjourned the meeting. Several members of the board detained Grace by slipping her an encouraging word.

She would simply smile and say, "It is not anything I have done. It is what God has done."

Albert Jameston intentionally lingered to walk out with Grace. "Grace, keep it up, " he smiled.

"I will try, sir." She smiled the smile that won every heart she met.

He continued, "I have done some investigating on my own into your work."

She looked at him in surprise. "Oh? Is something wrong, Sir?"

"Very." He knew he was making her suffer. "I have noticed over the years, that the funding you request

244

seems a mere pittance. I do not recall it ever having increased, as I know it should with the cost of living. How come that is, do you suppose?"

"I am sure I don't know, sir. We try to be economical in our spending. Speaking of which, it is a waste for you to reserve me a suite. I do not take up that much room to spend that kind of money. Also, you need to stop booking me on first class flights." She had forgotten that she was the one under rebuke. "I always trade the first class tickets in for economy. Do you realize how many supplies can be bought with the extra money?"

"Now, that is what I am talking about. I found out that someone is spending out of her own pocket for company expenses, and I want to know why? I would gladly give any amount of funding you need. I know what I pay you, and frankly, I do not see how you manage it." He directed her from the conference room into the hall.

"Sir, you pay me more than enough. Do not worry about that. If anybody, Ruth and Isaiah should get more than I pay them, but that is my fault. I could not survive without them. That is something I need to remedy right away. Thank you for bringing it to my attention."

Jameston shook his head. "You are incorrigible. Why not let me payroll them? They are doing a service for me. If I did not have someone taking care of my best employee, think of all the money I would lose." He reached in his breast pocket and pulled forth an envelope to hand to Grace. "This is something for you. I can never repay you for all you have accomplished. This is a small bonus to make up for some of what I owe."

Grace pushed his hand away from her. "No sir. I will not take that."

"But you have not heard my complete proposal. I want to start up two more advocacy foundations. The work you have done is so beneficial to the northwest area. I feel the need to set one up in the Midwest and one on the east coast. I would like for you to take on that extra responsibility of starting them up for me. You will go and interview for qualified individuals to head each one, show them the ropes, and basically get them started. I know you carry a full load, but do you not think we need to reach more?"

They came into the lobby, where Renee was eagerly

waiting. "Of course I do. Mr. Jameston, I would like you to meet my dear friend, Renee Winston. Renee, this is Mr. Jameston, my boss."

The two shook hands in greeting with a mutual, "Nice to meet you."

Grace continued. "I am trying to persuade Renee to come to Oregon. My assistant left me holding the fort alone, and Renee would fill in perfectly. I am just having trouble getting her to commit to it."

"Well young lady, is there any good reason why you cannot accept this job?"

"No sir." The intimidating figure did not have time to mess around and was straight to the point. "I honestly can't think of one."

Grace encouraged. "I have the utmost confidence, sir, that with the additional work you request of me, Renee will be perfectly capable of handling the foundation in my stead."

"Sounds to me like it is settled. Since Grace refuses this, I will give it to you, young lady for moving expenses. Grace, I will get with you soon with more specifics. Good day, ladies." Jameston handed Renee the envelope Grace had refused.

"Grace, what just happened?" asked a bewildered Renee.

Appointing Grace

"I believe you were offered a job you cannot refuse by the big boss, himself."

"What do you think? I don't know if I should leave Travis. We have been there for each other for so long. I would hate to desert him when he really needs me."

Grace placed her hand on Renee's shoulder, directing her toward the elevator. "Your brother is a grown man, perfectly capable of fending for himself. I do not see that it is desertion. The question is, do you want to pack up everything, move across country, and begin a whole new life?"

"You know, you are right. My brother loves you. If he has his way, I believe he'll be moving to Oregon before long, leaving me stranded. I do want to do it. I will! I am moving to Oregon, Grace."

The excitement kept building with every sentence she spoke.

"Great! Thanks partner. You are a life saver."

"Now, I am getting excited. We'll have so much fun."

Grace had been thinking. "We can build you your

own apartment at the back of the house, so you can have your own privacy. You will be a much-needed relief. I know you will love this job."

The two ladies spent the evening shopping. Grace ordered the charm for Amy's bracelet, which required them to pick it up on the morrow. Ruth was easy to buy for. She had dreamed of the day, when she could visit New York and buy some fancy French perfume. The delicate fragrance she chose was fitting for her Scottish queen. Isaiah was slightly more difficult to buy for. For him, she picked out a Scottish tweed suit. The ensemble was not complete without a matching cap and pipe.

Grace did not leave out her long time friend. It would not serve any purpose, though, to get him something that could be misconstrued. Deciding on a beautiful overcoat was hard, but became the satisfactory choice. Renee reaffirmed, he had never owned anything of this sort before which pleased Grace.

Good fundamental Bible believing churches were not to be found in New York. Grace looked, but to no avail, so they ate a late supper and retired for the night. It had truly been a long exhausting day. The suite was fully furnished with anything they could have wanted. They felt like two fairies in fairyland.

Around three thirty that morning, Grace was awakened from the depths of sleep. A quick passing of sadness seemed to have taken her breath away. "Peace, be still, and know that I am God," were the comforting words from her Master, and the knowledge came to her that her dearly beloved had gone on to eternity. Then, a Peace that surpasses all understanding enveloped her, and she slept soundly once more. The precious jewel of their last moments together was treasured until her death.

After a full day of touring the Statue of Liberty and the Empire State Building, the two weary adventurers flew back. Travis, who did not mind the lateness of the hour, because she was coming back to him, met their plane. They had at least one more day together.

Renee was not blind to the fact that her brother looked straight through her, or that his face lit up like a Christmas tree, when he saw Grace. She truly did not mind. Her brother was happier than she had ever seen him before. Grace had done that, just like she had turned Renee's life around. Yep, she could see it now. Those two were destined to be married. It would not be long before her brother was living in Oregon with them. Things were falling into place.

Being that she was a lady and he a gentleman, Travis refrained from exhibiting public affections. His respect for her would not allow him to break the code of etiquette, so he briefly placed his arm around her, delivering a peck on her cheek.

"Do you want to go to the hospital?" he asked gently.

The love of his life put forth a forlorn smile. "There is no need. He is no longer there."

"Oh, I am sorry." He choked the words, unable to speak any others.

"Do not be. He is no longer in any pain. He is walking with his Savior on the streets of gold as we speak."

"When are the arrangements?" he asked.

"I am not sure. I have not spoken to anyone, yet. I shall call in the morning."

Renee tried to lighten the mood. "Tonight, we are dead on our feet. Take us home brother, dear."

Expiring Grace

The rain began floating from the heavens, cooling the air quicker than anticipated, which left Grace underdressed for the weather. The dismal day reflected the attitudes of most attendants at the funeral, all but Grace. She knew where her beloved was going. He was now in Glory in a whole new body and she would not wish him back here for anything.

Grandmother, followed by Claudia, led the procession under the tent. Brothers and sisters, then nephews and nieces followed suit. Lynette and her family did not come to the funeral at all. Grace remained on the arm of her escort. The feeling of never belonging had bore through Grace for many years, and the cold condescending looks from several cousins and aunts confirmed the feeling.

Because of his newly found salvation, coupled with the fact that Claudia was not saved, they forewent a church service. They simply met at the graveside for some preacher to pray over him. Grace's heart wept. She wanted to cry aloud for the indiscretion against her loved one. He who had fought and ultimately died for his country, his family, for her and her rights of freedom, to be buried as a criminal pauper. They could not even extend to his memory, the common decency of a soldier's burial.

No songs were sung, no generic courtesies, just a few words and a prayer from the man calling himself a preacher. The umbrella was being held over the red curls, but it did not stop the tears from drenching her broken heart. Uncle Jerry had struggled and sacrificed for years to provide worldly possessions to his family and if a man were measured by his earthly wealth, he would be considered rich. Fortunately, he was rich in the Heavenly measurement, which was the one that counted. This sham of a funeral was a dishonor.

When the last amen was spoken, the couple under the umbrella shifted further from the stream of traffic. Two aunts, a cousin, and the remaining uncle ventured toward them to acknowledge Grace. Grandmother showed her severe disapproval of Grace not staying at her house by ignoring her completely. The fabric of this family had begun to unravel years ago, leaving only the tattered remnants laying on the wayside. Grace was not the only black sheep, but she was the only one that did not force a relationship upon the others. This family was only a family in name.

After the last person left, she paid her final respects to the shell which once contained the soul of her uncle. She knew he was no longer there, but she needed to put closure on a precious relationship in memory of all he had been to her.

Travis had failed to keep her dry. Her movements were too fast for him to keep up with, which resulted in the both of them getting soaked, regardless of the jacket Renee had loaned to Grace. The overcoat she bought for Travis in New York was placed lovingly around her shoulders, followed by a strong arm. Her mind was elsewhere when he escorted her to the car.

The man was disheartened when Grace asked for use of his car. He wanted to be the one to comfort her, but she rejected him. He sulked the first couple of hours, then graduated to pacing at her continual absence. Where could she be? Maybe she went to visit her family. He thought better of that idea. The last place she would go for any kind of help was her family.

Finding Grace

Grace drove the few miles down the road to the favorite little church she loved so much. Procuring permission and the keys from the pastor, she went to the only Source for comfort. Upon her knees in humble adoration to the Son of God, she prayed to the Father. So much had landed on her shoulders in the last little while and being away from home, she was unable to visit her prayer garden. The solution to this problem was to leave it all at the Savior's feet. There was nothing too great in which He could not bear.

Obtaining forgiveness was the first order of prayer. Once all her sins were covered under the Blood, then she submitted first one object, then another.

Michelle was the first object and possibly the most important. She prayed for the child's safety and salvation. Grace could remember the haunting in the ten-year-old's eyes. Michelle needed God's grace in order to survive the trauma of her childhood. She prayed for a long time over this one child, until the Lord lifted it away, leaving a peace in its stead.

Next, she prayed for Amy. Oh, how she longed to

make the golden girl her very own. Again, she prayed until the Lord lifted the burden from her.

She asked for grace to comfort her loss, and victory prevailed. It was hard to be sad at his passing, because he was in Glory now, yet she knew that she would miss the opportunity to visit him on this earth. Once again, God shed His mercy on her.

The last burden laid down was a dual one. The prayer for the two lost souls of Travis and Renee burdened her heavily. She was not praying for her gain, that she may love this man, but because she could not stand the thought of these two so dear to her going to hell. When one has the perfect love of Christ in their heart, they have the desire to see all saved. A peace did not come at first, so she prayed more. When at long last, she prayed through and the burden was lifted, she stood in awe at His wonderful power.

It was a smile that adorned her lips, not tears from her eyes. It was contentment in her heart, not resentment. She had communed with the most Holy. She had dined at the Throne of grace, which filled her soul with a much needed balm.

Leaving Grace

Renee was surprised to see Travis pacing in the darkened living room. "What are you doing here?"

"Last time I checked, I live here," he grumbled.

Renee rebuked, "Don't be such a grouch, Travis. That's no way to impress a woman. Where is your car?"

"Grace needed it. I don't know why or where she went."

"I can't help you with the why, but I know the where."

"What do you mean?" demanded the man.

"I saw your car at that church down the road. I thought you and Grace might have some good news for me. That is why I was not expecting you to be home."

The church! That is where she went. He should have expected something like that. He never thought about the church. How could he compete with God?

"What exactly were you thinking we would be doing at a church?"

"Okay, I confess. I thought you may have been getting married or at least talking about it."

"Don't you think you are rushing it, like a lot?"

"No. You love her, and she loves you. Why waste time? You have felt this way all your adult life. How is that rushing? Please explain that to me." The sister commanded from him.

"Yes, I love her, but I am not sure the feeling is mutual."

"Of course it is. What makes you think that?"

"Because she won't say it to me."

"Do you tell her?"

Travis sighed, "Time and time again, but she never says it back."

"I don't pretend to know why, but I do know that she loves you. I can see it in her face whenever she sees you. I can see the adoration in her eyes." Renee walked to the window at the sound of a car pulling in the driveway. "She is home. Stop being a grouch now, or you'll run her off."

Grace entered carrying a pizza box. "I brought home supper, so you wouldn't have to cook for me. Do you still like pepperoni and mushrooms, Travis?"

He exchanged a mysterious glance with his sister.

She gave him a 'see what I was talking about' look. "I do," Renee shouted with a waving of her hand. "You weren't supposed to do this. We are supposed to be the ones taking care of you."

"Nonsense. You two have done so much for me. Let me repay you before I leave."

He had forgotten she was leaving him. He was not ready for her to go. Suddenly, his appetite faded. She was going to walk out of his life indefinitely. Could Renee be right? Could he honestly think about such a serious move as marriage this early? Would she marry him?

Renee was the one to respond to Grace's reminder. "What time does the plane leave?"

"Seven fifteen. I still have my things packed, so that will save some time. Come on you two and eat. Travis, I know you have not eaten anything since this morning. Come on."

"I will in a minute. You two start without me." He retreated to his room in silence. He was debating inside whether it was really too soon to think on such serious questions. He listened carefully to the conversation in the next room, hoping to get the slightest bit of encouragement.

"You really shouldn't have done this," his sister was saying.

"Please, allow me one pleasure. You have catered to my every need since I have been here, plus you accompanied me on my trip, not to mention you are moving to Oregon to be a tremendous help to me."

"I am beginning to get excited about it. I haven't had a chance to tell Travis yet. I will miss him and Wendy. I wish you could have met her. You'll like her."

"If she is anything like her dad, I am sure I will."

What was his sister talking about? Renee was moving to Oregon? Since when? How come no one told him she was moving? He had to smile at the way Grace mentioned his daughter. He was sure Wendy would like her, if she ever could meet up with her.

Renee was continuing. "Grace, are you okay? I mean, I know your uncle just died and all."

"Thank you friend, but I am better than fine. I shall never forget how you and your brother have been there for me today."

"And I shall never forget the flowers and card you sent when Grandmother died and then when Mom died. It meant so much to me that you would think of us, when we had not seen each other in years. You didn't leave a return address, so I couldn't send you a thank you." Renee patted her hand between mouthfuls.

Flowers, card, when did she do this? How come Renee never told him about it? Dear sweet Grace. The intoxication of her presence was addictive. The tenderness expressed in her voice was drawing him against his will. He did not want to go in with her and watch her flee away from him, but he could not resist the addiction to her nearness.

"A thank you was never necessary," she was saying when he came in the room. "Travis, I sure wish you would eat something. You'll be sick from hunger if you don't."

"Well, maybe I could eat one piece. Thanks." He placed his body next to hers on the floor.

"What about you, Grace?" asked Renee. "Aren't you going to eat something?"

"Not before I get on the plane. I will be sick for

sure." She turned appealing eyes toward Travis. A glimpse of hope was detected. "Will you take me to the airport? I can call a cab, if it is not convenient."

No, it was not convenient. It was not convenient for her to leave at all. No, he did not want to take her anywhere. He wanted her to stay forever. Instead, "Sure. Renee, have you talked to that daughter of mine? I wanted her to meet Grace. This may be the last chance for a while."

"I have not heard from her since day before yesterday. She sure is acting strange."

Parting Grace

The two women, then, explained to Travis how Renee had agreed to move to Oregon and work with Grace. He was dumbstruck, even though he had heard the information earlier. He and Renee had always been there for each other. When Linda had died, Renee willingly moved back in with him to take care of him. After her first marriage, his home had been a refuge for her. Things were moving too fast and beyond his control, now. He did not want Renee to move there, he wanted Grace to move here.

Renee opted to wait until the first weekend in October to make the move. This would give her sufficient time to settle all things on this end of the country. She would have her belongings shipped to her by movers. Travis agreed to accompany her on the initial move, giving him another excuse to see Grace. They would fly to Oregon on the first Friday of October, and he, alone, would return on Sunday. Well, at least that was something to look forward to.

At the airport, Travis grew more exceedingly broken hearted. How could he say goodbye to her? She was in his blood, pumping through his veins into his very heart. October was a long month away. He dared to broach the subject he had on his mind since talking to Renee, but was cut short of asking.

"Grace, I know we talked about this on the Ferris wheel the other night, but I do not understand what your answer is."

"My friend," she picked up, "someday, I pray you will understand. Things should not change as they are now. You have a life here. Your happiness and daughter are here. I have my life across the country. I cannot leave Oregon. You have no right to ask me to leave, nor do I have the right to ask you to leave. It would not be fair to Wendy."

"You are not asking me to leave. I want to be with you. Don't you understand that?"

How could she explain to him without his acting without understanding? She knew if she flat out told him she could not be with him because he was not a Christian, then he would 'become' a Christian just to please her. He had to come to know Jesus as his Savior of his own choosing, because he came to the realization that he was lost, dying, and going to hell, not because he loved her.

"I understand that you think that is how you feel. You never know what may change those feelings. We have tried the test of time before and failed. I think time is the one thing we need. If we cannot pass the test of time, then it is not meant to be."

The voice of a woman burst forth in the air announcing the boarding of Grace's flight. God must have sent that just in the knick of time. She gathered what bags she had not checked in and readied to leave. The pitiful rejection on his face was almost more than she could bear.

"I must go. You will come with Renee next month, right?"

"Yes."

"What about Thanksgiving? Will you come for Thanksgiving?"

"Anything you want, I will do for you." He took her free hand in his. "Do you not get it? I will do anything you ask me to do. Just name it."

"I have to go. They are calling my flight again. If

you truly want to do something for me, keep going to my little church. I shall pray that you will get out of it what I have."

"I will do it. When I come in October, you and I will sit down for a serious talk. I am sure you have an idea of what I want to discuss, and I will expect an invariable answer. Go ahead, or you will miss the plane." Hoping against hope, he threw an "I love you" toward her to no avail, but she did not respond.

Preparing Grace

Springfield awaited its lost love with the problems of before. Grace had yielded to the mighty power of her Master which rendered her heart free from these problems. Michelle had fit in well at the farm. Grace had procured all the necessities they could possibly need before coming east, so Ruth and Isaiah were able to stay in seclusion to protect the girl. If trouble had come flirting with their gate, they never knew, because they did not turn the system off one time.

Grace did not announce her return. She quietly went about her daily business, working double hard for the arrival of Renee. She met with a contactor about designing her friend's apartment and sent the plans to Renee for approval before consenting the start. Then, she met with Judge Moore to start the proceedings for adopting Amy. Of course, he was not the one to process her request, but ultimately, he would have final say.

Travis ventured to call her at the beginning of the week, but the two decided for the purpose of expenses, it would be better to correspond by mail, instead. He was faithful to write her daily. Sometimes, he would continue the same letter the next day before sending it. He always ensured his feelings for her. She in turn would send letters of calculated wording in order to not encourage the man in something that may never happen. God may have lifted the burden for his soul, but He had not okayed the relationship thus far. Grace continually prayed for wisdom and strength in this matter.

The second week Grace was home, Mr. Jameston sent her to Virginia. Virginia was the place of choice for the eastern location of the two additional foundations he wanted to start. It was more neutral than most any other place. He wanted Grace to go over on Thursday, dig up some real estate and hopefully begin a search for someone as qualified as she.

Having heard Grace's request, Jameston did not book her on a first class trip to Virginia, nor did he put her in a posh hotel. Instead, he called on an old friend, who owned his own airline. The friend was in need of a favor from Jameston and was only too happy to oblige one little seat on a private flight. The smaller plane made Grace nervous. It was less quiet, and the turbulence could be felt a lot more. Once her feet touched ground on the other side, she determined it was not so bad after all.

She met with a realtor Thursday evening, which promised to take her all day on Friday to explore all possible places, but Grace was not one to sit around waiting for someone else to make something happen. She rented a car and explored on her own. There were too many good spots for an office. She would have to shop with the realtor about which would be the best one.

Next, she drove a little to the outskirts of town. She was trying to find a suitable spot for the group home. They needed something large enough to house the necessary children. An old warehouse, or something of the sort, would be perfect. The settings on the outskirts of town were usually better places to locate these homes.

It was about dusk when she chanced upon a curious site. It appeared to be an old school of some sort. The wild overgrown weeds prevented her from seeing a lot of the groundwork. She quickly pulled the car over to investigate her find. It was not a very large school, for that was, indeed, what it was. It had "Eastside School" faintly painted across the top. The grass touched her chest in some places, because it was so high. An antiquated wooden swing set fell in various places, where the elements of time had taken their toll on the play piece. A rusted old fence surrounded the property with "No Trespassing" signs attached.

The windows had boards nailed preventing her from being able to see inside the building, but she estimated the size of the building to be sufficiently large enough for her need. Tomorrow, she would ask Mr. Russell about this property.

Mr. Whitmire's Grace

After obtaining the owner's name to whom the school belonged, she went to the office of Whitmire and Whitmire to negotiate the land. Russell had informed her in no uncertain terms that Whitmire would not be interested in selling that parcel of land, but that would not stop the stubborn Irish girl.

"Good morning. I would like to speak with Mr. Whitmire please." She entered with her most charming smile, her hand held out in greeting.

The forty something gentleman smiled amusedly at this waif of a girl coming in here as if she could conquer the world. He doubted she could even conquer her checkbook. He eyed her under scrutiny, trying to figure her angle. Her handshake was firm which was impressive for a woman.

"I am Mr. Whitmire. How can I help you?" he asked arrogantly. She must be with one of the women's clubs, soliciting for a charitable contribution.

"I should like to inquire about a parcel of land in which you own."

He was slightly taken aback, "Oh. And which parcel

is that?"

"The one in which the old Eastside School sits on."

The dramatic change in facial expression was noticeable. The tone altered to match the coldness of his face. "I am sorry. My father owns that land, and I can tell you right now, it is not for sale, not for any price. Goodbye, Miss..."

"Please just call me Grace. Maybe if I explained to your father our purpose for it, he would change his mind."

"I am afraid you are wasting your time, Grace, was it? He is not interested in selling it, but if you insist in making a fool of yourself, he will be in the office later. Good day."

He turned to show this meeting was over. Grace took her cue and left to collect Mr. Jameston from the airport to take him to see her final choice for the office. Naturally, he was pleased with Grace's choice. Mr. Russell met the two with a hired contractor, who had thrown some plans together that morning. Grace excused herself while her boss met with the other two men.

"Mr. Jameston, will you excuse me for a few minutes. I should like to call Mr. Whitmire's office to see if he is in yet."

"Sure, go ahead." he dismissed, and then turned to Russell and the contractor. "What does my assistant think of these plans?"

Grace ran across the street to the pay phone. Receiving the curt, "no", she returned to the waiting gentlemen a little distracted.

"What do you think, Grace? Do these plans meet your approval?"

She stepped in to look them over, "What is this here?" she pointed.

"Executive restrooms," answered the contractor, "This will be the inner office sanctum. Here will..."

Grace separated from the group, accentuating with gestures as she walked in demonstration of her wishes. "The restrooms are suitable as is. We do not need fancy makings. We do not need a second story built on. It would be a waste of resources. You put an office here and here. They would be very spacious, then the lobby would work perfectly well right here. We do not plan on serving multitudes of people here. We do not usually get many parents wanting to come in and chat with us. It is mainly for the use of the workers."

Jameston smiled confidently, "You heard her boss. She knows her business. Any questions?"

"We should be able to complete this task inside two weeks, then. It will not be very hard at all." The contractor was speaking mainly to Grace, now. The other two gentlemen wandered off still talking. "I could not help overhearing you earlier. You were looking for Whitmire?"

"Oh, do you know him?" cheered Grace.

"Well, sort of. He is a contractor, and I am a contractor. We have come across each other's path. You are not thinking of trading my services in for another, are you?"

"No." He enjoyed hearing her laugh. "I wanted to ask him about buying a piece of land on the outskirts of town for the group home. I spoke to his son. He seems to think his dad would never part with it. I suppose I could be wrong in asking."

"His son is right. He would never be interested in

selling it."

"It is too bad. That old school would be perfect."

"That is what old man Whitmire thought, some twenty years ago."

Grace looked at him curiously, "What do you mean?"

The man explained, "He designed and built that school. It was his pride and joy; that is until the fire. Seventeen children died at his hand. He was never the same again."

"Oh goodness. He must have been devastated, but I do not see how it was his fault."

"There was not sufficient fire exits. Somehow, they were blocked or something. Anyway, the whole town blamed him. He boarded up the old place and never looked at it again."

Grace protested, "They were wrong. How come when something tragic happens, one person must be responsible. Sometimes, God allows things to happen for His own purposes."

"Well, they did. To make things worse, his daughter was killed in the fire. His wife left him, because she could not bear to look at her child's murderer."

"Oh, that poor man," Grace shook her head sadly. "He lost everything he had."

"Yep. Anyway, throw your proposal at him, you never know. You do need it for a good cause. When will you be able to return for inspection of the new office?"

"I am going to trust that into your capable hands. I am not sure exactly when I shall be able to get back. I have a grueling schedule back in Oregon."

Grace spent the rest of the evening searching for a suitable head for the foundation. The phone book provided the names of preachers in which she intended to interview for names of possibilities. She hoped to find one experienced in this line of work, who could understand the job fully. She met with several preachers before it grew too late. She only sifted one plausible candidate out of the whole evening.

Wearily, she dragged her tired limbs into her room. She recalled the pitiful story of Mr. Whitmire all evening. She knew she could no longer even think about confronting the man for her selfish wants. Then God gave her a peaceful solution.

She phoned the number to the man's office, "Mr. Whitmire, I know you do not know me, but the Lord has laid you on my mind, and I wanted to tell you I am praying for you." She hung up the phone in time to answer the knock at her door. "Who could that be this late at night?"

"I could not resist the chance to see you. Are you surprised?"

Enduring Grace

Upon receiving Grace's return letter, in which she informed him of her trip to Virginia, Travis left as soon as his workday ended on Friday and drove the distance to surprise her. When the door was opened, Grace was startled. Bedraggled from a hard day's work and feeling ashamed at her appearance, she surveyed the handsome man before her, wearing his blue flannel shirt and jeans. His cologne had an intoxicating effect on her fatigued senses. It was not long before she fell asleep on his shoulder. He covered her cautiously prior to exiting to his own room.

Travis was tickled when Grace desired to stay over till Sunday. He was, however, not too thrilled at the idea of going to church. It was one thing to attend the one back home, but these strange ones; that was a different story. Grace wanted to meet at least one of the candidates in person before going back home. She had a particular one in mind to attend. The woman Grace intended to interview was not in attendance that morning, therefore, she would have to make a second trip later. There were no specific reservations for her home trip, so Travis convinced her to ride back to North Carolina and leave on an evening flight from there. They left as soon as church was out. Things were going his way, which made him happy.

The clear sunny sky warmed the riders in the vehicle, giving them a pleasant trip. Travis valued the fellowship with his Irish beauty very much, but he pulled into the airport with regrets of having to say goodbye. Even Grace lingered as long as possible before leaving. She was getting into this much deeper than she wanted. She could not afford to be in a relationship with a man who was not a Christian.

Plenty of work awaited the wanderer upon her arrival home. The progress on Renee's apartment was steady, because Isaiah had taken good charge over the project. His keen wit left him with a great head for this type of work.

Amy and Michelle were growing too close for comfort. Grace knew it was only a matter of time before the child would be returned to the system, and Amy would be devastated. They both would. She prayed for the Lord's will to be done with Michelle, begging Him to not let her fall in love with the girl, only to have her ripped from her heart. It would more than she could stand.

Her new task in Virginia did not stop simply because she was no longer in Virginia. She still had to sift out the perfect director for the east coast foundation. Jameston had already begun negotiating on the central foundation. He was looking more toward Oklahoma or Arkansas and promised to wait until she had Virginia up and running before proceeding too far into the central. He knew how industrious Grace was.

A typical case popped up in California prior to her DC trip. There was enough to keep the woman too busy to allow her heart to fall hopelessly. It had not registered in her mind that she had fallen wholly when the two were young lovers. She thought she could deny the truth, but the angels watched from above, adorned with their version of a smile, knowing their Creator had control.

The main focus after the Virginia trip was preparing for the Senate Hearing next week. Along with the

California case, a quick business trip to Washington State to investigate a case crossing the border from Canada, intervened her schedule, forcing her to procrastinate till the last minute to finalize the details of her speech. Stephanie double-checked her speech for her, and Grace felt safe in a faux security that she could present a flawless case, void of any havoc.

Misconstructing Grace

In truth, her woes began before she left for DC. Nervousness reared its ugly head in a familiar way. The symptoms of before came back ten-fold. The only consolation in the whole nightmare was that she was booked on a small private flight, free from James Nicholson.

In her hotel room, amidst a bout of nausea, a knock on the door disrupted her misery. To her dismay, it proved to be James, who announced his room was the adjoining room with hers. Beholding the vision before him, James felt sympathy for his friendly opposition. He almost called off his plan to charm her, almost. His carefully laid plan was working.

When he found out that the red splotches plaguing her face were from nerves, he tried to calm her by offering his help. This was a start. She opened up to him about her fears, as she asked him to proof her speech, which he did. He pointed out the opposition's argument. He could think from the lawyer's point of view and tell her how they would twist her words around to suit their own purpose.

Then, Grace reread it herself. How could she be so stupid? He was right. They could walk through the holes in it. Grateful that he had discovered this before she humiliated herself in front of all those people, Grace tore up her speech and agreed to allow him to assist her in making another, much to his joy.

She did not touch a bite of the dinner he ordered for fear of not being able to keep it down. She was not aware when he shut the door between their rooms in hopes of secluding her solely to him. The good part about sitting up all night doing this was, that it took her mind from her affliction. They worked, then reworked, and then reworked again. Daybreak was upon them when they completed a feasible speech. James had insured her that the opposition may fight a good fight, but they could not tear down what she had prepared. His friendship was purely precious in this incident.

Hoping to regain strength and poise, Grace pleaded off to shower and wash the night's troubles away. He followed her back to her room and used her phone to order breakfast. He hesitated when the phone began ringing, and since Grace was in the shower, he answered it for her.

"Grace Sorenson's room."

"Where is Grace?"

"She is in the shower. Can I take a message?" he offered.

"I tried to call her all night. Is she alright?"

"Oh yeah," laughed James, "she has been with me all night. We..."

"Who is this?"

"James Nicholson, who is this?" but the answer to his question was the dial tone. Whomever had been on the other end had hung up.

The breakfast was delivered before the lady returned from her preparations. James set his ordered flowers in specific array to impress the lady; however, she scratched her arms continually throughout the meal, not paying a bit of attention to his gestures. Somehow, he was determined to make her notice he was alive.

Accepting Grace

The dreaded hour drew nigh. Grace contemplated calling Travis. She wanted to hear his voice, but that defied all she believed in. Proper etiquette would never allow a lady to call a man. She wished he had called her last night. She had become more dependent on him than she had realized. He could give her something she needed. Oh well, she could understand why he did not. He probably did not even realize she was in Washington DC on that particular day.

She went into the courtroom with little confidence. The huge room contained hundreds of prominent lawmakers and professionals scrutinizing her every move. When, at long last, her appointed time was at hand, the woman stood on wobbly legs, presented a strong voice, and sent forth her plea. No one in the room would have ever guessed this lady was petrified to the point of almost tears. Even James became enraptured in her words, in spite of the fact he helped write them.

Grace mesmerized the crowd, and then returned to her seat to allow the other side to present their opinion. Conversely, she left the hearing much dejected, because her mission had failed. She had not made her point. She had let all the Shannon's down. She had failed them all.

She left the room, went straight to acquire her

belongings, and then caught the first flight out of DC. She did not wait for James to escort her. She did not even wait to tell him she was leaving.

This let down sent her into a working frenzy. She had to make up the difference to these kids. She could not be superwoman, yet she tried to personally protect everyone by herself. This wearied her fast, and to top it off, the love and support from Travis was far removed. She received neither letters nor calls for the entire week, before Renee's move.

The apartment would be finished around Thanksgiving, so Grace readied the attic room with bright sunny windows washed and curtained. Amy offered to bunk with Grace, leaving Renee her room, if Renee took offense to the attic room.

The office had been long waiting its new manager. Grace made all the possible adjustments easy for her old friend. Starting the new fiscal year allotted a fresh start for the newcomer. Grace had sent some information to her to review, so she would not be walking blindly in. She could go ahead and familiarize herself with the impending cases.

Renee did not mention anything out of the ordinary about her brother. Grace realized she must be overreacting. Of course the man could not continue to write her everyday. He was a very busy man. She was juvenile to expect it. By the day of Renee's impending arrival, Grace had been elevated. Finally, she was going to see him. She counted the moments till his arrival in order to give him the letters she held for him. She could not send them until he wrote to her first, so she planned on giving them to him in person.

Only, when Renee came, she came bearing the news that Travis, without explanation, refused to accompany her. He had made some excuse of having to work overtime. Other than that, Renee's arrival brought a new zestful life. Oregon was beautiful. The golding of the leaves was somewhat different than the tourist-attracting quilt of many colors from the Blue Ridge Parkway.

Renee had sold her old car in North Carolina, and with the money from Jameston, bought a new Jeep in Springfield. She settled into the third story room gladly. The chameleon-like creature fit perfectly into her new life. She was knowledgeable of the pending cases at work, enabling her to glide in without rippling the water too much.

Amy loved Renee from the very beginning. She was so much like her brother, and Amy loved him especially. Despite her insistence that kids hated her, Renee won the heart of Michelle too. She filled the role of aunt perfectly.

The snow set in, showing the alien beauty anew. Renee was going to spend her first Thanksgiving in memory with snow all around. Christmas brought snow, sometimes, but not Thanksgiving.

When Travis rejected the invitation to spend the holiday with them, Grace wondered at the sudden change. What had made him stop all communications with her? Had she broken his spirit with her inability to commit? Had he found another? He had broken his promise to her again. She had vacillated too long. Oh well, God had answered her prayer.

She would rather have not seen him at the class reunion at all, as opposed to renewing these old feelings, then losing him all over. Now, her prayers had to change. "God, help me forget him."

Renee moved into her newly completed apartment. She said nothing of her brother to Grace. She had noticed he had been lacking in communication with her boss. He had not even talked to her as much as she had expected. Had the two had a fight? Surely, Grace would have said something if they had separated. Renee made a mental note to ask Travis the next time she spoke with him.

A large envelope was delivered in the mail, which Renee hoped was from her brother. It was face down on the entrance table when she came in, but this was not her house to pry.

Grace was working longer hours, and though Ruth still insisted on her joining them for supper every night, many meals were taken without Grace. Amy would watch her drive in, then wander over, knock on her door, and wait for her to get ready to eat.

Favoring Grace

Grace didn't mind working over. She had to do everything in her power to keep these children safe. The curious envelope must wait for the morning to be opened, because of the extremely late hour in which she arrived home this particular night, so Amy brought it to her over the breakfast table. She adored Grace's "Thank you".

They all watched in anticipation, even Isaiah, although he would never show the outward appearance of it, but Grace did not volunteer an explanation. They could see the postmark, which told them the envelope was mailed from Virginia, much to their disappointment.

Enclosed was a stack of legal documents, including a deed and a letter to Grace:

Miss Sorenson,

Please accept this contribution for the purpose of building the home for your children. The deed is legally signed into your name. You will find that enclosed. Also enclosed is the description from the title search. Please consider this an early Christmas present.

She fingered the documents in disbelief. Mr.
Whitmire had signed and notarized the wanted property
in her name. How did he know? She had not told his
son who she was, nor mentioned her name to anyone
that she could remember. This must truly be a gift from
God. He knows what we need and when we need it.

Grace could not write a letter of thanks for such a
sweet gesture, so she executed a short trip to the Virginia
spot. She left the office in Renee's capable hands,
which was the whole purpose of Renee being hired on.
This trip did not include a preparatory call to Mr.
Jameston. She left all on her own. Besides, there was
no point in sitting around waiting for no letter to arrive
from Travis.

The idea of traveling by train had a seductive pull,
but time was of the essence, so she declined this method
of transport. Flying was the best route, so she booked a
flight on a small commercial airline.

The weather was a reminder of years gone by,
bringing memories of watching the sledders tramp up

the huge hill, in order to blast a new path with their sleds. Before she knew it, a smile had perched sweetly on her lips, making the few other passengers curious about the cause.

The plan was to bee line it to Whitmire's office or house, whichever he proved to be at, extend her sincere thanks and return home. The hearing for Michelle's placement was to be held first thing day after tomorrow, so she must be back by tomorrow evening.

Whitmire junior was the only one present at the office. His handshake lingered longer this time, while he tried to determine what kind of creature this was. He had tried for years to get the old man to relinquish that land over to him to build condominiums on, but his dad had never wavered. Now, for some cute redhead, he not only sold it to her, he gave it to her, lock, stock, and barrel. What power did she have over the old man? Well, she would not pull any funny stuff with him. He would see to that.

"Is your father in?" she greeted.

"No. Quite frankly, I am not sure exactly when he will be in."

"I shall wait for him, if that is alright with you."

He shrugged carelessly, "Suit yourself. It could be late."

She placed her petite figure in a comfortable chair, not with the intentions of intimidating the man, but doing so, nonetheless. He watched her shrewdly over the pretense of working. The satisfied smile made him nervous. For almost three hours, she waited, while he shot side glances in her direction. What was her angle? He would like to be a fly on the wall for the conversation between her and his father.

The door opened and the Jameston contractor stepped through. Grace stood in greeting. "Hi, fancy meeting you here. I was going to get your number from Mr. Jameston and call you while I was in town."

"Grace, right?" he shook her hand, grinning boyishly. "Are you not satisfied with the office?"

"Oh no. It was perfect. You did such a superb job; I was interested in hiring your services again. You will never believe it. God has supplied the land for the home. It is the most incredible miracle. Maybe, later today, you might be able to ride with me out to it. It would be awesome to get it going. We could have it up and overflowing with children by Easter."

"Well, what is wrong with right now?" asked the gentle man.

"I was waiting for Mr. Whitmire to come in. I hate to miss him again. He was so generous, I would not feel right unless I made a point to thank him in person."

He held his finger in gesture to hold on a minute, "Anthony, when is your old man coming in?"

"I do not know," was the reply, "I figure sometime late this evening."

"Tell him not to leave this office until I get a chance to see him." The man commanded a reverence because of his age and wisdom. "Shall we?" He held his elbow out in order to escort the lady.

Searching Grace

Grace sang the praises of a man she had never met for the entire trip to the land. The older man delighted to watch her lady-like gestures as she told of her immeasurable gratitude. At last her eyes feasted on the dilapidated old school.

Where before, the tall grass reached chest high in places, it was now manicured to the minutest detail. The old wooden swing set was nowhere to be seen. It had been replaced with a new state of the art aluminum, play set. It was three times larger than the old one, with a slide, monkey bars, a tunnel, and much more. A chain link fence was in the middle of being set up around the property. Sand was boxed in around the play area. Boards had released their hold on the windows and doors. Grace stood dumbfounded outside the car.

"I cannot believe Mr. Whitmire did all this for us. Can we walk down?"

"It is yours, you can do as you like," he helped her through the old wooden fence. Watch your step."

The closer they approached the building; the details of the structure became more defined. "The artwork is beautiful. See the trimming, I do not think I have ever seen such a technique before."

He pulled her arm gently, "If you like that, wait till you see this." Inside, he pointed to the ceiling. It contained a hand painted mural, alive with the description of the era in which it was painted. "My daughter painted some of it. Carrie was to be in the first class to graduate."

"You rarely see such raw talent this detailed. She interpreted youth uniquely. Does she still paint?"

"No. She was one of the seventeen killed in the fire."

"Please tell me you did not condemn Mr. Whitmire, like everyone else," she searched his eyes.

"I am afraid I was probably the worst one. Anyway, what do you think about the building?"

She proceeded through the halls, pronouncing what this room could be, that room could be, until they found their way to the cafeteria. Outside it, gaping holes told the horror story of years gone by. Grace concluded to leave the upstairs as the bedrooms, while leaving some of the rooms downstairs in tact, to open a school for the children staying for long periods of time. Lastly, she was led into the black room in which her partner knocked until the boards fell down.

Seventeen faded wreaths still lay, marking the memorial of the lives lost. The second story floor had fallen through, leaving a mess of debris in its wake. The stench of stale smoke almost made the cries of death audible, all these years later.

"The fire started in the chemistry lab next door. The explosion completely destroyed this wall. This was the theatre. It was small, but it was a small school, they did not need a big one." He must be reliving the trauma all over. He was no longer talking as much to Grace, as he was himself. They could not get out. The fire exit was on the back wall. They could not get out. I do not understand why they could not get out." Sadness enveloped him.

Grace had listened carefully to him all day. Something was beginning to register in her brain. Of course, why had she not thought of it before? It all made sense. She could not remember getting an introduction to him.

Her kind words soothed his guilt stricken soul. "Mr.

Whitmire, how long will you condemn yourself for something you had no control over?"

"I should have done something different. I could have given life, instead of taking it."

"You could not have changed an inkling of what happened any more than I could change it. God is the only One that can dictate the events that occur. It was His will. His reasons are pure and holy. It is not ours to ask why."

"What could be pure or holy from seventeen children being burned alive?"

Grace was speaking equally with her hands. "Right this minute is pure and holy. If Carrie had to die, then let her death account for something. Had it not been for her death, then her father would not be standing before me this minute, learning how to be saved. Mr. Whitmire, you have a hope of Redemption, but only you can choose it. You must decide your future. Christ is knocking at your heart's door. It may be the last time He ever will. The life that begins after this one ends will last for an eternity."

She explained, "I do not pretend to know Carrie's

heart, but I can say, if she was born again, you can join her again in a land where there is no more pain or death. A perfect home with streets of the purest gold, clear as crystal, walls made from the most precious of stones, and twelve gates made of twelve perfect pearls. I imagine the Light of the world creating many never before seen colors which permeate by His mere presence. No guilt will be found there, for sin cannot enter There. The price has already been paid. The One knocking paid it that you may be with Him forever and ever and ever."

"But, I have been a really mean man. For years I have ignored my son. His mother took off with him after Carrie died, and I am afraid I resented him, as if he had a choice."

"There is nothing He will not forgive you for. *If thou shalt confess with thy mouth, He is faithful and just to forgive us our sins.* You must come with child-like faith. You must believe in His virgin birth, that He lay down His life for our sins, and that on the third day; He rose from the grave and ascended to the right hand of God the Father. Let Him in your heart to guide you in

His path."

He had seen enough religious ceremonies to know that you must kneel to the ground. Ignoring the years of soot and grime that had built on the floor beneath his neatly pressed pants, he fell to his knees. He grasped Grace's arm, pulling her to her knees. They both prayed amid the ashes that stood as a reminder of the tragedy so long ago; one came up renewed, the other came up reborn.

To make his decision perfect, Grace explained how they would convert the full two stories of this room into a chapel for the home. They would take the original wreaths and place them under a picture of each of the seventeen victims. The chapel would be named after Carrie as a memorial.

Depressing Grace

While she had been gone, Harris had been busy. He had taken advantage of her being gone to throw a monkey wrench into the sweet harmony. He was unable to turn Moore's ruling, but he did the next best thing. With the father's permission, she had been taken from the farm and shipped to a boarding school, under the provision that the father came nowhere near her. For Harris, the important thing was that they had her away from the troublemaker.

As soon as she found out, Grace flew to the school to investigate the situation. She wanted to make sure the officials did not allow Bradley anywhere near Michelle. She was not happy at all about the whole arrangement, but had no choice but to comply. She promised Michelle to make periodic visits to keep check on her. Michelle, in return, promised to call Grace should she need her for anything.

This brought further discouragement to Grace, when she went through the proper channels to bring Michelle home for Christmas, but her dad had seen to it she could no longer get visitation rights. She wanted all her loved ones safe with her.

When Thanksgiving passed without hearing from Travis, she secretly wished he would come for Christmas. Deep in her heart, she felt he would not be there. God had answered her prayers and she was just not liking the answer.

The third heart-breaking ordeal was when James

Nicholson decided to invite himself to spend Christmas with them via Renee. Ruth would never turn anyone away from her table, even if the person was the maleficent man Grace told her about.

Renee considered his presence at Grace's house for the holiday. Did he play a part in her brother not communicating with Grace anymore? Could he and Grace have some relationship going on? She did not believe Grace would do that to Travis, but something had come between them, and this guy was certainly shadowing Grace's every move.

His being there was only a minor setback for the hostess. She waited for the perfect chance to slip out unseen late in the afternoon. James had excused himself to the restroom when she made her escape. She knew where to go so he would not find her.

Isaiah had taken Amy out in her new sled, where he promised to pull her behind the tractor in the field. Ruth was flitting around cleaning an imaginary mess, which was not there, and Renee had taken the quiet moment to call her brother, who distractedly dismissed her before quickly hanging up.

When James returned from washing his hands he asked the only person there, "Where is Grace?"

"I am not sure, but probably she is out in her prayer garden." The dutiful sister decided to probe.

The man looked confused, "Her prayer garden?"

"Don't ask. You know how Grace is," she laughed.

"I obviously don't, but you seem to know her pretty well. Can I ask you a question?"

"Sure."

"What is her deal? I mean, I have tried everything I know to get her to go out with me, and she turns me down flat. When I ask her out, she laughs it off as a joke. I have tried everything in my power to get her to look at me the same way. Tell me please, do I stand a chance?"

"Quite honestly, it sounds to me as if she is trying politely to let you down. If you have tried that many different ways, and she has not responded, then it is safe to say you need to move on." Renee realized that this man could have very well have effected her brother's sudden reclusion. However, it did sound like Grace did not encourage him.

The guest began to wander the grounds in hope of finding the prodigal beauty. He found her in the cold snow, on her knees and she did not budge as he approached her. Something was wrong with her. The ungodly man did not understand the concept of prayer or a prayer garden. The would-be suitor tread carefully up to her, lifted her high, and began walking while ignoring her protests. He didn't stop until he reached the shelter of the barn."

"How dare you!" she spat angrily. "Have you taken full leave of your sense?"

"What? I thought you were hurt. You are going to yell at me for helping you? Thanks a lot."

"No, James. I am sorry. I should never have yelled. I have a lot on my mind. It is no excuse, I know. Please forgive me."

"Now I feel bad. I am sorry, too. I should have asked if you needed help before acting like a brute."

"There was no harm done," Grace suggested, "Shall we both forget it happened?"

"I will, if you will answer me a question, Grace."

Grace patted Samson's head, because of his insistent

snorting for attention. "If I can, I will."

"What is it going to take to get you to notice how I feel about you? I have tried for years to show you how incredible I think you are. I mean, I know we butt heads professionally, but you still have to know. Could you ever feel the same about me?"

She touched his arm, "That is dear of you to say, but James, I tried to never encourage these feelings in you."

"I know. That is the problem."

"I am sorry you wasted your time on me. I have been committed to another man for all my adult life. I could never betray that love. I'm truly sorry if I misled you in any way."

He hung his head sadly, "I appreciate you being honest with me. I feel really foolish."

"I wish you would not. We have been friends for so long. I would hate to think something like this would destroy our friendship."

"Friends?" he accepted with outstretched hand.

"Friends," she reiterated with a hug.

This ended the chase for James Nicholson. Grace was relieved that this one problem was solved. The other problem, which was imperative to solve, was Michelle's situation. Something must be done soon. She was afraid that if she procrastinated too long, Michelle would be in danger again. Stephanie was working on a plan to reverse Harris's judgment, but it would be near impossible.

Exploring Grace

Jameston called at the end of the first week of January for a special request. In her own homeland, Ireland, her specialty was in need. They offered to pay her to come and council a group of children in dire need. It was out of the ordinary for Grace to travel this far, but she would travel any length, for a child.

Albert Jameston called on his airline friend, Graham Singleton for the arrangements. Singleton replied by offering a private charter plane with a highly reduced airfare. Singleton's son, who was attending Oxford University, was flying home about the same time Grace was and stated he would appreciate the company for his son's return.

Grace made ready for the exciting new trip. Traveling overseas, whether for business or pleasure, was something she never imagined she'd be doing. She was tempted to take Amy with her, and had it not been for school, she would have. This would've been an incredible learning experience for them both. Naturally, Amy was devastated when Grace refused her travel rights.

In an effort to assess all the things that needed to be finished as soon as possible after her return, Grace started placing the irons in the fire. Isaiah and Grace slipped out early one morning for a routine fishing date. This was their haven of bonding. The two fished without exchanging converse. They did not need voluble words to communicate.

One commitment Grace made was to the overworked Scotsman. She promised to relieve him by taking on the duties of the farm work more. She knew he was wearing the tired eyes with pale skin, but Isaiah was almost as stubborn as Lamby, and refused to go to the doctor. Ruth promised to watch him extra careful during Grace's absence. Though they did not know it, this would be their last fishing trip together like this.

Then, there was the trip to England. The simple joy of riding down the streets of London was insightful enough. Her sightseeing was accomplished from the car window on the way to visit Oxford University.

Graham Sinclair's son and Grace became instant friends. David had expected an older, much more subdued woman; but instead, he was pleasantly surprised. Much to his disappointment, he was forced to take a rain check on her dinner offer in order to work on finishing his class work.

David Sinclair was an intelligent young man studying to become a lawyer. He had held off coming home for Christmas break in order to complete a crucial thesis for one of his classes. He was very articulate and very much a perfectionist. He would not leave school until a perfect work was turned in, which he foresaw would be at least three more days. The plans included his flying to Ireland to pick her up, when he was finished with his thesis.

The beautiful green mountains could be seen from the low altitude of the plane, but that was as much of them that Grace could see. Ireland's once beautiful city was filled with terror stricken residents and angry government officials. The civil war, which had ravaged its glory, raged on indefinitely. Many children had been orphaned in the cruelty of this battle.

The young children she spoke to broke her heart anew. Some did not look as if they could fend themselves from a fly, let alone a perpetrator of the cruelest measures. Grace could have taken every one of them home with her.

In three days, Grace had done all she could do, as a new type of discouragement befell her. Her definition of success had not even been within her grasp. The allotted time passed too quickly for the need. She planned to make a second trip later to complete her mission.

Home was inviting the wanderer back. She did not realize how homesick she was, until she thought about bringing Amy on the next trip. Grace intended to try and spend more time at home from now on. It seemed like ever since Amy had come to live with her, she was hardly ever home. Amy needed a mom, and whereas Ruth was the best, she had not signed on for that particular job.

Her dainty hand touched the circled charm on the end of the chain she wore around her neck. The distance across the ocean caused a separation that the miles across one country did not. At least in Springfield she felt closer to the man she loved, even if he would not allow her close enough to touch.

Had he not renewed these emotions which were

locked away deep inside, she would have been spared this new torment. At least, before he walked back into her life, she knew why he could have nothing to do with her. This time, she was oblivious to his instant dismissal. Could it be that he found a way to stop loving her? As it were, even going home would not mend her broken spirit.

David met her at the appointed time with having completed all his work. Grace had left immediately from the conference to pick him up at the airport. Grace offered him to drive. He was used to the busy streets, whereas, she was not. It would not pay her to wreck the rental car.

David took her to dinner, introducing her to the elite cuisine of the foreign country. He watched her graceful movements with pleasure. He never had a sister, but this older lady had all the qualities he would desire in one. She did not treat him like a child. She allowed him to treat her like a gentleman should treat a lady, instead of little schoolboy, like the usual accompaniment his dad sent. They were condescending to him, but Grace challenged his intellect.

Of course, Grace made sure the topic came around to her Savior at some point or another. David spoke respectfully of his faith. He had been raised a devout Catholic. Grace explained that it is not religion that saves you. It is not because you are Catholic, Baptist, Lutheran, or anything. The only way to Heaven is through Jesus Christ, the Son of God. It was He who died on the cross that we might live. This was an interesting revelation, yet he did not clearly understand it all.

As they drove toward the house Grace was staying at, they both marveled at the unreal scenery, which had rolled out a black velvet carpet before them. The car seemed to be going fast, but Grace did not mind. She looked over to see a look of pleasure on the young student's face, which assured her that she was doing the right thing. The boy obviously could handle the car.

Very little was said. Neither wanted to spoil the quiet wind blowing through the open windows. An occasional pointing out of something rare or beautiful was the extent of conversation.

Grace closed her eyes, laid her head back, and let the

air relax her for a while. A strong desire for sleep overwhelmed her, until she felt a sudden uneasiness. The motion of the car seemed rougher, now. She bolted. They were speeding through a pasture! They were going to hit that barn!

Without a second thought, she pulled the steering wheel into the opposite direction of the barn. The process of saving a collision with the barn had caused a side effect. The car hit an object, whether it was a rock, hole, or what, Grace was not sure, but the car took flight and landed on its top. Then, after two flips, it rocked on the caved in roof, while smoke and dust prohibited any vision.

Grace lay silently, double-checking her whereabouts. She had to verify she was not in Heaven just yet. Finally, her senses came back. Her head was in pain. She could feel the blood trickling down her temple. David! She still could not see a thing, and it took quite a bit of strength to get out of the vehicle. The side had been dented, preventing the door from opening. The caved in roof prevented her from being able to crawl through the open window.

With one hand trying to feel what was going on with her head, she pulled herself by the steering wheel to the driver's seat. It was vacant! Where was David? His door was completely missing. It was a struggle, but Grace managed to scrape her way through the small hole. She could see small flames licking. Her only thought was to find David. She dragged her trembling legs away from the car.

She could see a little, now that the dust had settled. The path of the car was becoming visible. Patches of grass had been uprooted in the wake of the skidded car. Grass was still attached to the fender and indentations of the roof. All the tires were bent on the axel, while two of them were flat.

An oddity caught her eye. On the bottom of the car, there were what appeared to be guns, somehow attached. This gave more urgency. The combination of those flames and those guns, the car was sure to blow. She must find David. At this point, she was crawling on hands and knees, for her strength had given out. It felt like hours, before Grace spotted a heap lying several hundred yards away from the wreckage.

She reached it after a painful passage on her knees. First, she checked his pulse. Then, she flipped him over. His eyes were rolled back into his head. He was seizing! Next, she checked out his mouth where she found a swelling tongue. Her hands were filthy and covered in blood, so she dared not touch his mouth, so she rolled him to his side in hopes of keeping the air passage open. She had nothing to place under his head except her battered legs. They both lay as such until the young man regained consciousness. Grace was struggling between the two worlds during this time. The car had thrown David far enough away from it, she thought, to be safe.

Neither was aware of the small explosion of the gas tank, followed by the snap snaps of the ammunition, which they would have expected to be much louder. It must have happened while Grace had momentarily lost her fight to stay awake, because, the next thing she knew the car was in roaring flames. She watched the flames, while waiting on her friend to come to.

The question of the purpose of the guns under the car kept crossing her thoughts. Why would they be there? Why this particular car? That barn belonged to someone; surely there must be a house nearby.

Once again, Grace closed her eyes in oblivion. When she awakened this time, she was in the arms of a strange man and could hear David's weak voice. The old gentleman smiled into her questioning glance.

"Aye, Lassie, I see you've awakened," came his thick rich accent, which was barely understandable.

"Oh, is she awake now?" asked David.

"I can walk," she barely whispered.

"We're almost to the house, wee one."

A tiny older woman met them on the stairs. "What did ye find Edward?"

"This young couple wrecked their car."

The woman's speech was equally accented to her husband's. "Aye, then bring them in. I'll get them cleaned up."

Grace looked at David, then at the gentleman. Had either seen the guns? What if they thought the weapons belonged to her? Neither looked at her strangely, so she forgot about it for the time being.

The sweet Irish woman bathed the wounded red head. A chunk of glass was pulled from the backside of her skull. The bleeding around the temple came from a gash above her eye. The elderly woman had a gentle touch as she cleaned first the wounds on her head, then the ones on her shoulders. After cleaning her hands, the woman finished by putting the soapy cloth to her burning knees.

"This isn't much. Ye be needing stitches, deary. That gash on your head, plus the place on the back. I am not sure about the shoulder. It looks a mite deep, if ye ask me."

Grace was not listening, though. The two men speaking in low tones captured her attention. David had the appearance of being agitated. He kept glancing toward her with a funny expression. The woman was going to make the preparations for taking the injured girl to the doctor when her husband walked in and quietly guided her through the door.

Accusing Grace

Grace searched David for the answer, "What is going on?"

"You tell me," he accused.

"I beg your pardon?"

David began with a regretful sigh, "What were those rifles doing on your car?"

"What? Surely, you do not mean to say you think those were my doing?"

"I must ask. You forget where we are. There is a civil war between the people and the government here. Mr. Monaghan made it plain that if the authorities find them, we will not be going anywhere any time soon."

"I tell you, I know nothing of those guns. I simply rented that car, as is. I did not think I needed to search it for hidden weapons."

Showing his manhood, David took charge, "Then we are to assume the rental company is filtering weapons in through these cars. There is no way to prove our innocence to the government. I will go back out and try to remove them, before anyone else does. Mr. Monaghan respectfully asked us to move on. He does not want to be a part of this, and I do not blame him."

"This is crazy! They cannot accuse us of something without a chance to prove our innocence," Grace retaliated.

"You forget, we are no longer in the land of the free, home of the brave. We have no rights here. If we go to trial on this, I guarantee you we will spend time in their prison system. I must hurry. I will be back. Be ready to go when I return."

Grace paced wearily back and forth. A more nervous Irish lady reentered the room with a box. "Edward tells me you and the lad are in trouble. If ye can tolerate, I have some of Edward's fishing line. I could tack up those cuts. I'm no expert, but we can't have ye running around bleeding all over the place."

"That is fine. I will try to hold still," Grace replied, while a heavy burden weighted down upon her.

The woman washed the needle and line in alcohol before beginning her dreaded task. Grace was not sure whether it was because the place was numb, or if God had just taken her pain, but she felt nothing of the first set of stitches. However, the second set stung as she touched the alcohol to her head. This one was a little more difficult because of the hair. She was not able to touch the shoulder, because they were interrupted by David's return.

He was breathing heavy from the fast run, "Too late. They are already on the scene. There were dozens of men out there. The firemen were hosing it down. They were all in huddles and pointing. They must know by now. Come on Grace. We must go now. Thank you both for your generosity."

The old man showed them through the back door, "Go to the other side of the woods. When ye get to the edge, follow it south until ye reach the next town. Hopefully, ye can lose yourself in a crowd before the authorities find ye."

"Here ye go," Mrs. Monaghan handed them a canvas bag, "ye may need this on the way. Mind ye to take care of yourselves, now. Gubbye. Please, don't think we're horrid for turning you out this way."

"Thank you so for your kindness," Grace hugged them. "May God reward you for what you have done."

David shook Edward Monaghan's hand, "I am sorry

if we brought trouble to you."

They did not linger any longer. On the lightest possible foot, the two were out of sight in the woods instantly. Grace's weary limbs threatened to forsake her. She felt as if she couldn't go on any further. She must stop. But no, the consequences were too dire if she stopped.

The beautiful sunlight that had warmed her face in the car had now renounced its friendly smile. Left in its stead, were the shadows of the evening dancing mysteriously, yet threatening the imaginations of paranoia. Grace thought the edge would never come. Her head was pounding, "Please God, give me the strength," she prayed, without realization. David was half pulling her by this time.

"Come on. We cannot get slack, now."

"David, you go on. You had nothing to do with this. This is my mess. I cannot expect you to be arrested for something I did. I will not let them involve you. Please, I cannot go on."

"Nonsense. I am not leaving you. Besides, what will I do? My passport was in that car. I can no longer go home."

Grace continued to argue. "But, you can contact your dad. With one of us on the outside, we have a better chance of getting out of this mess. If we both are in custody, then neither of us will be able to get help. Go on. Contact your dad. I lost my passport as well. My purse and personal belongings, along with all my money was in that car. I am sure by now, they have found out the car was registered in my name and have searched the place I was staying. This may be our only chance to get out of this mess. Go on in to town and see about getting a new passport. I will go in the opposite direction and avoid the authorities as long as possible. Can you remember my phone number?"

"You may be right, but I do not feel right leaving a lady in distress."

"Do not argue with me. We do not have time for it. If you value our freedom, you will go, no argument."

David shook his head, "I hope I am doing the right thing. I have a notepad and pen. You can write down all your information. I will find you again. Here." He handed her the pocket sized pad and pen. They were dirty, but that did not matter.

Grace took the items with trembling hands. She quickly scribbled a note to Isaiah and Ruth, pleading for their immediate attention to her plight. She folded it, wrote the address on the outside and asked David to mail it for her. Quickly, she wrote another note and address, asking him to mail it as well. Finally, she wrote down Mr. Jameston's phone number and address. If anyone could help her out, it would be him. He had the kind of power it took to deal with this situation.

David kissed her on the forehead. "Grace, you stay hidden until I can return. Do not let them find you. Maybe you can find an old barn or something to hide in. Do not stop until daybreak. I mean it Grace. Do not let them find you before I do. I will be back as soon as possible with your passport and way out."

"I will try. You remember, David, if they catch up with you, you never met me."

"Do not worry about me. Go. Quickly!"

They both ran as fast as their weary legs could go in opposite directions. Another quick prayer went up for the Monaghan's, "Please God, keep them safe, along with David."

Grace did not mind the orders of her young companion. Her battered body had given completely out. She found a tree, full of needles, and climbed to the top. There, she nestled in the branches safely to get some much-needed sleep.

The early morning rays of sunlight crept silently in, but what awakened the sleeping girl were the sounds of the distant barking of dogs. Grace wasted no time in scurrying down the tree. Her limbs were bruised and tender, and with each step, a new ache announced itself. Were those dogs for her?

At last, she reached the edge of the woods. Across the way, she could see a highway or road of some sort. She made a hasty crossing, after a careful searching for oncoming traffic. Once she safely passed the road, she came upon a small waterfall, leading into a good-sized river. An old trick she had learned was that if one was ever lost, find water and follow it down. The problem was passing the glen before her without letting the dogs catch up. She did not waste a second. Swiftly, Grace ran, almost as if she had wings, across the open. For a moment, the barking seemed closer, and then it grew fainter again. Yes, she had made it. Instead of running parallel to the river, she jumped in quickly. Each movement was made with graceful rapidity because of the urgency of maintaining her freedom. The cool water soothed her burning skull as she swam downstream toward the other side. Maybe they would lose her scent some. She exited the water when she came upon another forest and proceeded to disappear into the thick trees.

Once again on dry land, she was able to quickly resume her flight. She was no longer hearing any sounds, except for the calls of the wild. Once again, she breathed easier.

Running on Grace

Meanwhile, David had run nonstop to the village Edward had told him about. He pushed the hunger in his stomach out of his thoughts in order to accomplish his goal. His first task was to call his dad.

The operator spoke through her nose, "I have a person to person collect call to Graham Sinclair from David Sinclair. Will you accept the charges?"

"Just a minute please," came the reply.

Minutes later, Graham retrieved the phone, "This is Graham Sinclair."

"I have a person to person collect call from David Sinclair, will you accept the charges?" Reiterated the nasal tone.

"Yes, operator."

"Your call is being connected."

"Thank you ma'am." He waited long enough to hear his son's voice, "David, where are you? I was expecting you home in a few hours. Is everything alright?"

David set to explaining about the accident, the guns, and the authorities. He described how they had lost all their paperwork in the fire. He could imagine the frown his father was wearing on the other end of the line. Graham Sinclair promised to be over the next day, hopefully with two new passports. He could not guarantee success with Grace's, but he knew he could get his. No matter, he would be there for his son first thing. David felt much safer having confided in his dad.

Next, he called Jameston, who promised to be there as soon as possible for Grace. Lastly, he mailed the two letters. Finding postage and envelopes was slightly hard, when he only had a few cents in his pocket. There was a beguiling woman that lent him the money on the street outside the post. He promised the lady of the evening to repay in full, but she was in doubt of that ever happening.

David was starving. It was not until then that he realized he had taken off with the canvas bag Mrs. Monaghan had prepared for them. Inside were sandwiches, which had been hastily thrown together. Bless the dear woman's heart. He also found some currency in the front pocket. Why had he taken the bag? Grace would be without any means of getting food. He was such an idiot. Well, at least he could pay back the borrowed money. He would make sure the Monaghans were paid back some day.

There was enough money to procure a room for the night, but his guilt of leaving Grace without would not allow him the pleasure. He pondered to whom he might ask the important private questions in which he needed answers. If Grace were caught, where would they likely take her? Would it be the nearest town? Was there a central place in which they took all suspected rebels?

He would just have to wait on his dad to arrive. He would know what to do.

The long night seemed endless. The chair where he perched was uncomfortable, but he would not allow himself comfort while his friend was running for her life. He wanted to find her, but declined on the grounds that his father would not find him if he did.

Pursuing Grace

As soon as they arrived, Jameston and Sinclair found the address David disclosed as his whereabouts. Mr. Sinclair hugged his boy with great relief, while David reiterated quickly the story from the beginning for both men.

"Have they caught up with her, yet?" asked Jameston.

"I haven't heard. I wanted to search for her after I called you, but I needed to meet you. I think we would know if they had caught her."

Jameston studied the boy carefully. He looked like his father. He was not sure about honor of the boy leaving Grace to fend for herself, but that judgment would come later. He took command for his girl, "Then, I suggest we begin back at the beginning. Do you remember where the wreck was?"

"I think so. I will have to retrace my steps from the airport, though. I do not even know where I am at this very moment."

"What are we waiting for?" Graham Sinclair clasped his hand on his son's shoulder.

At the crash site, the only remains from the wreck were the skid marks in the field, and a few broken pieces of metal and glass. Upon approaching the Monaghan house, Edward greeted them with a stern glare and acting as if he had never met David before.

"Mr. Monaghan, this is my father, Graham Sinclair. We have come back to…"

"Sorry lad, ye must have the wrong fellow. I don't believe we have met." As he spoke in a low gruff tone, the man gave a semi frightened glance toward the house.

Jameston stuck his strong hand out, "My name is Jameston. I am looking to buy some land and was wondering if you would be interested in selling that lot over there." He pointed in a general direction.

The young Sinclair looked at the man in confusion.

"There is some acreage out behind the barn. Would ye be for looking at it?

"Yes, please."

The conversation was not of much importance, just questions about the weather in this part of the country and all. It was not until the group was completely in solitude behind the barn that Monaghan spoke of the accident.

"They are watching my house. They assumed ye'd come back to salvage yere personal belongings." He explained, "They have not left since arriving yesterday. Martha is a nervous wreck. I am glad to see thee and the lass made it to safety."

"We did not. That is why we are here. The lass insisted we split up so I could contact some help. We are hoping to catch up with her before the authorities do. Do they know anything?"

"They know very little. Martha told them she knew nothing. I told them I saw someone running into the woods, but I could not tell how many there were. They arrived later with the blood hounds."

Jameston tried to expedite the conversation. "What is the town south of the opposite side of the woods?"

"Castlepolland," was the reply.

"That is where you picked me up this morning," informed David. "When we split, she went in the opposite direction. What is the closest town?"

Albert interpolated, "If I know that girl, she will not go near a town. She will manage without being seen.

Can we drive to a location close to where they separated?" he asked the Irishman.

"Aye, some close, but you will have to walk a kilometer or so," he responded.

"Well go back to your business and pretend to be contacting a lawyer about selling some partial of land. Maybe they will not suspect a thing. Can you just direct us in the right direction?"

"Aye. There be some good size mountains to cross. I doubt a lassie would be able to trek such a journey. Maybe she waited and turned back later to follow the lad."

"You do not know my girl, Mr. Monaghan," chuckled Jameston. "Ready Graham? Or would you prefer to take your son back to the states?"

The father and son exchanged a mutual glance. "We are staying until the girl can fly home with us."

"Good, let us go."

Graham Sinclair gave the Irishman a handshake, while subtly slipping him some money as repayment for helping his son.

After a long day's search for the missing girl, the men

met at the evening meal hour. Though none desired to eat, thinking of the girl who was sure to be starving by now, they made an appearance of supping. They took up the search again after the meal. When the darkness blanketed the earth with cold, the two older men called it quits for the night. David, however, refused to give up. It was his fault she was out there, and he could not sleep until she was found.

Questioning Grace

Grace ran until her tired, starving body denied her access anymore. She had traveled much ground before collapsing into a fatigued heap. She no longer heard the sounds of the wild about her. She did not realize that only yards away, at the edge of the woods, a cozy town slept peacefully.

Exhaustion, mixed with physical injury prohibited her consciousness. In fact, she had more fainted than fallen asleep. The pain in her head had become blinding. This was one of the worst headaches she had ever experienced, and she had some bad ones.

She lay in a dream world where everything was so white and bright that it hurt her eyes. She was riding in a car with a strange man, then it flipped over and over and over. It would not stop. She became dizzy, yet it would not stop. She was going to be sick. Would it ever stop? "Help me Father!" she uttered. "Please make it stop." Then out of the sky an armless hand touched the car with one finger, and set it upright. Who turned the radio on? They were not listening to it. Now, it was blaring loudly. She reached to turn it off. Still, it played on. She looked at the driver. Why did he not mind the awful music? The wreck must have broken the doggone thing. She put her hands over her ears, but she could still hear it. Now, where was that shrill coming from? She did not see anyone around.

"Wake up, I say!"

Somebody was sleeping. The driver was not asleep. There was no one else around. Who were they talking to, and who was talking?

"I do not care. I want her to answer my questions."

Suddenly, the brightness turned to pitch black.

"Wake up. You must wake up."

Grace's eyes fluttered open. Where was she? This was not familiar. What was the last thing she remembered? Her head hurt too much to think.

"Good, you awake. Kellner wants to talk to ye. Here, sit up and drink this."

Grace wrapped her tiny cold fingers around the warm mug. She hated tea, but right now, it was the best thing she had ever tasted. She became steadier as she drank some of the medicinal drink. She was in a room with bars; she was in jail! How? When? Oh drat!

"What are ye doing carrying weapons into our country?" demanded a short red haired man.

Grace puzzled briefly. How could she explain what she did not know? She tried, "They were not mine. It was a rental car. I suggest you ask them."

"Of course not. No one ever admits they are murderers and terrorists. We deal harshly with rebels in this country. Ye yanks are spoiled. Ye think ye can do anything, but ye'll see. It's time ye learned you lesson. Now, I ask again. What are ye doing smuggling weapons into our country? Who is yere contact? It'll go a lot easier on ye, if ye tell us what we want to know," a very rich accent demanded.

She shook her head, "I cannot tell you; I did not even know they were in my car until the accident. I suggest you speak with the rental company."

The short man became angry, "Tell me who ye were taking the guns to!"

The fiery red Irish lass became equally stubborn. She stared him eye to eye. "Well, I suppose if you are too stupid to know the truth when you see it, then you deserve this rental company and all the guns they

338

smuggle in."

Grace had crossed the line in her delirium. How dare she speak to an officer of the law like that? He ordered, "Send her over to O'Malley. He will deal with her justly. Merry stinking Christmas," he laughed weakly.

Grace was taken to another town. This one seemed bigger than the one they had just come from. People on the streets stared into the car as it cruised through town. After another hour's interrogation, which revealed nothing new, Grace was taken downstairs to a damp cold cell. Contrary to her surroundings, she treasured the opportunity to sleep once again. She did not even care that they had not bothered to feed her. Her brain's calling for rest overruled her stomach's calling for nourishment.

Trial Of Grace

The morning brought no news on the whereabouts of the lost one for the three searchers. None paid any attention to the fact that it was Christmas Day. They scrutinized wearily every possible wooded area and valley she could have been. David was kicking himself for having separated from her. Although, no one said anything out loud, his father and especially Jameston were agitated with the boy as well. Albert may even have gone as far as blaming the boy for her disappearance. The lack of sleep was showing on all three faces.

A little after noon, they met back at Castlepolland. David spoke weary, tired words. "I tell you dad. She could not have disappeared of the face of the earth."

Mr. Jameston presented a strong voice. "She is a smart girl. If she is hiding from the authorities, she will not come out until she is ready. You said her head was cut real bad?"

However, David was no longer listening. He had easily been distracted by something else.

"David, Albert asked you a question," his father

spoke sternly.

Both Jameston and Sinclair turned to see what held his attention. It was a picture of Grace on the small television, which sat on the counter. They could not hear all the words, but the scene of their loved one in handcuffs spoke volumes. No wonder they could not find her.

"Excuse me," Jameston grabbed the passing waitress. "Could you tell me about that news reel on the television?"

"Oh, that? Haven't ye heard? It's been all over the telie all day. They've done caught them an American trying to smuggle weapons to the rebels."

David asked excitedly, "Where have they taken her?"

"Don't know exactly. They may have taken her to Dublin, but I can't say for sure. She was arrested in Coole. Why, do ye know her?"

The posse was already en route. Jameston threw a handful of bills on the table, and they were gone. They drove as fast as possible to Dublin to no avail, because she was not there. They were told a man named Kellner was the one who arrested her.

Once they arrived in Coole, Kellner was no kinder to them than he had been with Grace. He refused any knowledge about her or her whereabouts. He sneered at their audacity and boldness.

"I can help ye, some," a quiet young man in uniform told them, as they were about to get in the car. "Ye will please overlook the boss. The wee lass made him real mad calling him 'stupid'. I don't know why, but I believed what she was saying. I have sort of investigated the rental company a little. I don't suppose I could find as much as ye. Ireland isn't very big, and everybody knows practically everybody. I heard them say something about taking her to Clifden. There's a real tiger officer over there by the name of Byrne. Kellner thought, perhaps, he could get her to talk."

"What have you found out about the rental company?" asked Jameston.

"Not much. They started the company seven months ago. They have been squeaky clean. That worries me. Nobody is that clean."

Sinclair inquired, "What is the name of the rental company?"

"Red Hot Rentals. I must go. Kellner is hollering for me."

"Thank you so much officer," David shook the man's hand.

The three men separated once again. The young man went with Jameston to find Grace, while Graham Sinclair went to investigate the rental company. Clifden authorities proclaimed that although Grace had been there, she was no longer in their custody. She had been sent to Mayo. The search, then, led the duo to the next stage of the chase. They were angry about getting the run around.

Exiting Grace

Grace was unable to stay alert during most of the passing hours. Her head ached profusely, and they refused her any medication. They believed her to be faking the pain. Her world was filled with confusion. She was not aware of what happened to her in the last forty-eight hours. Disorientation had taken its toll. She may have been awake, but she was oblivious to most of her surroundings. The closed mouth routine was causing her more trouble than she had bargained for, only it was not because she was not willing to talk; she knew nothing. Her mind could not remember her own name at this point.

Upon arriving at Mayo, she came into the custody of a kinder gentleman. He ordered a visit from the doctor, who confirmed the girl was sick. Infection had set in, causing her a terrible fever. This is how Albert and David found her. Her face was sunk in from dehydration, and her complexion was pale. It was obvious her fire had blown out.

Graham worked hard, but it took two more days before he could prove the weapons were being smuggled by the Rental Company and not Grace. Fortunately, for her, Grace was placed in the infirmary of the jail, instead of the cold hard cell.

David's father brought a new passport for his son, but Grace had to wait longer. Ruth had to conjure a way to lay hands on another passport. It was not an easy undertaking without the actual person.

By the time they headed back to the states on Sinclair's plane, without an apology from the Irish government, Grace was not sure if it was worth coming back to Ireland again, and the government was not sure they would allow her back in.

Although the infection was under control by the antibiotics, a shadow had fallen on the fire that once burned so brightly. The color in her cheeks refused to return. Her tiny wrists seemed to be getting even smaller. The brightness of her curls had dimmed. She was almost a shell of what she used to be.

David looked on with guilt, feeling helpless, hopeless, and ashamed. This was his fault. This was his doing. Had he taken his medicine as he should have, this would have never happened. He knew he was epileptic, but he was embarrassed to take his medicine in front of Grace. He had wanted her to like him, so he simply did not take it, so he shame-facedly explained this to his father. Graham Sinclair was not one to excuse his son's actions. He knew the time would come that David would have to confess his error in judgment and take responsibility for his actions, but for the time being, they both kept it to themselves.

Jameston coddled the young lady. She was only one of thousands of employees, but his heart fell hard for her. Grace was different. She was real and selfless. There was Something about her that imbedded in his big heart to make him love her like a daughter, as Grace loved him equally.

To his delight, she allowed him to hover over protectively; not for her own selfishness, but because it made him feel useful and appreciated. He had come all the way to Ireland to rescue her. It was the least she could do.

Both the Sinclair men had fallen under her spell. Neither could deny her a thing. David was glad to be going home, but knew he had spent all his vacation and must return to school within a day or two. He really could not afford to wait that long, but found it necessary. Grace watched him as he sat quietly during the flight back. He was not so sure of himself anymore. He was quiet and withdrawn. Her questions to him were answered with nods and one-word answers. She realized something was burdening him and sent a prayer up for her new friend.

The surprise waiting for her at the New York airport was almost too much excitement. Upon seeing *him* there for her, Grace lost strength in her legs. She noticed something was different with him. He had a peculiar glow on his face. The girl did not need to be told what it was from, she already knew. She, too, had experienced that glow years ago. Could her life get any better? The only thing missing now was Amy. Boy, how she had missed that child, her child.

Ruth welcomed her with a hug and lots of kisses, preventing Isaiah from getting near her, but the exchange of glances between the two was enough. Suddenly, Grace saw something disturbing. She had noticed it before, but could never quite put a finger on what it was. Her beloved Isaiah was ill. He would never worry her by telling, but she could see it. Oh, she would have to take special care of him. He was thinner than when she left. She must make him see the doctor.

Travis's supportive arm around her waist gave her chills. This was something she had desired for so long, but honestly thought would never come to pass. He was saved! God had worked His miracle. Now, she could be free to love him. God was so good!

Broken Grace

The night before the senate hearing, Travis had called Grace repeatedly. Knowing the severity of her nerves when it came to orating, he wanted to be an encouragement to her. Also, enough time had passed since he had been enchanted with the sound of her angelic voice. He just wanted to hear her say his name.

When, at three o'clock in the morning, there was still no answer in her room, his frustration reached its zenith. A combination of worry and aggravation did not mix well. Work came in four more hours; he must get some sleep, yet all he could manage was a lot of tossing and turning.

When the alarm sounded at six, he was already wide-awake. Instinctively, he reached for the phone to dial the number, which was seared into his brain. There was still no answer. Could she have not made it to New York? Where could she be? Amidst his brain spewing out possible scenarios, his fingers impulsively redialed again. It was busy!

At least she was there. He would try again and again. Finally, after what seemed forever, there was an answer.

It took a few seconds for his brain to register the answer on the line. He was glad to reach her at long last; no that must be the wrong number. No, the voice answered under Grace's name. All these thoughts, plus more, crossed his mind, before he spoke the first word.

"Who is this?" brought him an answer he never would have fathomed. James Nicholson! The scoundrel who was plotting to win Grace? He remembered what the creep said in the men's room that day at the courthouse. How could Grace fall for his tricks? Not Grace, no. Not his Grace. All night with this creep? Did she not know? How could she do this to him? Is that why she could not tell him she loved him? She tried to say it was because of her religion. Well, curse the blasted woman, and curse her God. Now, he knew the truth. She had been lying to him all along. Did his own sister know? Could even she be keeping this sordid secret from him?

Sickness swept over his whole being. It felt as if someone had ripped his heart completely from the arteries that pumped the very life into him. He tried to scream, but the lump in his throat prevented it. All he could manage was a pitiful cry of despair. He was tempted to take a sick day, but decided against that. He would not let any woman cause him to do that. He got over her once, and he could do it again.

But liberation did not come to Travis Winston, who found it was not so easy the second time around, to exorcise this creature from his heart. He wrote a letter expressing his disgust in what she had done, telling of his hatred toward her, and cursing her on behalf of her betrayal. Instead of mailing it, though, he ripped it to shreds. No, he would not give her the satisfaction of gloating over the ability to make him hurt. If she were trying to pay him back for not meeting her twenty years ago, and for getting married, then she most certainly had accomplished what she set out to, only he would not give her the pleasure of knowing it. He fell into the reclusive shell as he had lived pre Grace.

When it came time for Renee to move to Oregon, he conveniently had to work, disengaging him from his commitment. Renee protested and fussed, but he held his ground. He knew Grace would never call him. This lady-like quality had been an enticement to her attractiveness. On the other hand, what she did in New York was much worse.

Whatever he tried to do, he could not stop her smile from burning in his brain, or the touch of her fingers on his hair from sending chilling reminders of who owned his heart. Another Pulling had continually drawn at his heart's door. A Force beyond his comprehension kept drawing him back to the little country church Grace had taken him to. He would keep his word in spite of her.

Wendy was enthralled when the intruder became a part of her dad's life, no more. Now that Renee had moved away, she had Daddy all to herself, and she was crafty enough to keep a close watch on every move her father made. She did, however, refuse to go to that creepy old church when he went. She did not understand why he insisted on going.

Redeeming Grace

For three months, Travis spiraled into an illusion of desolation in which he created for himself. According to his way of thinking, he had been betrayed by the two women he loved more than life, the would-be-lover, that never was, and his sister. Was there anyone he could trust? Even Wendy could not provide what he needed. There were rope burns on his hands where he was sliding fast to the end of his rope. Christmas was upon them and he lacked the desire to even live.

He made his plans carefully. He would make Wendy attend church with him on Christmas. This would serve as a good final day together. After church, he would disappear into the big country. There was nothing to hold him here anymore. He would free himself from this miserable existence once and for all. It would not hurt anybody. If he wanted, to drink, he was the only one who would suffer. He could sell his car, buy a motorcycle, and work jobs from town to town. He could survive. Wendy was almost twenty, which was old enough to live alone. It was set.

The reason Wendy consented to go along with him to

what she assumed was an occult, was the strange look he wore in his eyes. Even at her mother's death, she never recalled having seen it before. She was, in fact, a little worried about him.

The narrated Christmas play was called; *Can you pay Sin's Price?* From the first words, the parallel to his own life brought him to full awareness. The main character was being told how sin brings you to places you should not be. The thought of his plans after this service was over seemed to sting him to the quick. Then, the preacher in the play said sin would make you do things you really do not mean to do. There was a whole lifetime of things he regretted doing and never intended on doing.

When the play's preacher came around to the price you are forced to pay, the words jumped out in real living characters. "The price of sin includes money, health, and for some, it could cost them a child or parent, a spouse or a brother. The wages of sin is eternal death in the lake of fire, where the worm dieth not, and the fire is not quenched. Is the pleasure in sin for a season worth losing your soul for an eternity of time?" Then he went on to say that redemption was free to man. Jesus Christ paid the price so it could be free to us. Believing in Christ was not enough; you must be born again.

The young man had been primed. The moment of choice was at hand. God had extended His hand of mercy on Travis Winston one more time, as Christ Jesus knocked on his heart's door. It was a choice in which only he could make. None other could impact him in any way.

He fidgeted in his seat, contrary to Wendy's chagrin. She wished if she had to be here at all in the first place, he would sit still and stop making a scene. In her ultimate dismay, her father pressed passed her with tears streaming as if he did not care, when the music began playing after the curtain fell. How embarrassing! Could he be any more humiliating?

Grace, Renee, James, Wendy, and all the sorrows of the recent past were no longer on his mind. The only object of thought in the man's mind was that he was lost and on his way to hell. Sin had cost him enough. He was not willing to pay any more. God opened blinded eyes to see how sin crippled his heart. The longing in his soul was not for Grace. It was a longing for the Savior to set up residence. The loneliness he had become so adjusted to escaped him. He was not desolate, nor forlorn. He was filled with the Holy Ghost, Who promised to never leave nor forsake him.

He was relishing in the newfound Love. The newborn babe supped on the nectar of the Word of God, allowing it to fill his spiritual appetite. Oh how sweet It was. He understood, now, what Grace had been talking about. He could finally understand the previously foreign language he had been alien to. He met some fellow Christian brothers at work, who met at break to pray, and he quickly joined in the celebration of his Savior. His life changed forever.

The forgotten problem about the woman he loved was solved by the problem Solver. He was not concerned about Grace's faithfulness. Deep down, he knew there was some explanation for what happened that night, but she was no longer the main focus in his life. There was Someone new and exciting to get acquainted with. Soon, he would make things right with his twice-lost love, but today it did not matter.

Letters of Grace

Over the next few days, he collated a love letter of a different kind. In it, he told of the greatest love story ever lived. It was about One who loved him enough to give His own life for his wretchedness. Of course, Grace was well aware of the story, but it was exciting to share it with the one he knew had been praying for him. By the time it was completed, it was the longest letter he had ever written. He was not sure of what to expect from Grace next, and at this point did not care. He had left it all in the hands of his Savior to complete His will.

He patted his hip pocket all day to ensure the envelope was still present, then he dropped it in the mail on his way home from work.

The first day back to work after Christmas had been another long day with overtime, and he was just content to be home to relax. His lonely life had been so drab, since Wendy had gone to the beach with his cousin, Brad, and Renee was living in Oregon. He threw a piece of bologna between two slices of bread, calling it supper. Physical food did not seem to satisfy his hunger. It was the reading of the Word, the spiritual food, which he desired.

He turned the water on in the shower and returned to his room to undress. It always took a few minutes for the water to heat up. He absent-mindedly shuffled through the mail before sitting down on the bed to remove his shoes and slip his shirt from his body. That was as far undressing as he got. One of the envelopes had strange handwriting on it, and it was from overseas. That was unusual. All the bills were typed. That was odd. It would not do him, until he satisfied the curiosity. He retrieved the object one more time. Who could it be from? He opened it cautiously, and a tiny piece of paper fluttered to the ground. Travis's heart fluttered as well, when he recognized the writing on the paper. That was Grace's!

Travis,

Since I may never have the opportunity again, I love you. I should have told you so many times before. You deserve better than I gave. Please take care of Amy. Goodbye.

You have always had my heart,

Grace

He sank to the side of the bed where his body rested, while he pondered the words. There was so much mystery in it. Something was wrong. A sickening feeling in the pit of his stomach confirmed this fear. Something was wrong. He could feel it.

He totally forgot about the shower still spraying cold water full blast in the other room. He would call Ruth. She would know if something were wrong. He trusted the old Scottish woman.

"Renee?" he spoke after hearing her voice.

"Travis!" she could not keep the sheer delight from betraying her. "It is you. It's about time you called your little sister. What is going on?"

"That is what I was hoping you could tell me. I received a letter from Grace in the mail today. Something is wrong. I am not sure what, but I know there is."

"Well, all I can say is something is going on, although, I do not know what. Mr. Jameston called the other day and flew Ruth and Isaiah to New York. Something was wrong, but he would not say over the phone. I was waiting to hear from them. It is a good sign if she wrote you. Did she say when she would be home?"

"No. It sounded a little like she was saying goodbye. She even went as far as to ask me to watch Amy."

"Well, Amy is fine. I would never imagine her leaving Amy. If I hear anything, I'll let you know."

"Please do. I will call you if I hear anything as well."

Travis began to worry, and then he remembered, he now had a heavenly Father who owned the whole world and was in control of it all. Down to his knees he slid in prayer, "Oh God, keep her safe please. If it be Thy will, bring her back to me, so I may keep her safe for the rest of her life. Help me to help her, according to Thy will."

It was after he had finished making his request of the Father that he realized the water was still running full. Instead of being able to shower now, he brushed his teeth and reclined on the bed for the water to heat up again. Sleep was far from his mind. He replayed the words over in his head. What was she trying to tell him?

None of this other stuff was as important as her telling him she loved him. Now, he could not wait to see her face to face to hear it straight from her precious lips, while gazing into her intoxicating eyes.

At some point, he must have fallen asleep, because the screaming phone awakened him. The clock told him the hour was between three and four.

Anticipating Grace

"Hello," he answered alertly.

"Oh Laddie, this is your old friend Ruth. I joost heard from your sister. She said you were asking about Lamby. Mr. Jameston called. There's been a problem in the home country. I don't know mooch, boot there was something about goons and a wreck."

The news dropped his heart seventeen floors. "Is she safe?"

"Don't know. We are expecting a call froom them at any time. Mr. Jameston is in Ireland as we speak. He arrived there day before yesterday. Isaiah and me are waiting to hear word."

"I will be there as soon as I can. Where shall we meet? I am sorry I do not know a thing about New York. Would I be able to find your hotel?"

"I soopose so Laddie. We are at the Regency Hotel."

After securing the information, Travis called for plane reservations. He threw some items in a bag, took a fast shower, and ran a razor over his handsome face. Then, he was ready to go. He was too anxious to sleep on the flight, which seemed to last forever. All he knew was that this plane was flying him closer to the one he loved.

The beautiful manmade objects of New York fell on unconcerned eyes. His heart was full of praying. Ruth and Isaiah were not due to meet him at the airport, but they surprised him by meeting him there. They took him to the hotel and checked him in as well.

"Have you heard anything," he asked.

"No news," the little Scottish mother-like creature said. He noticed the darkened areas under her twinkling eyes. It was evident she had been sleepless all night. Isaiah faired little better in appearance.

Once in their room, Travis showed the letter to the couple. They were told by Jameston to wait for further information, but none were tired enough to sleep. Neither Isaiah nor Ruth was any more astute in figuring out the cryptic message.

The young man was the first to fall asleep, because his eyes refused to stay open any longer, so Ruth covered him with a blanket and let him be.

They all slept later than they wanted, but no word had come from Jameston as of yet, and all were tired. None were hungry and all refused to eat a bite, until around the noon hour, when they finally heard from Albert, who sent a messenger to have them meet in his office.

Once they were gathered in his office, he placed a call from overseas. He spoke with Travis, who relayed the message to the Scottish couple. He explained how David and Grace were in an accident. He discreetly told him that there had been some trouble getting the officials to let them leave, since their passports were destroyed in the accident. He reported that they were on their way home as soon as possible. The borders were very particular about letting people in and out, but it was his job to get Grace home safely.

Ruth, Travis, and even Isaiah were with closed eyes, praying to Jesus Christ the advocate, knowing He would hear and answer their prayers.

Later that day, Ruth received a phone call from Renee, who announced that they had received the other letter from Grace. In it, she explained she was safe and would be home as soon as possible. She also asked them to help Mr. Jameston get a new passport for her.

The three waited prayerfully. Ruth and Isaiah

worked on getting Grace's new passport in working order and mailed all the necessary papers to the post office Albert had given. As each day passed, they grew more concerned about not hearing anything from Jameston. Why had he not called? He said he would call soon. Had they found trouble getting out of the country?

They holed up in Jameston's office to wait. When the phone finally rang, a sigh of relief went around the room. They were on their way!

Falling Grace

"There is her plane!" Travis shouted excitedly. "It is taxiing down the runway."

Ruth and Isaiah followed obediently, "Let's get our Lamby," confirmed Ruth.

All were taken aback at the girl that emerged from the plane. It was not their Grace, although it did look like her. Where was their Grace? Who was this imposter? The mutual understanding between Grace and Isaiah was shared without words. She was sick. Something was seriously wrong. He understood she had been through a lot, but the hollowness of her eyes could not lie.

The only thing Travis saw was the most beautiful creature ever made, and she loved *him*. He could not wait to tell her about his salvation. He honestly understood why she hesitated in loving him. God was an awesome God, who had worked all this out so wonderfully. If he had only accepted the call from the Father sooner, they may have had years of happiness together already.

Travis supported her back when she faltered in step. Her whole body was shaking. Had they been alone, he would have swept her off her feet and carried her. This was when he noticed a weakness in her voice. Now that he looked at her, she looked weak. Well, she had been through the ringer over there.

He had not told Ruth and Isaiah the part of the conversation about her being in jail, but he could see it had taken a toll on her. He would make it his job to make sure she got plenty of rest and recuperation. He was going to take care of her from this point on. She was wearing his ring, which entitled him to that right.

Jameston insisted on both Grace and David getting checked out. David protested, but his father vetoed his vote. They had both been through an ordeal that could be detrimental to their health.

While waiting for the results on the kids, Graham confided in Albert that the wreck was caused from David having a grand maul seizure behind the wheel. He wanted to approach Grace about it, but wanted confirmation from his good friend on how to do that. Jameston assured him Grace would understand, although he was not pleased with the boy's irresponsible behavior.

"Family of Grace Sorenson?" A man in green scrubs approached the crowd, which stood in response to his question. "I am Dr. Mills. I made the initial examination on Miss Sorenson. As you may be aware, an accident of this nature can be fatal. Miss Sorenson is lucky to be alive. She was thrown around quite a bit. Besides major bruising and contusions, there is only one point of concern."

Travis could not hold back any more, "Is she alright? Will she be okay?"

"Well," the doctor continued, "We found what we believe is a cerebellar astrocytoma. This is a usually benign, cystic, and slow-growing tumor. In Miss Sorenson's case, it has been present a long time, possibly since childhood, which is odd, because she should have suffered some major signs. Now, I am not a cancer specialist, but from my experience and its appearance, there is the possibility of malignancy. Some contusions to the head aggravated it during the crash. Dr. Williams is in with her now. He is a specialist. He will be taking over her case. He will be able to give you more information after he examines her. He will better answer your questions. I suggest you write down any questions you think of while waiting, so you do not forget anything you want to ask."

"How long will it take the other doctor to examine Grace?" asked Albert.

He responded, "It will be a while. When I left, they were preparing her for some CAT scans. It may include taking a biopsy as well. It just depends on what the scans show. She lost consciousness right after being brought in, and she has not come to yet. That was the reason we began looking for reasons."

"Thank you Dr. Mills. You have been helpful," Jameston shook his hand goodbye.

It was not long before another doctor entered to inform Mr. Sinclair of the results of his son. David had broken a collarbone. He had not mentioned one word of pain for himself this whole time. He had suffered silently.

Much time passed before the others were allowed to see Grace. Because the results of the tests would not be back before tomorrow, Dr. Williams had left before meeting with Ruth, Isaiah, Travis, and Albert. Jameston stayed every minute the others did, as if the Irish lass were his very own child.

Healing Grace

The sleep that fallen on the beauty lasted all night. The healing fluids pumped into the petite body, slowly working on recovering her to full potential. As he sat vigil beside her bed, Travis fingered the circle that was wrapped around the fourth finger of her left hand. Isaiah and Albert sat silently watching the happenings outside the window as Ruth and Travis took turns kneeling over their loved one.

The Father, Who answered them according to His will, heard the many prayers sent up that night, and the coma broke as the morning did. It was Ruth who comprehended the mumbled words of her Lamby, pleading for the lights to be turned off. She complied, and then went to the nurse's station for assistance.

The nurses called for Dr. Williams, followed Ruth back to the room, and took her vital signs, recording them according to regulations. Dr. Williams came in, without introduction, to examine Grace.

"Miss Sorenson, I need you to wake up now. Can you open your eyes? Miss Sorenson? Grace? Can you open your eyes?" Viewing her attempt to open them unsuccessfully, the doctor shone his penlight into first one pupil, then the other. "Grace, I know it is painful, but open your eyes. I will set you up a morphine pump for the pain, but for now, I need to explain some things to you."

The violet overshadowed by the dilated black fluttered, slowly, painfully being forced to stay open. Even the darkness was too bright for their sensitivity.

The doctor pushed, "How do you feel, Grace?"

"I have a headache. I do not think it has ever hurt this bad," she mumbled through rubber lips.

Williams grunted, "I guess not. This is not a regular headache. You were in a car wreck, I hear. Do you remember it? Tell me the last thing you remember."

"I remember the wreck. David and I were running, and then I woke up in a jail cell. They told me I had been out for days." The more words she spoke, the more control she gained over her functions, because she did not want to take the morphine. Ruth looked at her in surprise. Jail, no one had said anything about jail.

"Do you remember your flight home?"

"I do. How is David?" she suddenly remembered her

young friend.

"Do you know what day this is?" asked the doctor, ignoring her question.

Grace thought, "Is it morning or night?"

"Morning."

"Is it Thursday?"

"Friday," Dr. Williams examined her head carefully. "The problem we are facing, Grace, is you have a tumor on the back of your brain. It appears it has been there for many years, which puzzles me as to how come you were never diagnosed and treated for this sooner. You have not had any clumsiness of one hand, stumbling to one side, headache, or vomiting? These are the symptoms you should have been experiencing."

Ruth intercepted the question, "Lamby doos get headaches, soomething horrible. Vomiting too. I couldn't be too sure about any clumsiness. Isaiah and I tried to get Lamby to see the doctor about it, boot she is a hard headed Lamby."

"You ignored some pretty serious signs, Grace. You must have known something was wrong with you. When someone experiences blatant signs of illness like that, there is no reason for not getting examined."

"I suppose that is why I did not go to the doctor. No news is good news, is that not what they say?" Grace excused quietly, while holding her white hand over her squinting eyes.

"Not in this case. There is a thirty-eight to ninety-four percent cure rate if treated in time. Each year that percentage decreases."

"What are the options of treatment, doctor?" Travis stepped in.

"And you are?"

"Travis. I am Grace's fiancé," he held her dainty hand in a position to show the ring.

"Then you are an important factor in her treatment. The cornerstone of treatment is surgical resection. If complete resection is not possible, radiation therapy may be beneficial."

"What about chemo? Will she have to go through that?" asked the lover.

"Chemotherapy is usually reserved for the unrespectable, progressive cases. There is a strong possibility it will be necessary, but we cannot know anything until the pathologist sends back the results of the biopsy. From what I have heard, she is strong, rendering her a best case scenario."

Ruth questioned, "Are you saying she will recuperate?"

"As it stands, I do not see why not. I do not foresee any complications in the surgical resection. I will be in contact with you as soon as the results come in. Please remember, the information I have shared with you is a preliminary verdict. Without the results, I cannot be positive. Are there any more questions?"

For the first time, Isaiah spoke in his purposely enunciated English, "Worst case scenario, how long doos she have to live?"

He ignored the shocked gazes of the others as the doctor answered, "And who are you?"

Grace intervened, "He and Ruth are my guardians." This answer received a funny look from the surgeon. A thirty something woman needed a guardian?

"Worst case, I would venture a guess, mind you only a guess, of less than five years. If she had treated this as a child, this would not even be an issue at this point."

Indebting Grace

Even as they spoke, an elder gentleman was making the necessary arrangements to pay the girl's hospital bill. His son was responsible for this whole mess; the least he could do is take the financial burden off of her shoulders. The young accountant smiled. This was the second man trying to assume responsibility for this one patient. That was definitely a first.

The next day, Graham Sinclair entered with his overcoat draping in a neat fold, over his arm and reaching his hand for hers. He was very distinguished, somewhat like Mr. Jameston.

"Miss Sorenson, it is my displeasure to formally meet you under these circumstances. Albert and David speak so highly of you, I feel as if I know you already. I would have loved to meet you without a tragedy. What you did for my son leaves me eternally grateful. David told me everything you did during his seizure. You saved his life. I must say I am impressed. Thank you so much."

"I did nothing on my own. Give God the glory. He is the One that saved your son's life."

"I am so terribly sorry about the crash. Even sorrier about the results of your diagnosis. Is there anything I could do for you?"

"Thank you, no."

He had a kind, soft voice, filled with true remorse, "I feel responsible for..."

"You are not responsible for anything. You did not put this tumor in my head."

"Maybe not, but we are responsible for the accident."

"Not to be contrary, sir, but you are not even responsible for that. It was all in God's hands. Do you not realize? He has a reason for all He does, whether we deem it a tragedy or a victory? How do you figure that you are responsible? You would do nothing to harm your son, neither would my Father do anything to harm His child. This too, shall pass."

"I do not understand your reasoning. I would understand completely, if you desired to take me to the cleaners. You are a nice young woman, and I would not hold it against you."

"I will not sue. How can I sue you for something God did? We were never out of His care. No. That is not the answer. You stop worrying about all that and concentrate on David. If anyone is responsible for this accident, it is me. Maybe this was God's way of making this stubborn girl go to the doctor to get her head examined."

Sustaining Grace

Grace opened her eyes, she did not see the man she loved smiling deep into her eyes. She was only conscious of the excruciating migraine she was having. This was the worst one yet. They had never hurt like this before. Where was she? She must have passed out. That was new. She had never done that before. The room was so bright. It hurt to open her eyes. She lifted her hand to massage the pounding skull, but her arms were suddenly leaden. What was wrong with her? She must stop and think. The last thing she remembered was... a bright light blinded her. She could hear a voice speaking to her.

"Can you turn off the lights, please?" she tried to speak with all her might. In her mind, the words were spoken clearly, but to the others, they were mumbled and barely sensible. When she opened her eyes again, the lights had been darkened.

"It is about time you woke up, sleepyhead," a softened version of Travis's voice was heard, even though she could not see a clear picture with her eyes.

She felt his lips on her forehead, and his warm hands

clasped securely around her right one. This felt so good. She was so cold, while he was warm. She tried to speak again, but her mouth would not function at her command. She grew frustrated and angry. Not only could she not see, she could not talk.

Shortly, the lights were blaring again. She did not have to open her eyes to know this. She felt the brightness through her lids. Several voices were muffled in her ears. This must be one doozy of a headache to receive all this commotion.

Cold hands and utensils replaced the warm ones of before. They were forcing her eyes open. The light sent sharp pains extending vindictively in every direction of her head.

The muffled male voice became clearer as she forced herself into full awareness. The stranger kept calling her name commanding her to open her eyes. Oh, if he only knew how hard she was trying. The lids were just too heavy to budge. Morphine pump? She did not want any morphine. What was going on here, anyway? All she wanted to do was sleep this pain into oblivion.

He was asking how she felt? If her lips would move,

she would tell him she felt like she had been thrown in front of a truck. "I have a headache," was complicated enough to utter. Trying to explain her memories was near impossible, but she must respond or get the morphine. Her strength built with each sentence, and even more so with listening to the doctor's explanation of what was happening to her.

The words did not scare Grace Sorenson. She had longed to cross over to the celestial home many times. She was homesick for that Country for which her eyes have never beheld. The thought of dying was welcome. Tumors; cancer; it was something she did not particularly want to live with, but what person ever had the choice?

She contemplated the eyes of each person standing around her bed. Isaiah's held pride. Confidence in the healing power of God permeated his solid jaw. Ruth had prayer in hers. The continual prayers of this sainted lady had seen Grace through many hard times, as it would see her through this. The doctor's eyes were different. His held the knowledge of the worldly nature. All he could see was the failure from a doctor's point of view. There was no concept that all was in the hand of One mightier than he. Then, she looked in the eyes of the man she held dear for so long. They were different, now. The last time she was looking in them, they contained a lacking, which was not here now.

She was so engrossed in her scrutiny; she did not hear the doctor's final words. If she did, no one could tell. It did not change her expression one iota. Travis retook her delicate hand, while taking his turn at looking into her eyes. Ruth and Isaiah slipped quietly away, allowing the young lovers to be alone.

"You have something to tell me, young lady?" Travis whispered gently, "I want to hear it come straight from your lips. You are wearing my ring, which delights me to no end, but I need to see it in your eyes and hear it from your own real life voice. Tell me."

Grace forced a faint smile. The pain was so bad, her jaw clenched tightly, disabling her natural charming smile to come forth. She had opened this can of worms, and there was no way of closing it up, until they all crawled out, so she better make it the best.

Slowly, more reading her lips than hearing the words,

she whispered with a clenched jaw, "I love you."

Without a word, the young man gently kissed both eyes, cheeks, then lips. "You don't know how I have wanted to hear you say that. I honestly began to think you didn't. You go to sleep now. I will be here when you wake up."

But Grace was incapable of sleeping as someone watched on. Her burning eyes followed the handsome lover's motions. His fixed, firm jaw showed determination and strength, while his soft brown eyes displayed sheer love and compassion. He smiled when he caught her watching him.

"You are supposed to be sleeping. Do you need something for pain?" he asked her gently.

She gently shook her head no. Talking was too complicated. The sound of her own breath was magnified and contributing to the aching in her head. Her teeth were clenched in an attempt to survive the agony, which was constant.

"You are a sight for these sore eyes, Miss Sorenson. You gave me quite a scare. By the way, if you ever do that to me again, I am never going to speak to you again," Travis softy teased. "I have missed you."

She managed a bitter smile, while relishing in the warmth of his touch. They were contented to smile into each other's eyes, quietly, without words until Isaiah and Ruth reentered the room.

"Lamby, why aren't you asleep yet? " Ruth fussed amiably, while her husband smiled tremendously with a twinkle in his eyes. Even though he was a man of few words, he spoke volumes to Grace. He was the father Grace never had. He could not have loved her more, or been more proud of her, had she been his very own.

Two nurses came in with more equipment to attach, "We are here to hook up your morphine pump, Grace."

Ignoring the pain, Grace protested, "I do not want that."

"Oh Lamby, it'll be fine. It will help ease the pain," the surrogate mother insisted.

Grace took on an expression of fear. Isaiah spoke up in his strong learned voice, "For heaven sakes, woman, if she does not want it, she does not want it. Do not try to force her. She knows her own limits."

"Dr. Williams ordered it. You will feel a lot better.

It will ease your pain," the nurse explained.

"No, I do not want it." She threw a grateful smile to her advocate.

"Okay, but if you decide to change your mind, just press the button." The two nurses stayed long enough to take her vital signs, before leaving.

"Laddie, we can stay with Lamby, if you want to go to the hotel and clean oop."

"No, thank you, Ruth. I do not plan on leaving her side again.

"I am fine," Grace assured. "Go ahead. I will be here when you get back."

"Maybe later. Right now, I plan on staying. I will, however, call Renee and Amy to check in."

Since the young man became occupied with something besides watching Grace, she was able to fall fast asleep. It was a welcomed rest, the first natural sleep in days. The longer she could sleep, the quicker the pain would go away. At first, she tried to replenish the knowledge the doctor reported. The tumor, cancer, biopsy, chemo, surgery, she was not sure of the outcome, but she knew her Healer had control of it all.

385

The pain would not allow her to remember the rest of the words, but one phrase from a song played over and over in her head, until she was deep in slumber, *"I'm a winner either way, if I go, or if I stay."*

Diagnosing Grace

Travis did go to the hotel and shower, while she slept. When he returned, Ruth and Isaiah retired for the night, promising to be back up bright and early in the morning. The young man made himself comfortable in a chair beside his beloved, holding desperately to her bantam arm. Grace had always been the epitome of strength, inner, as well as outer. This was the first time he had ever seen her in a weakened state. Maybe now, she would learn to lean on him just a little. He understood about her leaning on the Father, but the flesh wanted her to need him.

That night Grace slept soundly, only awakening when the nurses poke and prodded her arms, mouth and head. This was, indeed, the best medicine. By morning, the headache was more tolerable.

"Good morning, Sunshine. How are you feeling this morning?" greeted her betrothed, when the first signs of violet appeared.

The smile was still forced, but slightly brighter, "I feel like going home."

Dr. Williams's loud boisterous voice intruded, "You

are not going anywhere just yet. You have a long way to go, first. How are you feeling this morning, besides homesick?"

"Better."

"No pain?"

"Some."

"Why did you refuse the morphine pump?" the doctor inquired.

She explained, "I do not want or need it."

"We will see about that later. Do you understand everything I explained to you yesterday?"

"Yes."

"Good. Now that you have had time to sleep on it, are there any questions you would like to ask?"

"I do not think so."

Travis stepped in, "I do. When will we get the results of the biopsy?"

"It will be a few days. There is also some blood work being done, which will take a few days, as well. I will be perfectly honest with you both. From what I saw inside that head of yours, we are looking at having that surgery before you leave here. We should think about going ahead and scheduling it."

"What are my chances of beating this thing with the surgery?" Grace asked slowly. "You were saying yesterday, that chemotherapy could be required if the surgery did not take. What are my chances of it not taking?"

"At this point, I cannot answer that question. I will be honest with you, had you come in twenty or thirty years ago, it would have been a simple procedure. The longer you waited, the larger it grew, while becoming more entwined with the nerves. I do not understand how you were allowed to grow up without having this discovered."

"I was a pretty healthy kid. I didn't frequent the doctor's office often."

Dr. Williams looked confused, "Healthy? How do you explain the massive scar tissue I found? The x-rays showed several broken bones that do not appear to have been set properly, if set at all."

Grace glanced nervously at Travis, "Would you mind going and getting me a cup of cocoa?"

"Can she have that doctor?" he asked for permission.

The physician understood the patient's desire for privacy. "Sure. Go ahead." He waited till the man left the room before continuing, "How about it? How do you explain that?"

"Well, I'll be. Oop already, Lamby? Isaiah and me saw your young man, and Isaiah went with him." Then, she realized her intrusion by the sincere gaze exchanged between the two occupants of the room. "Oh, pardon me." She came to Grace's side, taking hold to her hand.

Grace continued, "I was sort of clumsy growing up. It was never any big deal, so I never suspected having broken anything,"

"Clumsy? And I suppose you are going to tell me that whatever walloped you in the back of the head to give you this tumor was just some clumsy fall?" When she refused to answer, he added with a touch of abruptness. "Please do not insult my intelligence"

"It's okay, Lamby. He can't help you, if you don't be honest with him." Grace gave her a withering glance. "The Lamby don't like talking about the past. You understand?"

"I don't remember what I was hit with. It could have

been a crowbar. That is the last thing I remember seeing."

"There is proof of multiple traumas to your skull. How many times have you been hit in the head?" pushed the doctor.

"I do not know. Is that what caused this tumor?"

"It certainly looks that way. You suffered a tremendous trauma to a very delicate place. You were not taken to the doctor afterward? Your parent's could not tell a difference? How did your mom explain it away? Your teachers did not notice anything different in your behavior? No one noticed?"

"My mother died when I was young. No one noticed, because things just went on as usual. That is all ancient history. We need to look forward, not backward. We cannot undo what has already been done."

"Be that as it may, I would like to know how this went untreated for so long." He grew angry, when he realized Grace was finished talking about it.

Even though, the arrangements were made to operate on Grace, Dr. Williams insisted on waiting to get the results back from all the lab work before proceeding.

That was an important factor in the cure.

Operating Grace

In the next days prior to the surgery, Travis reveled in his newfound Grace and love. The grace of God had been extended to him immeasurably, and achieving lifelong love was one extension. He, of course, did most of the talking, while Grace lay in discomfort, listening to his planning of the wedding which would definitely follow her going home. Grace simply smiled on all his suggestions.

Ruth and Isaiah were continually close at hand, with Ruth assisting in Grace's many walks. She would not leave Lamby's side. Since being privy to the secreted past, Ruth kept mum about her revealed knowledge. Instead, she took what she had learned and allowed her heart to weave utmost compassion for her little girl. She and Isaiah had known Lamby long enough to know something had gone much awry in her youth, but neither had ever asked, while Grace had never volunteered. This one horror, she kept from even her husband. God help the man, Isaiah would wring his neck with his bare hands for what he did to the Lamby. Not to include, the other suspicions Ruth held secluded.

The groom-to-be arrived every morning in elation, hiding his worry and concern. His beloved was not improving as he thought she should. The color was not returning to the natural blushed cheeks. Hollow eyes peered weakly, where the fiery violet once shone. He tried relentlessly to encourage her strengthening. Doctor Williams convinced the awaiting crew that after surgery, recovery was sure to be quicker, so each rallied around their Grace, while waiting for it to come to pass.

A routine developed for the patient. For therapy, the patient insisted on walking. She could not afford to lose her virility, or sense of it, anyway. If Grace Sorenson was not able to be busy, then there was no point in living. Blessed Ruth would take her by the arm and guide her through the halls of the massive hospital. Isaiah would, at times follow behind, holding on for an opportunity to offer aid.

She found some solace in the pediatrics, where her heart cried out for the pitiful little ones whose bodies had been ravaged with this hideous cancer. She would talk to them, while offering a witness. A special closeness enshrouded. They would open up to Grace and express their fears and angers. This relationship with the children made the days pass by quicker for all. If the doctor, or anyone else, wanted to find her, all they would have to do is go to the pediatrics section. Sometimes her loved ones would stand outside the room and watch through the window. They could not bear to see the little ones suffer.

Forbearing Grace

Mr. Sinclair visited her again to stress his desire to make some sort of financial settlement for the trauma she had been through. Of course, Grace refused any such nonsense. She thanked him kindly, but dismissed his worry.

She was doubly pleased when David made a special trip from England just to see her. He slipped a handful of colorful flowers through the door as a sort of peace offering, first. He was greeted with a sweet Scottish burr, instead of the small quiet voice he expected. Ruth explained where Grace would be, so he followed instructions to find her. He watched her momentarily through the window, but when she turned toward his direction, he tapped on the window.

Grace smiled a welcome and immediately excused herself from the present conversation on who was cooler, Mickey Mouse or Barney.

"Grace, look at you. How are you healing?"

"I am fine. How about you? I see you are still wearing that cast. Are you in a lot of pain?"

"Oh that. It does not hurt," he laughed.

"Would you like to take a walk?" Grace asked.

"Sure would. Are you able?"

"Try and stop me." Grace slipped her hand in the bend of his offered elbow. "What are you doing home? I thought you would be studying hard in school again."

It was a grim smile in which he faced her, "I needed to take a special leave. I got permission from my professors. I needed to take care of something here, before I could ever dream of accomplishing any school."

"Well, I am sure they were only too happy to comply after everything you have been through."

"That is sort of what I wanted to talk to you about."

Grace gave him a look of confusion, "You mean you came all the way here to talk to me? What on earth for? Certainly it could have waited until you returned to the States."

"Oh no it wouldn't. I have a confession to make. It is really rather embarrassing. I am so ashamed at what I have done."

"Well, I am sure whatever it was, you had a good reason, and all is well; so do not worry another thing about it. Do you understand?" she dismissed.

"No. I cannot. You see…"

Grace stopped in her step, "David, I do not have to know anything. You owe me no explanations."

"The car wreck was all my fault. You see, I wanted to impress you. I did not want to seem like a little boy to you, so I deliberately did not take my medicine. I am an epileptic. I must have seized, because I do not remember one thing about the actual wreck."

"Yes, I know," the smile on her face did not even flinch. "Thank the Lord, you were thrown from the car quite a good way. You were full blown by the time I found you."

"Then you saved my life, and for that, I now owe you."

She shook her head, "No, nothing so grand as that. You would probably have been fine without me."

"I don't think so. My doctor says it was a grand maul. You saved my life."

"Stop talking like that, or I am not going to listen to you anymore. Now, when do you return to school?"

She had done it again. She had made him feel like a man, instead of a boy. The old friendly feeling had returned between them.

"I must return as soon as possible. Listen, Grace, thanks for being so great about all this. I wouldn't blame you if you resented me and hated my guts. I don't know what I would have done, if the shoe was on the other foot. I am responsible for you being here. If I had taken my medication when I should have, you wouldn't be in the hospital."

"David, you listen to me and listen well. My hospitalization has not one thing to do with you. The reason I am here is because of something you had nothing to do with. I am not angry, nor shall I be. This is what God has in His plans for me; therefore, I shall do His will. Just pray that I do it with grace coupled with faith in order to not let Him down."

She embraced his neck to seal the understanding betwixt them, when she became shaky and weak. Maybe she had pushed the walk too far. Grace realized that she was guilty of the same thing as David. She did not want to be embarrassed over not being able to take a simple walk, and let it get the best of her. She understood his position.

"Are you alright?" he questioned. "You look mighty pale."

"I'll be fine, but I must head back to my room. Would you care to walk me?"

David held his arm to escort with a smile, "My pleasure, me lady."

Upon returning to the room, Ruth scurried the patient back into bed. "The doctor's been in here to talk to Lamby, twice."

Grace laughed, "It is okay Ruth. It is not like I am going anywhere any time soon." She bid her farewells to her newest friend, and then climbed obediently into her bed.

Doctoring Grace

"The nurse told me you passed her station." the doctor's voice boomed. "I have been looking for you. We received the results of your blood work. It is worse than we thought. Have you ever heard of a condition called aplastic anemia?"

"Yes, my uncle and grandfather had it," she responded.

"Why didn't you say so sooner?"

"I did not think it was pertinent."

"Yes, Grace, it is. It is hereditary. The problem is, now on top of the other surgery you need, you need to consider a bone marrow transplant. It is rare to find a match, but we do find one sometimes. However, if you have a sibling, it would increase your chances tremendously."

"Then that is no problem. I have no siblings, so let it be."

"I am afraid I do not understand what you mean." The doctor looked confused.

"I mean, don't plan on a transplant. The chances are rare, and I would just as soon not get my hopes up only to have them shattered. I am ready to meet my Lord. If it is my time to die, then I shall do so with grace."

"I don't believe that is an option, young lady. Your name has already been put on the waiting list. As soon as it comes, you will be as good as new. That is, you will be after the surgery. We have to remove the tumor, if there is any hope of recovery."

"That is another thing. Just cancel the surgery. I will go home as soon as you release me." Grace had seen her uncle die from this. It was neither pleasant nor quick. If she was to die this way, she wanted to do so in the comfort of her own home. There was no point in deluding herself or anyone else. Another thought came to her mind. She could not let Travis become trapped in a relationship that was to be short lived. It must not have been God's will for them to spend a lifetime together, after all. This was the proof. She must make him go.

The doctor shook his head, "I think you are making a big mistake. You have a fighting chance. Do not throw it away. Take a few days to think on it. Please reconsider."

"A few days, a few months, it will not matter. My mind is made up. "

To emphasize that the conversation was over, Grace turned toward the window and began humming. The doctor threw a look to the Scottish woman in a plea for help, before leaving.

"Lamby, what's going on?" Ruth wrapped her arms around the slender body.

"It is no use Ruth. You cannot change my mind. First, I do not have the money to have the surgery or the bone marrow thing. Second, my chances of recovery are slim. Third, I must make this as easy on Amy as I can. She will not like seeing me fight a losing battle, only to have to say goodbye to me in the end."

"You are wrong, Lamby. She will want you to live as long as you can. What about Laddie? He will insist you do it."

"Well, that is easy to solve. Travis simply will not be told, by anyone." The fire was in her eyes once again. "As for Amy, the best thing would be for the courts to refuse me adoption. Then, she could find her a permanent home. I mean it Ruth, not a word."

"Oh, but Lamby. Y…"

"No buts about it. I mean it."

"What are you butting heads about in here?" Travis demanded, as he and Isaiah came back. "You two look like we interrupted something important. Should we leave, again?"

"No, as a matter of fact, I want to speak to you privately. If Isaiah and Ruth do not mind, that is." She ignored the withering glance being thrown her way by Ruth.

The faithful caregiver hugged her neck and whispered, "You'll regret this, Lamby. Don't do it."

When Travis and Grace were alone, she suddenly did not know what to say. She fumbled, "I think you should go home. You have stayed out of work too long for me. I am sorry I embroiled you in this mess in the first place. I believe the best thing for all involved is to get on with our own lives."

Puzzled, he frowned, "I have made my choice. I am not returning to my old job. Actually, I plan to secure a job in Oregon, so that I can return there as your husband."

There was coldness in her voice. "I did not make myself clear. I do not want you in Oregon. I do not want to be your wife. I want to be alone."

"You are being silly. Of course you want to be my wife. We have it all planned."

"Then it is time to change your plans. Now, if you will excuse me, I have somewhere to be." Grace pulled the door open.

"Wait!" he commanded. "You cannot say that and just leave. You are not going to marry me? Boy, you are confusing. I love you, and you love me. What do you mean?"

Without turning, lest he see the tears about to fill her eyes, Grace just answered, "I do not love you. Now, please leave." Then, without hesitation, she left.

Contradicting Grace

Travis stood there dumbfounded. What was going on? Of course she loved him. Maybe it was the medication she was on. All he knew was that she was going to be his wife, whether she liked it or not. He had her words, close to his heart, plus burned in his memory. He knew she loved him. The bitter words stung his heart.

Grace fought back the stinging tears. She would not allow herself tears. That would just make things worse, and she knew she was doing the right thing. She was doing this for his own good. She could hear him calling her name. She walked briskly to get away from the piteous sound. She blindly passed Ruth and Isaiah in her flight. It was Isaiah that won the debate of who should follow her.

He need not say a word. His arms encircled his child with understanding and comfort. Grace gave him a grateful smile. "You understand why I am doing this, do you not? Do you think I am wrong?"

"Follow your heart, Grace." The only time his Scottish burr came out was when he was agitated or excited, but now, he was calm. "Your head will tell you things that are not true."

"Would you want Ruth to devote all her life to you, if you knew you were going to die any day?

"It would not be my decision. It would be up to that woman. You could not tell her not to love."

"Indeed. Well, I shall not waiver. What is done is done. He is young. He needs to find a young wife to spend his life with. I will not be here long enough. You do not hate me, do you Isaiah?"

The only answer he gave, or she needed, was a warm embrace. She knew he could never hate her. He may not agree with all the choices she made, but he would always love her.

The two sat in silent thought until Ruth set out to hunt them. She had consoled the heartbroken man to the best of her ability without breaking Grace's trust. She did, however, insinuate that Grace was under a lot of stress and made hasty decisions, which she thought were the best. She had left the young man alone to ponder his thoughts.

He was doing just that. He tried desperately to

deduce the facts in which she could have possibly uttered those four cruel words. He knew it was not true. He knew she was lying. Only how could he find out what was going on?

"I am sorry. I was looking for Miss Sorenson. Am I in the right room? I believe I saw you with her before. My name is Graham Sinclair." His thoughts were interrupted.

"Travis Winston. Nice to meet you," Travis replied.

"Oh yes, you are the fiancé."

"Yes. That is I was, until ten minutes ago."

"I am sorry. Have I interrupted something?"

"No, Grace should be back in a while. Hopefully with her senses in better shape. Feel free to stay. I'll come back later."

He left with a heavy heart. Sinclair saw how the broken spirit consumed the man. He waited a few moments, until Ruth forced Grace back in bed.

Offering Grace

"Mr. Sinclair, how nice to see you again," she smiled as if nothing had happened.

"Grace, I have come here in hopes of stealing you

away from Albert. His business is good, and you have someone replacing you in Oregon. Why not move here and work for me? I could use you. I would pay you well. You would not want for anything."

Grace smiled half of her normal charm. "Thank you for the kindness, sir, but I do not think I could leave Mr. Jameston, even if I thought for a moment that you were serious."

"Well then, I figured you for a loyal kind. It is rare to find loyalty these days. Just know you have a job waiting for you at any time."

"That is so kind of you sir. Thank you. Did David get back to school alright?"

"He did, thanks for asking. I will leave you with your loved ones." He spoke while approaching the door. "By the way, your young man, the fiancé, I like him. He seems to adore you. I hope you know what a rare treasure that is anymore. If I were you I would hold on to him tightly."

He knew none of the details of the problem, only that there was a problem. So he left his words of wisdom, hoping she would heed his suggestions. He closed the door behind him without giving her a chance to respond.

"See Lamby, he even knows your wrong," Ruth protested.

"For heaven sakes, woman, leave her alone. She is a grown adult," Isaiah interpolated.

"But Loovey, we can't sit by and watch them throw away a life."

"Ruth, I am not throwing away anything. I am dying. As soon as you accept that, you will understand. I love him too much to make him suffer needlessly through an illness that could last a long time, then a death that could equal in time. That is cruel beyond belief. He does not deserve that."

The two argued until Grace became ill and tired. Then, Ruth fussed at herself for letting Grace overdo it. Maybe Grace was right. She would have to accept that Lamby was dying. No, she would most certainly not. The doctor said there could be help in the transplant and surgery. No, Grace was being unreasonable, by giving up. She had a Physician that had the power to heal Grace, if He wanted to.

That night Travis came back to the room, but Grace

was asleep. Her tired features told him a story of how much help she needed. Why was she being so stubborn? Should he shake her from her sleep until she came to her senses? Was she trying to save him from the long fight with cancer? Well, she would not even know what she had until the surgery. He made himself comfortable to stay the night. She could not get rid of him that easily.

She woke briefly when the nurse came in to check her vitals, but Travis slipped out of the room, in case she should see him and get upset. He paced down the hall until one of the nurses asked if he needed something.

"No thank you. I was just waiting for the nurse to do her checks," he responded.

"It should not take long. What is the patient's name?" the nurse prodded nosily.

"Grace Sorenson."

"Oh." The woman gave a sad note. "It is such a shame about her. She is so young, too. I do not know what I would do if I was told I only had a few months to live. I know I certainly would not refuse any help that would prolong my time."

Travis looked at the woman as if she had lost her

mind. "Are we talking about the same person? I am with Grace Sorenson in room 719."

"Yeah, that's who I'm talking about. Dr. Williams was not happy having to release her A.M.A. As a matter of fact, I think that is why he insisted she stay till the morning, hoping she would change her mind." The expression of utter bewilderment made the woman shut up. Had she said something to someone she should not? She feared for her job, after revealing private information.

The young man stormed quietly into Grace's room. Fortunate for her sake, she had gone back to sleep after the nurse left. Things were beginning to make some sense. So what if she had this tumor in her skull, even if it is holding onto the brain. That was not a guarantee of her dying. Surely the doctor explained this to her. No, Grace may be stubborn, but she would not misunderstand that.

Travis remembered he could go to his newfound Father, so to his knees he went. All night he spent in prayer, seeking wisdom from above. When Grace woke in the morning, the first thing she saw was her lover knelt in prayer. How could she be angry with him for praying? This is what she had wanted for so long. It was funny how God had caused this all to happen this way. He must have a sense of humor to put the two of them together for a short time, before separating them for good. Only it was not funny to her.

Grace began a prayer of her own. "Dear Heavenly Father," she prayed, "I come to you in humble thanksgiving with a repentant heart. Please forgive me of my wretchedness. Please cover me with Thy blood. Make me as white as snow. I come to You to ask for strength from Above. I have not the strength of mine own volition to bear the burden before me; therefore, I beg for You to help me through this path You have chosen for me. I understand that it is Your will I travel it alone, with only You at my side. Thank You for never forsaking me. I pray only, that when the time comes, and the pain becomes unbearable, You help me to be brave in You. I ask these things in Thy precious, holy name. Amen."

Tears were rolling down the girl's face, yet she had no understanding as to why. They came against her command or will. She could not control them, nor stop them. Oh why was she bawling like a baby? Why could she not stop? Upon hearing Travis stir, she closed her eyes and pulled the cover over her face. She had to prepare for throwing him out. This was something she could not do, if he saw she had been crying. Yet, the tears continued to stain her face.

Travis had spent a sleepless night in prayer. He had heard the slightest gasp and completely stopped what he was doing. He then listened to the softest sounds of a sniffle. He quickly concluded his intercession with the Father. Out of the corner of his eye, he could see Grace's movement, as she pulled the cover over her. Venturing over to her side, he contemplated whether he should touch her hand in comfort, or would she still be angry with him, same as yesterday. Should he dare kiss the fiery tresses? Could she really have meant the hurtful words of yesterday? Somehow, he could not quite read what God was intending. In one aspect, he had a peace of being with this woman, but in another, he feared to stay.

"You best be leavin' Laddie, before she wakes. It

wouldn't do anywoon any good to get her all fired up. Isaiah's gone to fetch soom tea, if you want to join him," Ruth whispered as she entered the room.

"So you think she meant what she said yesterday?" Travis asked quietly.

"Afraid so Laddie. She's not thinking straight. When she gets home, she'll change her mind."

Travis hung his head as he left her room. How could this be real? On the way to find Isaiah, his thoughts drifted back to her sixteenth birthday, when she held him so dearly in her eyes. He could remember, just as if it were yesterday, how she watched him leave, how he thought he could not do it because of that look, and how that had been a mistake he could never undo, no matter how much he desired. Where was that Grace? Where was the Grace that met him in Oregon with gladness in her heart? What had happened in such a short time that would turn her completely? Oh, how he loved her so! She was his delight. No, he was not going to let her go so easily; not until God showed him it was His will.

He did not see Isaiah, however, but he met up with Graham Sinclair, who greeted him solemnly. "Beautiful

415

morning, Travis."

"Mr. Sinclair. It is nice to see you again. Are you on your way to see Grace?"

"After breakfast. I do not suppose you know how our young lady is doing this morning, do you?"

Travis countenance held sadness, "Frankly, I am not sure. I do not understand her abrupt dismissal toward me. Everything was fine until yesterday. We were planning our wedding. Now, she will not even see me." He shrugged his shoulders. "I just do not understand."

"I guess if I had been told I was going to die, I would not be thinking of marriage either. Surely you are not thinking of yourself at a time when she is facing all this."

"That is just it. She has not told me anything. No one has. I found out accidentally from a nurse that she was leaving today, and they only gave her a few months. That is all I know. If you could explain more to me, I wish you would."

Graham pondered momentarily. "I am not sure if I should share her personal affairs. I only learned of it from Albert. He said she was a very private person."

The older man watched the hope fade from the young man's features. He debated in his soul whether he should share the information or not. In the end, the desolation he was forced to see could not be overturned. "There are some complications with her cancer." He explained, "She has an unusual condition called aplastic anemia. It is a disease that attacks the white bloods cells, which fight off germs, diseases, etc. They can give her blood platelet transfusions, but until she receives a bone marrow transplant, she will not get any better. The impact of the latest news has discouraged her so that she refuses to have the tumor removed, now, but, you did not hear this from me."

"Then I will give her my bone marrow, and she will be fine. She can have the surgery, and then we can get on with our lives." He was hopeful, now that he understood.

"My boy, if it were only that simple, do you not think any one of us would have done it? You can be tested to see if you are a match, but the odds are not good. It is a shame she had no siblings. They are the perfect matches, having had the same DNA from both parents."

417

Travis brightened, "But she does have one. She has a brother."

"I don't understand. She said she did not have one." The gentleman became confused, until the meaning of Travis's statement sunk in. "She has a brother! That means she could have the bone marrow transplant and the surgery. Are you sure of this? How do you know?"

"She told me. I know it has been many years ago, but I believe I remember her telling me she had a brother. I am almost positive."

"If you can supply me with a location to where her family might be, I will search out to find this missing brother. I wonder why she did not mention him. Oh well, that is not important, now. We will find this biological sibling and convince her to have the surgery."

Travis shook his head, "Pardon me for being contrary, but I do not think you can convince that woman to have the surgery, once her mind is set."

"That, young man, is why you are the one to convince her. I have this job, and yours is to make her change her mind," Mr. Sinclair spoke with finality.

"Again, begging your pardon, sir, but how do you

propose I do that, when she is being stubborn and cantankerous. She will not even allow me in her room, when she is awake."

"Well, Mr. Winston, it depends completely on how bad you want this. I know if it were I, I would let absolutely nothing stand in my way. If she were your wife, you could consent for her medical emergencies. Are you beginning to get the picture, here?"

Travis was defeated before starting. He knew she would not speak to him, let alone marry him. It was great that Mr. Sinclair was helping, but he would have to back down and leave the rest to Ruth and Isaiah.

Sinclair rose from the table, throwing something on it and picking up the information Travis had scribbled down, while they talked. "I am on my way. A word of advice: Take this and give her whatever she wants, even if she wants the moon. Find a way," and with that, the man disappeared.

Stealing Grace

Ruth pampered Grace to the best of her ability, but it was Isaiah that brought the girl comfort. He mostly stood staring out the window, but his mere presence was solace. Grace felt that something terrible was wrong with her father figure. He would never complain nor speak of illness, but Grace could sense something was definitely wrong. She knew he would never confide this with her, if he thought she was in need, herself. The tired darkened eyes hardly held their sparkle anymore. The bounce in his step seemed gone. She could not put a finger on it, but something certainly was amiss.

When Dr. Williams came in for the morning rounds, he convinced Grace to stay just long enough to get the results of the biopsy. In truth, he already had the ominous results, but he was trying to prolong her stay enough for someone to convince her to have the surgery. With her agreement to stay for no longer than it took to receive the results, Dr. Williams was at peace.

During her routine visit in the pediatric unit, Grace sent a hand written note to Ruth insisting that she and Isaiah were to go out for dinner and sightseeing today and night. If she saw either face again today, she was going to be angry with them.

Surprisingly, the two obeyed, but not because of Grace's note, but because another had asked them for a night alone with the Irish beauty.

Taking advantage of the time alone, Grace could and did refuse the food the nurse brought her to eat. Now, she could suffer in peace, with no one to bother her. If she did not like the nasty food, fussy Ruth was not standing over her ordering her to eat it.

The only interruption all evening was by Mr. Jameston, who briefly stopped by. His words of encouragement failed to convince her to continue with the imperative surgery. For her, there was no point wasting time fixing the pot when the fire was gone out.

She had settled down with the Good Book for comfort reading, when she heard a faint tap on the door. Assuming it was the nurse coming for vitals, she admitted freely without looking. "Come in."

"A rose for the lady's hair." Grace bolted up at the voice. "A corsage for the lady. Finally, a song for the lady."

The sight to behold took her breath away. Travis stood before her dressed in a black tuxedo, appearing, as Grace Sorenson had never seen him. He had showered and shaven, and overall cleaned himself up very nicely. She had never see anyone so handsome in all her life. Her rebuke froze temporarily in her mind. Instead of rebuke, it was filled with awe. His brown locks did not fall so ruggedly as usual. He had transformed into a dream.

"What are you doing here?" she uttered.

"Quite simple, my lady." He sat a portable tape player on the sink, plugged it up, and turned it on. "If I remember correctly, there was a beautiful young lady on her way to her prom, when she was stood up by a certain fellow, due to circumstances beyond his control, I might add. I would like to present you with the prom you never had. A rose to adorn thy beauty." He crossed to her bed, putting the white blossom in her red curls. "My lady, your corsage. May I pin it? Huh uh uh uh uh, no arguing allowed. Save that for another time, please. Tonight is to be carefree and no fights." He pinned the white flowers to her hospital gown. "Now, your golden slippers, my lady?" He slipped a pair of shoes on her tiny feet, ignoring the protests she put forth. "Now, you are prepared for your royal ball, my lady."

Because she was in a state of disbelief, the only words Grace could form were, "I do not know how to dance. I do not dance." She had never seen her young man in a tuxedo before. He looked like some debonair movie star walking off the screen.

She could not argue when he drew her close to his breast, while the scent of his cologne teased her senses. The soft instrumental music in the background appealed to her sense of hearing. She could feel his heart beating beneath her soft cheek. It beat in perfect rhythm to the music.

"I do not know how to dance either," he whispered. The touch of his lips on her ear weakened her. For the brevity of a moment, she allowed Travis to sweep her into a dream. She forgot about pushing him away. The sweetness of his breath on her neck caused a yearning in her to forget that she was dying and forsake all caution and submit to him completely. The fact that neither was dancing mattered not.

The man did not dare speak one syllable to break the magic. He knew the moment was too sensitive for words to spoil. He too, had a yearning to forbid her to die, so he could sweep her to complete isolation. Somewhere in a cabin in the middle of the vast woods. Somewhere where no one could ever find them, especially death. Even in her hospital gown, adorned with his corsage, she was the loveliest sight his eyes could behold. If he could only capture this moment and keep it, how wonderful it all would be. He loved her so that his soul ached. If she rejected him this time, he thought that he might die, himself.

The music had stopped, but Grace had been content in his arms, and he was not about to move away to start the music again. It was not worth it to lose this moment. After talking to Mr. Sinclair, he understood more why Grace was pushing him away, but he was determined not to let her. The wise words of the elder gentleman did not fall on deaf ears. He would give her anything she wanted, but he would not be so easily pushed aside. She may be stubborn, but this time he would prevail.

Finally, he could no longer restrain from the intensity

of their closeness. He had drawn her face to his and could not resist kissing her. She briefly responded, before the spell was broken. In that time, a commitment of sorts was bonded. He knew she knew she was bound to him for life. Possibly, that is what caused her to retract.

"I think you better leave. You have been here long enough," she almost whispered. The words caught in her throat. This was no way to make him leave. She intended him to leave her for good, and she should not encourage him this way.

"I will leave, if I must, but I will be back in the morning."

Grace's fire strengthened. "No! I mean you better leave for good. Just go back home. Go back to work. Leave me alone. I do not want you here," she struggled to spit out the final lying words. "I do not love you. Find another to keep you happy and leave me alone."

Isaiah was wrong, she thought to herself, after Travis had left. He said to follow her heart, but her heart was calling out "You stupid fool! Call him back." That was not the best advice to follow. If anything, she should follow her head.

Behind a closed door, Travis spoke silently to himself, "I will leave you Grace Sorenson, for now, but in the morning, I will return. I'll not be swayed that easily." Then a quickened step led him toward his next plan.

Condemning Grace

Graham Sinclair's private plane landed in Grace's old home state. It was so much smaller than New York. The airport was maybe one-tenth the size of her hometown's. The people were not necessarily nicer; they just seemed to notice one more. He hired a car to take him to the courthouse, where he planned to obtain information about Grace's brother. He had set this mission to be one of his main priorities. His feelings for Grace were pretty strong. She had proven herself worthy to him. In a world where everyone was so quick to sue, it was refreshing to meet someone who chose a simple life, rather than one of luxury at another man's expense. Because of these reasons, Sinclair was bound to find a donor for this girl.

The courthouse employees were pleasant enough, only they had a peculiar manner when questioned about the name, Sorenson. They became hush hush and intentionally refused to speak with him any further. Nonetheless, Graham Sinclair was not one to be put off. He searched through court records dating within five years of the time Travis told him that Grace came to live with her uncle.

Travis also informed him how unhelpful the uncle's wife would be to divulge any information without nosing in and trying to take over. He remembered how she had kept Grace and him apart all those years ago. He knew she had an Aunt Janet, but did not know the last name.

Sinclair had taken his right hand man along to help do the grunt work. So together, the two worked through the lunch hour before hitting pay dirt. The allegations claimed by Grace seemed a far cry from the ruling of the judgment. It seemed that she had left directly after an incident which left bruises and open wounds, which the authorities took pictures of. Yet, the only declaration the judge made was neglect. As he read the court transcript from the hearing, he realized that the social services had the idea that she might have some medical repercussions at this point, but it appeared no follow up was ever ordered. If there was, he could not find record of it.

The social service office was the next stop, but he hit a brick wall. They were adamant about not letting anyone privy to someone else's records. He showed them selected copies of the court hearing and threatened to bring a lawsuit against the judge and social services, if they did not comply, because of their failure to protect the child and seek necessary medical help, they saw he had plenty of grounds.

There was no mention of the brother in either set of records. The medical questions had gone unanswered, but he found the reason for all the shut mouths. Byron Sorenson, Grace's birth father, had been a deputy sheriff in this county until he retired a few years back. They were protecting their own. It was the buddy system, and they would never turn on one after forty-five years of service.

The only other helpful information revealed was the name of the uncle and aunt in which Grace went to live with later on. Procuring a local phone book, he jotted down the number of the uncle and the dad. If worse came to worse, he would contact him.

A phone call to Claudia led him to the information that her husband was dead, so he scheduled an interview with the woman that afternoon. Time was of the essence. He was not sure how much longer Travis could con her into staying in the hospital. He needed success by tomorrow, at least.

"Who did you say you were, again?" Claudia inquired. She had a way of smelling the rich, therefore putting on her sweetest charm.

"My name is Graham Sinclair. I represent your niece, Grace Sorenson," he began to explain.

"Grace? What in the world is she up to? I always knew she would end up in some kind of trouble."

"You misunderstand me. She is in no trouble. I understand you have a daughter?"

"Exactly how do you represent her then, Mr. Sinclair?" The aunt eyed him cautiously.

"Grace is very sick. She needs a bone marrow transplant. I am trying to find a match for her."

Claudia became stern at the mention of this in relation with her daughter. "Lynette cannot donate any bone marrow. She has children. I am sorry, but you will find no help here." She turned to imply the conversation was finished.

Sinclair stood, towering over the widowed aunt, "I am not asking anything of you or your daughter.

However, if you have any information on Grace's brother, it would be much appreciated."

"Oh, is that all? Why did you not say so to begin with? That is simple. His name is Shawn Sorenson. He lives on the farm with his father and two children. But I must say, you will not likely receive any help from him after everything Grace did to his family. You know we tried with her, but it frightened me terribly that she might lie on my dear Jerry the same way she did her dad, bless his heart, but Jerry would not turn her away." Now that she found he did not want anything from her, she was willing to flap her jaws about every intimate detail concerning someone else.

"Does Shawn Sorenson work?" Graham asked.

"As far as I know, he lives off his dad. Mind you, it has been umpteen years since I have seen him. You want to see trouble, well, he stays in it. Are you a lawyer?" Her oversweet charm had come back.

"No. Thank you for your time. May I call you if I need any further assistance?"

"Sure," Claudia watched him leave, wishing she could have found out more about the man.

Graham's next stop brought him face to face with the former deputy. For the sake of the girl lying helplessly dying, he blinded himself to the information he accumulated from her social service report. Had he not been able to blind himself, he probably would have killed the man standing before him.

The old man explained that Shawn was picking his children up from school and would return shortly. He offered the guest to wait in the den. Sinclair, being in a hurry to complete his mission, agreed to wait. He had to fight to keep vile thoughts about this man from entering his head.

At last Shawn arrived, being followed by an arrogant boy and frightened girl, which were immediately ordered to go feed the animals. He uninvited the man from his home by drawing him outside to communicate.

"My father is fragile. He does not have too many more years to live. I prefer any serious conversations to take place away from his ears. What company do you represent? Never mind. I can't pay you what I don't have," the man spat out quickly.

"I do not represent a company, and I do not want

money," Sinclair began to explain as his dislike for Grace's brother grew. "I am here on behalf of your sister."

"My sister? I guess you have the wrong guy. I don't have a sister. Look, I don't want whatever it is you are trying to hang on me. So why don't you just leave?"

Again the gentleman tried to explain, "I have checked you out Mr. Sorenson. The reason I am here is because your sister needs a bone marrow transplant and you are the best one for a match. You both have similar DNA, having been born from the same parents."

"You really are a crazy old man. That stupid witch has destroyed my father and this family. What makes you think I'd lift one finger to help her? You didn't mention this to my dad, did you?"

"No, I needed to speak with you about it."

Again, Shawn interrupted, "I hope not. We have disowned that witch, and it would kill my father to hear her name mentioned again. Now, you need to go. Goodbye." He turned to leave Sinclair standing by the car. There was something funny about his stout shoulders. Maybe it was the yellow streak that ran between them. Suddenly, as an idea came to the man, he turned on heel. "Wait a minute. What's your name, and where is Gracie?"

"My name is Graham Sinclair. Grace is in the hospital. Are you going to test to see if you are a match or not? I would adjure you to do so."

The brother had an evil gleam in his eye. "I could be persuaded, maybe, for the right amount of cash. You look kind of rich. What are you, her sugar daddy or something?"

The distasted grew in Mr. Sinclair's mouth. "Or something. What is your price?"

"Let's say fifty thousand dollars. Twenty-five for testing, and twenty-five for donating, if I am a match. Is it a deal?"

"Fifty thousand? Fine, but you do not receive one dime until you have completed it. I will bring a cashier's check in the amount of twenty-five thousand the day you test, and another after you donate."

Shawn thought a moment about the arrangement before agreeing. "Where do I go?"

"Just meet me at the airport by seven o'clock tonight

or all bets are off." With a distinguished step, the gentleman finished the distance to his car door and left. He could understand why Grace did not feel she could come to this brother.

In New York, he prepared everything for the transplant. The donor would be coming in with him, and it was Ruth's job to get Grace's approval. They would try to arrange it for tomorrow.

Convincing Grace

Graham left Shawn safely tucked in his hotel room with the understanding that if he came out for any reason, the deal was off. The love of money was good enough reason to keep the man inside.

Quickly, Sinclair headed to the hospital to inform Dr. Williams of the possible donor. He would arrange for Shawn to be tested elsewhere. From what he had seen of the man, he did not want to risk contact between him and Grace. The man was pure evil.

The following morning, Dr. Williams made the trip to the local clinic to test the brother, and to their fortune, he was a match. Getting Grace to approve of the procedure was the next step. This needed the assistance of those near and dear to her.

Ruth and Isaiah were only told that a donor had been located. Graham did not feel right divulging personal information to anyone. The horrible revelations he had found in her records would remain his secret, even from Albert.

Travis was not around the first couple of days after Graham arrived back in New York. No one seemed to know where he had disappeared. They had all assumed he had gotten the hint and returned to his own life. This made the decision for Grace a lot easier. She must look at this thing objectively. When he was around, she could not do that. The yearning to live would win out every time.

It was Isaiah who finally persuaded her. "I can give you three good reasons to do this: Amy first. She has had enough heartache in one lifetime. She loves you, and you need to be there for her. Ruth second. I will not be around forever. Who will my wife have after I am gone? Thirdly, all those children that will suffer without you to intervene. How many will die, because you chose to die, yourself? Now, I think you are being selfish. I heard you say once, 'Dying is easy. You just stop living. It is living that is hard.' I never thought you to be a coward, Grace, but that is what I am seeing today."

"Isaiah, I hear what you are saying, but there are equally strong reasons why I should not. The main thing is that I have not the money for such an expensive procedure."

"That will work itself out. That is not a good excuse."

"Also, are my chances of living any longer going to change. It does not just end with this one transplant. They will have to follow this up with surgery to remove the tumor, along with only God knows what kind of chemotherapy and such"

"Then, I suggest you have that surgery, as well."

"On top of that, what if I do all this, and die anyway? Do you think Amy will benefit from that?"

"Grace, she will benefit froom you trying your best to live, if for no other reason, but her."

Grace understood that the slipping of the accent meant her beloved Isaiah was getting upset. She would not argue with him any further. He made sense. However, the final straw was when Travis showed up beside her bed the next day with Amy in his arms.

"Momma!" she cried upon seeing Grace. She had never called Grace that before. "Did you notice I called you Momma? That's because you are going to be my Momma. Travis talked to the lady. She said she sent you a letter of a...ap..."

"Approval," Travis helped.

"Yeah. She said I was going to be yours. And Travis told her he was going to marry you and be my dad! He has the papers and everything. Show them to her, Travis!"

"Indeed Miss Amy." Travis pulled out the copy of the new adoption request. "This is a copy. She said since you were already granted adoption, it should be no problem adding my name as father."

Grace looked beyond his triumphant look to Isaiah. Dear sweet old Isaiah, was he a man of wisdom? Perhaps he was right about the surgery, but neither was planning on this turn of events. Isaiah had a look of approval on his dear old face, but Grace disagreed. She may agree to have the surgery, but she did not sign on to marry anyone. She still wanted Travis to go back home. She would not see his heart get broken again.

"Let me see. Yes, it says here that you were legally adopted by me as of two weeks ago. Well, fancy that. Will you look at this Ruth? We have a new member of the family. Kill the fatted calf, Isaiah." Grace made a point of not acknowledging Travis's presence. "My question for you, young lady, is why are you not in school?"

"Oh Momma. Travis said it would not hurt to miss the rest of this week. He was hoping we could all go home before the weekend was up."

"He did? Well, we shall see about that. Right now, I insist you come here and give me a kiss. I have certainly missed you a lot."

Amy was happy to jump into her new mother's arms. However, she was not aware of how fragile her mom had become. Grace hid well the grimace of pain she received with Amy's pounce. The girl chatted nonstop for a good half hour, while perched contentedly on Isaiah's lap, leaving Grace to be relieved when Travis left the room with Ruth.

Staying Grace

By nightfall, Grace was worn out from all the excitement and had the beginnings of a headache. It was all she could do to keep her eyes open. She was not even sure if she had the strength to sustain the procedure in question. The papers still lay on her bed, awaiting her signature. Tomorrow was the deciding day. She would either agree to the transplant or head back to Oregon. She had already promised an answer to Dr. Williams by then.

When Travis and Ruth approached Isaiah with the idea, he had been very hesitant. Grace was his little girl. He was not keen on the idea of deceiving her. He prayed for wisdom in the choice he was about to make. His wife had the best intentions, but sometimes, she could let the female part of her take over, which may not be the best thing in this situation. The main thing was to do what was best for Grace.

He arrived in her room with a pretty new dress in tow for her to put on. He wore a navy suit, which was a far cry from the overalls Grace was used to seeing him wear. He waited outside, while the exhausted woman slipped into the dress he brought. He promised to explain to her the reason for his coming, when she finished.

The explanation, according to plan, was that Amy wanted to celebrate her adoption. She did not want to wait until they returned to Oregon. Grace wished she had picked another night to do this. She was really worn out, and her head hurt profusely. But Grace felt obligated. She would do nothing to embarrass this child in front of all her guests. This quality was the one Travis was counting on.

Her dear friend escorted her to the pediatric unit. She expected the room to be dark and desolate, but Amy had invited all the children from their rooms, plus Jameston, Sinclair, and their wives. There were a few others in which Grace never met.

Once they were in the room, Isaiah refused to let go of her arm. He escorted her to where Travis was standing with another gentleman. The smile he was wearing on his face showed that he was very pleased with her appearance. Isaiah gave Grace a kiss on the cheek before handing her hand to Travis.

"Forgive me, Grace. I did what I thought was best," he whispered in her ear.

A puzzled expression announced her ignorance to his comment, but when the man standing beside Travis began speaking, she began to understand.

"Dearly beloved…" he was saying.

She looked at Isaiah who dared not raise his eyes to her. He did not appear shameful of his actions. Well, she could always just turn and leave. She could run out. That would teach Travis Winston that he could not trick her. She meant for him to leave, and she was going to stand by it. Ruth watched on with admiration. She was of no help.

She felt a tug on her dress. "Momma, you are suppose to say, 'I do', now," Amy urged.

Grace could not refuse the pleading in the child's eyes. There was no way for her to flee now. It was not a matter of disgracing Travis, anymore. It would devastate her new child. Travis grew a little worried when the preacher had to ask the third time if Grace promised to love him until death. Surely she was not going to humiliate him. He had counted on her inability

443

to cause a scene. He felt comfortably sure she would not run off. "Just say the words," He was repeating in his head.

By now, even Isaiah was alert and watching to see what Grace was going to do. Amy kept pulling at her dress. All were praying.

Feeling trapped, Grace had no choice. "I do." She almost whispered while giving a withering glance at her husband. That was right, he was her husband. The preacher just said so. Prior to this moment, the only One Grace had ever submitted to was her Lord and Master. Now, she was to be in subjection to a man in which she was very angry with at the moment. Marriage was nothing to be taken lightly. It was for keeps. The trickery involved had not taken in consideration the longevity of this relationship in the chance that the bride was going to resent the groom for his tactics.

The applause aggravated Grace's already aching head. She barely looked at her husband, and did not speak to him at all. He understood that she might be angry and did not push her. Cake and ice cream circulated for everyone. Jameston and Sinclair brought their congratulations and introduced their wives.

The bride had not even taken the time to reflect in a mirror. The simple lines of the dress enhanced the tiny frame. It was no gown or grand gesture, yet no bride could have looked lovelier, and the groom was handsome. The bride did notice, but she would not even allow herself to look in his direction.

At last, she pleaded with Isaiah to take her to her room. She was hurting but did not want to admit it. She kissed Ruth goodnight. Upon receiving her kiss, Amy informed her mom that she wanted to stay with these children longer, at least until they finished cake and ice cream.

So with a "goodnight", she passed through the door. It was not Isaiah that joined her though. It was time for the new husband to bite the bullet and face the medicine he had coming, but Grace was too weary for even that pleasure. Instead of a protective arm behind her, Travis placed a possessive arm around her. She was his wife.

"Grace, please do not be too angry with us," he pleaded, once Grace was comfortably in her bed again. "I did not give the others much of a choice, so if you must be mad at someone, make it me, but I adjure you to please not be angry at all. You know how I feel about you. I also know that you love me. You do love me Grace." He gently turned her face to his.

Tears were on her cheeks. They burned the fragile flesh. They came because of the pain she was in, both physical and emotional. She was not so much angry with him as she was her own inept being. Why could she not promise him a long healthy life, with children and grandchildren? Why did she have to have this cancer now? Why couldn't she have found it last year, before she went to that stupid reunion? Why had she cursed his happiness with this kind of sorrow?

He whispered, "What is it, dearest?" He kissed her tears. His warm lips soothed her grief. "Why is it that you cry?"

The touch of her hand to his soft brown hair confirmed her love. Her voice was soft and gentle. "I am frightened."

"I understand, but I'll be with you, and you will get better, I know."

"I'm not frightened for the task that is before me. I

am frightened of failing you and Amy. I tried to protect you from…"

Travis interpolated, "I don't need protection from this. I have a right to choose." Her lashes covered her sad violet eyes, pushing the welled tears out. "I would rather love you, cherish you, and be with you for a short time of paradise, than to live a lifetime without ever having you near me. You are my choice. You are my love. Don't you get it? I am nothing without you. I never was, and I never will be. And as far as failing me, you could never do that. Amy is with me on this. She loves you as I do."

The comfort of his embrace caused her to sleep soundly all night, so that when the nurse came in to do the vital signs, she quickly retreated again. She could not intrude.

Made in the USA
Charleston, SC
27 May 2014